# Her Season Of Love

**Renee Bless**

I0671164

*I'd like to first thank you the reader, for picking up this book. Since I was twelve years old, I would get in my corner with my paper and my pen I would write poetry, short stories, and even songs. It has always been my dream to become a published author. I wanted to create a story that one could get lost within the pages. Hopefully this book will provide a get away for someone.*
*To my children Chris, Ya and Nej Bless, I love you and I hope you follow your dreams. To my hubby Mr. J Bless, thank you for always pushing me to keep going. I would like to thank my family a friends for all of their love, encouragement and support.Thanks a bunch to my readers I hope you enjoy.*

Enjoy,

Renee Bles

# Her Season of Love

## *The Beginning*

The summer before young A.J. started high school he and his best friend decided to play a game of truth or dare. Their parents weren't at home yet. Tim a cute boy who lived on the next street was A.J.'s best friend. He rubbed the peach fuzz growing on his chin while he sat on the porch with A.J. on that boring afternoon.

"I bet you won't ask the Williams cousins if they want to play." Tim asked with a look of mischief on his face.

"Why would they want to play Tim? Truth or dare requires willing participants." A.J. asked, as he was always up for a challenge but he just wasn't sure about this one. Tim crossed his arms as he looked across the yard at Cara, Shaia, and Terra sitting at their picnic table laughing.

"How do you know they won't participate if you don't ask?" Tim replied as he stepped off the porch and started walking across the yard to the picnic table. A.J. followed thinking that this boy was about to start some mess with these girls. Tim stood next to the picnic table rubbing his hands together.

"Yo! Who wants to play truth or dare?" Tim boldly asked. He didn't hold anything back. Shaia frowned as Tim and A.J. expected. Terra and Cara looked at each other, before saying in unison "okay."

So they played the game of truth or dare, and at first the teenagers played safe, by asking questions of truth, but then Tim got bored and decided to change the game.

"Okay, A.J. I dare you to kiss one of these girls." Tim challenged. A.J. was shocked, he looked at his friend with his eyes wide. When A.J. noticed everybody looking at him, he puffed out his chest and said,

"Alright, do I get to pick which one?"

Shaia piped in then, "No, I get to pick."

Her hazel eyes sparkled as she looked at her cousins Terra and Cara. She knew without a doubt that Terra would do it and she wouldn't think twice. Cara was always miss goody two shoes so she decided to put her on the spot.

"I double dare you to kiss Cara." She said while looking at her cousin.

Cara looked at her cousin and then looked at A.J. She knew what this was about and she wasn't going to back down even though she had never kissed anybody before. She looked at A.J., he stuffed his hands in his pockets and then he asked if they had to kiss in the open. Shaia told them to go to the back porch. "We will watch you to make sure you do it from over there by the tree." She pointed to the group of trees at the edge of their property line.

Cara and A.J. walked slowly to the back porch. She was nervous. So nervous that she looked around to make sure her parents hadn't pulled up into the driveway. A.J. saw her looking around so he whispered to her,

"You don't have to do this if you don't want to. I can just call it off." Cara shook her head no. If she backed down she'd never hear the end of it from her cousins.

When they reached the back porch, Cara took one last look around. Shaia, Terra and Tim all stood by the tree looking on. They didn't believe that the two of them were really going to kiss.

Cara stared at A.J.'s black, Patrick Ewing basketball shoes, and then she looked at his broad chest in his basketball jersey. Her heart was pounding in her chest. She had daydreamed of this moment but she had to tell him that she had never kissed anyone before and she didn't know what to do.

A.J. swallowed the lump that had formed in his throat. He knew she was innocent but he never imagined that he would be the first person she kissed. He cleared his throat then he answered,

"Its okay, I will show you."

A.J. was almost sixteen and he had kissed before. He looked at Cara's innocent face thinking how he had always thought she was cute, with her big hazel eyes and long hair. He never imagined that he would be standing where he was standing at that moment about to kiss her. He touched her hand, and slowly lifted her chin with his other hand. He leaned down looking into her beautiful hazel eyes he slowly kissed her lips.

Her lips were warm and soft against his and he could taste the flavor of bubble yum. He first kissed her softly, and then he paused so that she could pull away if she wanted to. He thought that she would pull away, but she surprised him when she didn't.

Cara lifted her lips closer to his, so that he could kiss her again. This time when he kissed her he held the kiss a little longer and she kissed him back.

They got lost for a moment, as he slipped his tongue between her lips she timidly touched his tongue with her own.

Cara liked kissing him.

They kept kissing until they heard Tim say a car was coming. They hurriedly stepped off the porch each going in a different direction.

Cara couldn't explain the feelings she had spiraling through her as he kissed her. She had all sorts of fluttering in her stomach as he stood near her.

In a daze as she walked back to the picnic table. She couldn't believe she had actually kissed the boy next door who was her secret crush.

Her cousins gathered around her asking a bunch of questions and giggling.

Tim put his arms around A.J.'s shoulders as they walked back across the yard to his house.

"Wow, you two were going at it." Tim stated.

A.J. touched his lips and reflected for a minute. He had always liked Cara the most out of the three Williams girls.

The kiss was special and he wouldn't forget it.

"You like her don't you? I knew it!" Tim teased, as he punched A.J. in the shoulder.

A.J. kept touching his lips and he just shook his head.

"No man, go ahead with that." A.J. tried to play it off.

He caught Cara's eye and she smiled at him. He smiled back. Then he tried to get Tim's mind off of the kiss by suggesting that he and Tim go play ball. It worked. They picked up his basketball and walked to the basketball courts around the corner.

Shaia and Terra didn't know what to say as they looked at their cousin. They dared her and she had done something that neither of them had been brave enough to do.

Terra broke the silence when she asked,

"So did you like it?"

"It was okay."

Cara blushed as they began to ask her so many questions about the kiss, that she almost gave her true feelings away. She couldn't wait to get to her diary so that she could write how she really felt.

She even thought about calling her Aunt Pam to tell her about it. Her Aunt Pam made it a point to try to talk to her nieces and her daughter about boys when she came home or when she called. No doubt she would have something to say about the dare. Cara wasn't worried, she didn't think that kissing A.J. was such a bad thing as long as she didn't go any further.

All through the summer, the kids went places together, laughed and played together. They didn't play truth or dare anymore, nor did they talk about the kiss.

"Call me, alright?" A.J. asked Cara when the summer was over and he was headed to high school. He knew that he wouldn't see Cara and her cousins as much as he used to. He had made his high school Varsity football team.

At the beginning of the school year, they talked on the phone almost every day at first, but soon A.J. became too busy and life took them in different directions.

A.J. followed his dream of becoming an engineer so he went off to one of the most prestigious colleges in the U.S. for engineering.

Terra went off to modeling school, while Cara and Shaia went to college for business and communication. Terra came home once a month, while Cara and Shaia went
into business together and saw each other daily. They were event planners, planning parties just like they had done when they were little. Except this time they planned parties for real. Their business was called,

"Every Occasion." They planned, weddings, large and small social events. Any event that you could name, they planned and they were so successful at it.

**\*Ten Years later\***
**\*All Grown Up\***

Gone were the French braids and pretty pink dresses. Gone was the innocence of being a child. Cara, Shaia, and Terra Williams were now strong beautiful, successful women.

Cara sat at her desk at the office of "Every Occasion" trying to decide if she should pick up her phone to speed dial *him* or just continue to sit still and wait for him to call.

She couldn't keep negative thoughts out of her head. She wondered if he was with someone else during the times he claimed to be with his children. If he didn't want to be involved with her anymore, why didn't he just leave her alone. How could you call yourself seeing someone and not contact them in several weeks when you had set the norm to communicate everyday by message or phone she wondered.

She had been thinking about it all day she couldn't say that she had been very productive with her time when she wasn't sitting directly in front of a client. She was glad that the workday had finally come to an end. She was ready to unwind. It was Wednesday. On Wednesdays, all three women would meet after work at the bar around for drinks.

Cara saved and closed the open files on her computer and then she shut her computer down. She made sure everything had been shut down in the office and then locked the door, set the security code and headed around the corner to the bar.

When Cara made it to the bar, her cousin Shaia, was already there. Her meetings had been outside of the office all day. Shaia was sitting at the bar, with her long lean legs crossed. She was wearing a chartreuse blue skirt that had a thigh high split. She smiled when she noticed Cara approaching. She smiled at the barmaid who had just placed a glass of cranberry juice in front of her. Cara sang her name as she approached. Shaia turned around to greet her, she stopped mid hello.

"Girl, that is a sexy dress, you must let me borrow or tell me where you got it from, and oh my goodness look at those shoes!" Shaia exclaimed.

Cara's dress was a simple black dress, with a plunging neckline that showed off just a hint of cleavage and it hung low in the back. She wore pearls to dress it up and long black hair was swept up into a neat bun.

"Thank you girl just give me a few minutes cause I gotta think about telling you all that." Cara teased.

The barmaid came over to take Cara's drink order. She ordered a "strawberry patron Rita" which was a marguerite with shots of patron and strawberry flavor. They chatted and relaxed. After twenty minutes, Terra sashayed into the bar dressed in a red pantsuit that hugged her model frame. She air kissed her cousins and then sat down beside Cara. As soon as she sat down the barmaid came to take Terra's drink order. She ordered a cosmopolitan. The barmaid informed them that the men that sat at opposite end of the bar wanted to put their drinks on their tab.

Cara sighed and nicely told the barmaid thank you but no thanks, she knew if they bought drinks most of the time they were looking for conversation. She had very little conversation for anyone besides her clients these days. Shaia felt the same.

"We only been sitting here like ten minutes and they can't help themselves." Shaia said while shaking her head with an amused smile. Terra frowned at her cousins, knowing that she wouldn't refuse the offer for a free drink or two. Shaia signaled to the barmaid that she was ready to order again.

"I'll have the same please, and tell those gentlemen I said thank you but, no thanks." Shaia said looking at her cousin, Terra.

Terra shook her head at her and then she raised her glass to the two fine men at the end of the bar. The two fine men raised their glasses back. She looked at her cousins like she were disgusted.

"You know Cara and Shaia you really should try something different for a change." Terra said with a frown.

Cara took a long sip of her drink and looked her cousin directly in the eye, she felt like she had to have the same conversation with her cousin every time they got together.

"Terra, I didn't come here to have conversation with any man, I came here to relax. I don't see anything wrong with that. Every time we get together I have to tell you the same thing." Cara said through clenched teeth. She took a deep breath to calm down, because she was so tired of her cousin trying to tell her how she should feel. She felt like she might lose hold of her tongue and curse her cousin out. She took another sip of her drink, emptying the glass and raised her hand to get the barmaids attention to order another glass.

"You don't need to get an attitude about it Cara, I am just saying. Give somebody the time of day besides Eric, I mean really. He isn't here to offer you a free drink or
conversation." Eric had been her boyfriend for the last two years. They're relationship had been rocky lately, so rocky that they were no longer together.

Terra didn't mean to say it so harsh, but she was tired of the way Cara's supposed boyfriend treated her cousin. She felt her cousin deserved so much better. Shaia agreed with Terra but she knew Cara didn't need to be reminded each time she saw her. Terra was sorry that she had said anything at that moment about it because Cara stopped talking. When the barmaid placed Cara's drink in front of her she sipped it down fast and then slipped off the bar stool.

"Can you watch my purse?" She asked not even looking at Shaia and Terra before walking away to the restroom. The men that had been watching at the end of the bar watched the gentle sway of her hips as she walked away. When Cara was out of ear shot she looked at Terra,

"Why do you have to start talking about Eric every chance you get, you act like you have all the answers when you don't even know what's going on." Shaia sipped her drink, trying her best not to show her irritation with her cousin for being so callous with her words.

"Well I am just saying the girl needs to know that Eric is no good for her. She should move on and these men that show her attention shouldn't be ignored. That's all I am saying. If I am wrong please excuse me." Terra opened up her purse to look for a cigarette. She had picked up the habit to calm her nerves while she was on the road. Shaia frowned at her she really didn't feel like smelling cigarettes. She really didn't feel like debating with her cousin either so she just turned her head. Terra didn't even notice as she found her lighter and lit up.

In the restroom, Cara washed her hands and looked at herself in the mirror. She loved her smooth honey brown skin and her big hazel eyes, her full kissable lips and long neck. She turned to the side to look at her hips, and she swayed slightly loving her curves. She could attract any man she wanted so why was she alone right now waiting to hear from one particular man who hadn't had the decency to call or send her a message in a few weeks? When Cara left the restroom and started back towards the bar she noticed the men that had offered the drinks were now standing beside Terra. She sighed to herself because no matter what her cousin had to say she wasn't there to make conversation with any man tonight. When Shaia saw her approaching she apologized to her cousin with her eyes. She apologized for the way Terra had spoken about her relationship so callously without knowing what was really going on.

Cara knew her cousin hadn't meant those words to hurt her feelings, so she gave them both a weak smile. As Cara stepped back to the bar, the men who had tried to buy her a drink wasted no time introducing themselves to her and her cousins. Michael and David Tyson were also cousins and both business partners at a prominent law firm they had also attended the same high school. They talked about their business and possibly needing an event planned. Shaia talked a little business with the guys and then she exchanged business cards with the men.

While everybody else talked, Cara absent mindedly stared at the door. When the jukebox started to play Rkellys, old school "Slow Dance", she started to sway, and sing to herself. Cara was in her own little zone. Michael smiled at her; he even reached out to move a stray piece of hair away from her eyes, as if they knew each other like that. Cara was thinking about Malek, her first love what this dude in front of her had just done didn't even phase her. Malek had been heavy on her mind a lot lately. She remembered how he used to sing that song to her and pull her close when it came on the radio. She had been spending time with Malek lately, and just like her exboyfriend Eric, he hadn't called in quite some time. She missed him.

As she swayed softly to the music, she glanced at the door, the door opened and she happened to lock eyes with a tall dark and handsome guy that was slowly walking in. Malek Jones. His jaws appeared to be set tight when he walked in, because the first thing he saw was Cara standing at the bar winding her hips and a man standing beside her not being discreet about looking at her hips at all. The man was being disrespectful to her and she didn't even notice or maybe she did, Malek didn't know.

He looked at the woman that stood at the bar, the woman that had once been his girlfriend in high school. She stood there swaying looking so sexy, he could feel himself getting turned on as he looked at her he was loving the way she wore that black dress and those heels. He didn't like that the dude at the bar stood so close to her. He didn't expect to see her in the bar, but he saw her car in the parking lot and knew that she had to be somewhere near by. As he passed the door of the bar he saw her inside with her cousins. He hadn't seen her in a while, he missed her and he needed to talk to her. So he stopped by.

When Cara looked up and saw Malek walking in she wanted to rush to his side and then kiss him. She wanted to tell him how much she had missed him the moment she saw him walk through the doors at the same time she wanted to pick up her purse and leave without even looking in his direction because he hadn't called her in a few weeks and dealing with him was too complicated. She just stood there like she was stuck, as she looked in his dark eyes she could feel her body start to react to him. She swayed from the effects of the Patron and the effect that the man who stood directly in front of her now had on her. The man who was standing beside her tried to start a conversation. As she watched Malek approaching she couldn't hear him. She closed her eyes for a second and when she opened her eyes Malek was standing directly in front of her reaching for her hand. She couldn't help being drawn to him, she let him take her hand and then he pulled her close whispering in her ear,

"I missed you."

She wanted to melt in his arms on site. The guy who was standing there beside her trying to start a conversation stopped talking when he recognized Malek. He stepped back.

"What's up man! Long time no see!" He reached out to give Malek a hand shake, and Malek shook his hand but he kept his eyes on her as he said,

"What's up man," and then he said to her, "Tell your family goodnight."

She started trembling as his breath caressed her ear she was in a zombie like trance as she grabbed her purse. She made eye contact with Shaia so that she would know that she was leaving. Shaia nodded and watched Malek lead her cousin out of the bar.

Terra looked at her cousin Shaia in question. Wondering why Cara was leaving with him yet knowing the only reason why she could be.

Cara slid into Malek's truck, while he held the door for her. Within minutes they were riding down the street away from the bar and towards Maleks apartment. She stared at the side of his face as he drove. Questions plagued her mind again. When they pulled to a stop in front of his apartment, he turned the truck off. Cara had no time to speak as he kissed her. His kiss possessed a hunger that had her sighing.

His hands were on her thighs, and under her dress touching her black lace thong. He stopped kissing her long enough to ask if he could keep going and when she nodded, he proceeded to lick his fingers and then he began his finger assault between her thighs.

Cara moaned softly. She had dreamed of him doing to her what he was doing right now. She had always held back because he was just a friend but this time there was no turning back, she couldn't stop what he was doing to her because she didn't want to.  Minutes passed and Cara had all but climbed over the center console and gear shift into his lap. He French kissed her, as he took his keys from the ignition and opened his car door. He helped her climb over the console and slide out of the drivers' side door. He held her hand as he opened the front door of his apartment.

When they were inside his apartment, he kicked the door shut behind him. When he pressed his body against her she could feel the heat rise between them. He lifted her dress over her head, and then he pulled the bobby pins from her hair to watch her hair fall to her shoulders. She had always been so beautiful to him, he kissed her senseless as she fiddled with his belt. He put his hands over hers and helped her take the belt off.  His slacks fell to the floor, and his red boxers followed. She massaged his manhood, causing him to groan. She suckled on his lower lip, and kissed his muscled arms and chest. He stood back from her and stood admiring her body. She had grown so much from the skinny little girl that he had loved when they were teenagers. She bit her bottom lip as he looked at her. Her breasts perfect round globes, he released them when he took off her bra. He rubbed her stomach thinking her skin was so smooth and he loved the voluptuous curves of her body, he thought to himself.

His conscience started to bother him as he kissed her sweet lips. He hadn't planned to kiss her like this and then end up in his living room like this. There they were standing naked in each others arms. He had wanted to talk to her about what had been going on in his life that had kept him away without so much as a message hello. He felt like he owed her that.

She stood in front of him on her tiptoes and she kissed him. She was driving him crazy with the way she was suckling on his lips. Malek placed his hands around her waist to pull her away from him. He knew he needed to say what we he needed to sa that he could say what he was going to say before it was too late. When he pulled away from her, she looked at him with those big hazel eyes in question.

"I'm sorry, we need to talk." He admitted to her. She heard him loud and clear, but she didn't know if she should blame it on the Patron for not caring what he had to talk to her about.

She was glad that he was there with her. It didn't matter that just an hour ago she felt so neglected she was going to send him a message to tell him not to worry about calling her again because she didn't have time to wait her turn. Right now as he looked all she wanted him to do was make love to her and make her forget their reality. She started kissing his hands and guided them across her soft skin. Malek shook his head and backed out of her reach he was struggling with this, decision that he had made a week ago even more now because he was staring into the beautiful eyes of the woman knew he would always love. He was drinking in her nakedness and drowning in her sweet kisses. He made a mistake by going inside the bar to get her. He should have left her alone he thought to himself.

"Cara please listen to me. I needed to tell you that I ended up back at home." He felt her stiffen, he tried to look into her eyes but she closed them tight. "Please, make love to me right now Malek." She begged. Malek couldn't deny that making love to her, is what he really wanted to do. She was the first woman he had ever truly loved. He wanted to make love to her to erase all the mistakes he had made when they were together. He wanted to close his eyes and when he reopened them, they would have been back at the time when she was his girl and he was her boyfriend.

He kept trying to explain his decision. Cara wouldn't listen to anything, she kissed his broad and bare shoulders, she tongue kissed his earlobe and every time he tried to say something she kept putting her finger to his lips to get him to be quiet. He felt bad because he knew that he had hurt her, but he still wanted her, and he needed to be her comforter right now.

He reached into his pant pocket to get a condom from his wallet but there was nothing there. She looked at him, and without a second thought she gripped his manhood in her hands and told him that it was okay.
"Are you sure Cara?" He asked.
All she did was nod. In the back of her mind, she was kicking herself because she knew better than to have sex without protection. It didn't matter how long she had known the naked man in front of her, because at that moment Cara didn't care. She closed her eyes when he picked her up off the floor as if she weighed only a few pounds, and then he leaned her against the wall with his manhood positioned at her center. She wrapped her legs around his waist.
 He held her up by her butt and plunged so deep into her moist center that she started trembling and mumbling something incoherent. She buried her nose against his neck and he continued to "long stroke" her.  With every stroke, she moaned softly. He knew she was climaxing already when she could barely hold on to him so he gently put her on the floor and then he turned her around and bent her over in front of him and then he instructed,
"Grab them ankles."
 She did. He entered her wet moistness once again from behind, gripping her hips to stroke her deep. It felt so good that she could feel herself folding. She wasn't thinking about anything but receiving his delicious deep strokes.
Malek demanded that she straighten her back and keep holding her ankles. She held on to her ankles and bucked against him stroke for stroke. Cara climaxed again and
could no longer move. He led them to the couch where she lie on her back and received him with her legs wrapped around his back. She cried out,
"I missed you."

He could barely respond because he was trying to stay focused. The only thing he could do was nod in agreement.

"I missed you too." He truly did.

He did the swerve of his hips hitting that spot that caused her to climax all over again. They climaxed together and he held her. He kissed her. Neither of them could find words for that moment. He rubbed her arms, squeezing them gently. He didn't notice her tears until he moved from the spooning position that they were in on the couch, he had moved to balance himself over her. She knew she needed to get up, get dressed and leave at that very moment but she couldn't, she felt stuck. He closed his eyes, because he hated to see her cry.

"I'm sorry Cara, please don't cry." The tears began to fall from her eyes like a silent stream in the middle of a secluded forest.

He kissed away her salty tears. He could feel her body trembling as she tried to hold back sobs. He felt bad, and he didn't want to let her go.

They heard a cell phone vibrating somewhere across the room. He dared to glance at the clock, he knew that it was his phone vibrating. He knew who was calling at that time.

"I think you need to get that." Cara said. The feeling of euphoria had left her. The person on the other end of that phone was what kept them from being the way they were
right now all the time and for all to see. It hurt her to think that they would never have more than a past and a few stolen moments behind closed doors in the present.

His phone vibrated again and he wished he had left that phone in his truck. Cara knew he was debating about answering the call. She stood to her feet slowly and then she moved away from the chair. She could feel him watching her. She avoided making eye contact with him as she went straight to his bathroom to clean herself up. Cara stood in front of the bathroom mirror staring at herself. She touched her kiss swollen lips, her wild hair, and sad hazel eyes. She was feeling lost. What was she doing here in his bathroom, with their love running down the inside of her thighs while he was sitting in the chair he had just had sex with her on possibly talking to the other female? She cried as she got into the shower. She turned the water on, and grabbed the shower gel that was hanging there. She stood in the shower until the water ran cold.

When she came out, wrapped in a towel, Malek just looked at her. He wanted to reach out and touch her but he didn't know what to say. He reached for her hand, and slowly she moved to stand in front of him.

"Are you going to be okay Cara?" He queried.

She took a moment to think about his question before she answered him.

"No." She responded.

He wasn't surprised by her response at all but, he questioned her anyway.

"No?" He raised his brows in question.

"Hell no, you told me that you had left your wife. You told me that you were done with her and all you care about is your children." She answered in aggravation.

Malek reached for her hands and he gently pulled her into his lap.

"I love you Cara." He admitted.

She looked into the eyes of the man who had been her first love. He was the man that she had dreamed of walking down the aisle with, the man that she had dreamed of having a home with, and raising children with. Even though she had fallen in love with Eric, Malek still had a place deep in her heart that couldn't be erased or denied. She sat on his lap and looked into his eyes,

"Malek, I love you, but I wish you had just left me alone."

He couldn't believe he was having this conversation with her. Things had been going so well that he didn't think this conversation would ever come up between them, but here it was slapping him in the face.

He had to be there for his kids, they shouldn't have to suffer for the mistake he made of marrying a woman that he didn't love. All he could do was think about was the look of happiness on his children's faces when he went home with his bags in his hand. He thought he was doing the right thing by his children, by going back home. He wasn't doing it for his wife, but he was doing it for his children.

Cara got up from his lap when he didn't say anything and then she started slipping on her dress, she grabbed her shoes and then she stepped to the front door.
"Can you take me back to my car please?" She demanded.
He tried to hold her hand but she pulled away.
"I'm sorry." Was all he had to say, repeatedly.

Cara looked at him and she felt her heart start to break again. She looked into Maleks eyes and she admitted her true feelings of regret. The regret that had been building up from the first time he kissed her. She knew she should have walked away then but being lonely and the feeling of familiarity, when she was around Malek kept her there.
 "I'm sorry too and I regret that I ever thought that it could be more between us then our past." She admitted.

 "You regret it Cara?" He had a pained expression on his face when he asked.
She took a deep breath as she looked directly into his eyes. The last couple of weeks she had felt alone again. He didn't bother to call or message her, she felt just like she had felt when she was a love sick teenager, waiting for him to call. She regretted every moment now.
"How stupid of me to believe that what we had yesterday could be more than what it is today. How stupid of me to believe that I would one day be more than just your friend." She stated.
He stood in front of her clenching and unclenching his jaw. It's what he did when he was upset.

"You are the best friend I have got, I can come to you when I can't go to anyone else, and you always know what to say."

Fresh tears started streaming down her cheeks at the word friend. She shook her head from side to side needing Malek to understand what bothered her the most.

"I am always there for you and you don't ever have to ask, but I have always had to beg you to make time for me." She reminded him.

He looked like he was trying hard to understand where she was coming from, so she continued to pour out her heart.

"You know I have never been hard to please. It doesn't take a lot to make me happy. You made me so happy when you just took the time to say hey, but you stopped taking time for that and do you know what really hurts the most right now Malek? I told you how Eric had been treating me, and I reminded you of how you had treated me sometimes when we were young. You acted like it bothered you so bad when I told you about Eric yet it has been so easy for you to do the same thing he did."

Malek sat back on the couch, upset with himself because he realized that he had hurt her again, and she didn't deserve it.

While Cara stood in front of Malek with a far off look in her eyes he realized what he had done wrong. Malek realized that he had stopped giving her the attention that she loved and he took it for granted that she promised to always be there for him whenever he called. He also forgot that he had come into her life again to heal her wounded heart not to break it all over again.

He had to tell her the truth he didn't want her to think he went back home for anything more than to be there for his children he explained,

"I went back home because she begged me back. She told me she needed me. Her mother even called to tell me how my not being there was affecting the kids. That is the last thing I wanted to do. I didn't know what else I could do except go home and be there for my kids."

Cara gave him a half smile. She felt used, she felt that he had conveniently lavished her with his attention and affection until he went back home to his family. Her heart swelled with hurt as she stood in front of him playing it over and over in her mind like a mental recorder, he said in so many words that he went back because "she"needed him. She realized despite the past "she" was the other woman. The past that they had together didn't matter because he had forgot about the past and given someone else his last name.

Suddenly the room felt stuffy, she needed some air, Cara didn't want to hear anymore he was still trying to explain so she stopped him mid sentence by raising her hand like she was in a classroom,

"Okay Malek, I understand. Can you please take me to my car?" She asked again, this time she moved toward the door. He reached for her hand,

"Don't be like that Cara."

When he reached for her this time she moved out of his reach. She wouldn't even look at him. He thought he could get her to see things his way no matter what he still loved her and she would always have a special place in his heart. He knew it definitely wasn't what she wanted to hear at the moment but he had to tell her the truth. He stood from the couch they had just had sex on,

"What about you Cara? Aren't I sharing you too?" She just stared at him as he continued to talk with his lips twisted, like he was upset.

"Are you going to leave that dude anytime soon? You are going home to him, after you leave here tonight aren't you?"

He set his jaw and looked into her eyes now.

Cara didn't say a word so he kept talking,

"You say you love me, but you can go home to be with him. I don't understand why you are sitting here right now telling me that you can't do this anymore?" He looked at her hard like he dared her to tell him different. What she would tell him next would blow his mind; she had no doubt. She turned around to look him directly in his eyes,

"Let me explain this to you Malek, not that it even matters right now but the moment you walked back into my life, I knew I couldn't keep sitting with him; letting him just treat me any kind of way. So I gave him his walking papers. He had to go. He is gone. Now let me ask you, does she know how you really feel Malek? I may be wrong but if she knew how you really felt she would let you go."

Cara could feel the tears welling up in her eyes again. She refused to cry again so she inhaled deeply and wiped away her tears. Malek was quiet as he watched her. He didn't know what to say. Cara looked at the ceiling, she chanted in her head that she wasn't going to let the tears fall this time. After a few moments, Malek finally stood to his feet, grabbed his clothes from the floor and disappeared to the bathroom. He came out fifteen minutes later with blood shot red eyes. He picked his keys up off the end table and went to the door.

"You ready?"

She nodded. She stood there looking up at him, just like she had done when they were younger and together. He didn't know what to say if he couldn't tell her what she wanted to hear. He got lost in her beautiful eyes; like he had been in a trance he shook his head, and looked away.

"Cara, baby I wish this was simple."

She looked away from him as he opened the apartment door and then pointed his clicker at the truck to unlock its doors. Cara didn't say another word as she got inside his truck and looked out the window. It seemed like the longest ride as he took her back to her car outside the bar. She didn't look at him until he pulled up in the parking space behind her car. They both looked around before she got out. He said,

"I love you Cara."

He meant it from the bottom of his heart. He just didn't know what else he could do at that moment except tell her that he loved her. He had to be there for his children. He watched a single tear fall from her eyes as she said,

"I love you too Malek."

His heart ached as he watched her settle into her car. He didn't pull off until he watched her pull out of her space and turn left. He couldn't believe how the night had turned out, as he moved from the parking space and turned to the right in the opposite direction.

## *Back at the bar*

Shaia finished her drink and looked at her cousin who was grinning into the eyes of one of the men who had sent them drinks.

"So Shaia, what are you doing tonight?" Terra asked her cousin.

"Nothing," She responded.

"I am just going to get my things ready for work tomorrow, what about you?"

Shaia looked at her watch for the time and then she looked at her cousin. She almost laughed aloud at the men who seemed to be hypnotized by Terra's grey eyes. Shaia just shook her head and slid off the stool.

Terra pouted as if she had lost her best friend.

"I guess go home to an empty apartment, I have no work tomorrow." She confessed.

On cue, the guy asked Terra if he could take her out to eat. He had taken Terra's bait. She wanted him to ask her if he could take her out. Shaia smiled to herself, because her cousin is a true pro at getting what she wants out of men. Shaia leaned over to hug her cousin.

"Goodnight Terra. Text me when you get home." Shaia said and then she began to walk out of the bar.

Terra nodded, before she turned her attention to the man waiting for her she smiled at Shaia and then she said,

"Oh and congratulations on getting that ring cousin."

Shaia looked at the ring on her left hand then she looked at her cousin. She left the bar shaking her head. She didn't know what was going on in her other cousin's love life and she didn't plan to talk about it because she didn't know and she had her own relationship issues going on. She dialed two on her cell phone to speed dial her boyfriend of almost six years. Everybody called him Bo. She had met Bo while she and Cara were in college. He swept her right off her feet, when they first met. He is every woman's dream man that you read about or see in the movies.

The perfect gentleman who opens doors, sends flowers and candy to his woman just because. Bo did all that. He listened to her dreams, and she listened to his. They seemed like they were meant to be from the moment they met and decided to become a couple while they were in college and a year after, but in the last year Shaia wasn't so sure. Bo seemed to have changed since he had proposed to her. Shaia remembered his proposal like it was just yesterday. He had taken her to a nice restaurant on the outskirts of town. Once they were inside he led her to a small table that he had reserved for them. Shaia could smell the aroma of good food wafting from the kitchen. She inhaled with her eyes closed, when she opened her eyes a waiter stood at the table beside a four wheeled cart, covered with a white cloth. On top of the cart was a

bucket of ice which held a bottle of champagne, and beside the bucket were two champagne glasses.

*"Good afternoon, my name is Todd and I will be serving you this evening. Here are your menus, I will give you a few moments to decide what you would like to order and I will be right back." The young man gave them a polite smile and then left the table. Shaia looked at Bo, wondering what he was up to. He met her gaze and smiled making her blush. She loved his dimpled smile. He reached across the table for her hands, and then he examined her French manicured fingers and fingered the gold promise ring he had given her for Christmas.*

"You know you mean a lot to me girl. You have been by my side *when my dreams were just dreams. When I had nothing but those dreams in my head I had no clue how to make those dreams a reality you knew it, and you stuck by me. I thank you for that." Shaia whispered that he was welcome. She wondered why he was telling her this again. He never took for granted that she had stood by him, he lavished her with cards that said thank you, and gifts that said I love you. She knew he was thankful that she had stayed by his side. She stayed by his side because she loved him. "Lets look over this menu before Todd comes back, he may not be so polite if we make* him wait." Shaia glanced around to see if the waiter was anywhere near by. He was placing plates on a table near them and no doubt he would be coming to them next to take their order. She opened up the menu and at first sight she knew she had to order the chicken parmesan.

"I needn't look anymore I know exactly what I will have this evening." She smiled at Bo and he returned her smile, "See that's why I love you because you are not hard to please at all. I would do anything in the world to please you." He kissed her hand as Todd the

waiter returned to their table to take their order. Bo hadn't even opened his menu he ordered the same thing that Shaia ordered with two salads and a glass of water. "So tell me about your day." Shaia shared with him about the clients that she had met with and the plans she had finalized that day. He gave her his undivided attention as he always did and she loved him so much for that.

One day after dinner, Todd the waiter, boxed up the champagne, and Bo took Shaia to the newest club in the city that he happened to design. The club was appropriately called "Club Center Stage." When they were inside the club, she was surprised to see so many familiar faces of people that she had gone to college and high school with. She smiled and she waved as Bo led her to a tall bar table right beside a mini stage. "I am going to get you something to drink love. Sit tight." He kissed her cheek and then he disappeared to the bar which happened to be a platform like a stage. The bar was lit up with lights giving it such a beautiful effect that you instantly fell in love with the aura that it created.

A waitress with a tray propped on her shoulder stopped at her table to offer her a variety of alcoholic shots. Shaia chose two shots, she smiled at the waitress and she rocked on the bar stool to the music. The D.J. was definitely playing some hot records, she couldn't be still. Shaia didn't realize how much time had passed since Bo had disappeared to the bar, she was busy people watching and feeling the music.

Then she heard a familiar voice over the sound system. His voice came from the speakers in the walls of the club. His voice had a surround sound effect. Shaia looked around to

see if she could see him in the crowd. When she turned around, he was there, in front of her holding a microphone. The spotlight was now shining directly on him,

"Tonight, I wanted to have you good people here to witness me ask this woman," The club grew quiet as everyone listened as Bo began to pour out his heart.

"Today I asked you here to witness me asking this woman, who has listened to my dreams, has she held my hand while I cried, because I couldn't yet figure out how to make my dreams a reality. This woman encouraged me, and she stuck by me until my dreams became real." Shaia covered her mouth as she listened to the man she loved.

The spotlight was now on her.

"I invited you good people here tonight to witness me get on my knees and hear me tell this woman I love her." He handed the microphone to the guy standing next to him, and then he pulled a blue velvet box from his pocket and got down on one knee in front of her. Women in the club started to tell her to say yes aloud, then some people started to clap, because they knew what he was going to ask next.

"Nashaia Nicole Williams, I want to spend the rest of my life with you. I need you. I can't live without you. Baby I love you. Please marry me. Be my wife." Shaia didn't even look at the ring he was holding for her to see, she slid off of the bar stool and cried out yes as she wrapped her arms around his neck. He somehow, managed to slip the ring onto her finger. She could hardly steady her trembling hands, but once the ring was on the middle finger of her left hand Bo *lifted her off the floor. He looked deep into her hazel eyes and then he kissed her.*


*"You make me so happy baby." He whispered into her ear, Shaia looked around at all the people, who clapped and cheered. She was so happy that she wanted to cry. The D.J. congratulated Mr. Bryan "Bo" Oden, and Miss Shaia Williams. Then he spun a track that had been the first song they ever slow danced to. Shaia couldn't believe that Bo had remembered it. Then again, she knew she shouldn't be too surprised because he was the type of man that paid attention to details and that's why she had fallen in love with him to begin with. They spent two more hours at the club, and then they thanked everyone for coming. Bo led Shaia outside where a white limousine was parked at the curb in front of the club. A chauffeur opened the car limousine door. Shaia looked at Bo, he smiled.*

*"I love you girl." He professed once more. She squeezed his hand as she got inside the limo. There was a bucket of champagne waiting on the mini bar. Bo slid inside beside Shaia, and before he could say a word, Shaia sat in his lap and gave him a long hot kiss. His hands were on her body, touching and kneading. Their breathing became labored.*

*It was all they could do to pull away from each other when the limo came to a stop and the driver announced that they had arrived at their destination. The driver caught a glimpse of the heated passion through his rear view mirror while he drove. He exited the car after he parked and then he waited five minutes, to give them time to get themselves together.*


*Bo had the key card to the room in his wallet. He led her to one of the three elevators in the hotels' lobby. To Shaia the elevator ride to the twelfth floor of the hotel was the longest. As soon as they were inside with the door shut and locked. Bo unbuttoned the four buttons* on the grey coat dress that Shaia wore, he pushed it off her shoulders exposing her grey Victoria's secret strapless bra and matching lace thong. Still standing he kissed a trail of fiery kisses from her chin to her collarbone, and then back up to her throat then down to her heaving breasts. Shaia closed her eyes thinking about how happy she was.

"I am so happy baby." Shaia said as she wiped at her happy tears. Bo took her by the hand and led her to the large bathroom. She gasped, when she saw that there were candles lit surrounding the Jacuzzi and on the counter, red rose petals were floating across the top of the water in the Jacuzzi. She wondered when he called to get someone to set the bathroom up. He was such a romantic man, that is why she loved him so much she thought to herself.

He poured the champagne he had brought in from the limo into two champagne flutes that were on the bathroom counter. He poured champagne, while she kissed the sides of his face with love. He placed the glasses beside the Jacuzzi with in their reach and then he began to undress himself, never taking his eyes off Shaia. She closed her eyes as he skillfully unbuttoned her bra and with one finger slipped her thong off. Once completely undressed they got into the Jacuzzi, as Bo kissed her neck she let her head fall

back, not caring that her hair was going to get wet. He stopped kissing her long enough to reach for the champagne flutes, after he handed her one he said,

"Let's toast."

Shaia raised her glass.

"To us, today, tomorrow, and forever." They both tossed the champagne back. He quickly put the glasses to the side so that he could give her all of his attention. He massaged her arms, her butt, and her back as he kissed her. He made love to her breasts with his mouth. Then he made love to the rest of her body slowly, his future wife.

So much had changed soon after that night.

When she got home that night, she tiptoed into the bedroom because she could see that Bo, was already in bed.

"Hey. I tried to call to see if you wanted anything, but you have your phone off." She whispered. He didn't answer although he was looking directly at her. She kicked off her shoes, picked them up and stepped into the bathroom. She wasn't in the mood to try to guess what mood he was in. She decided to take a shower, hoping that maybe he would speak to her when she came out.

Tonight she didn't feel like debating with him at all. Lately, that is all he seemed to do. She stayed in the bathroom for an hour. When she came out, Bo was still laying still in bed. She wanted to go back into the bathroom, but even in the dark she could tell that he was watching her. She climbed into bed, and when she lay down he wrapped his arms around her. She inhaled softly and closed her eyes tight so that she would soon fall asleep.

The guy, from the bar took Terra to a steak house. She enjoyed his company, but he wasn't someone that could keep her attention. At the end of the dinner, she thanked him. He asked for her number, and she told him that she would take his. He knew then that she didn't intend to call him. He wasn't upset, he was glad to get away from boring and have dinner with a beautiful woman like Terra who didn't want anything from him. He dropped her off in front of the bar as she had insisted. He was mesmerized by the sway of her hips as she disappeared down the street.

Terra wanted him to watch her, she loved the attention so she made sure to put an extra but natural sway in her hips for his pleasure. When she got to her 2009 C-class Mercedes Coupe, she made a call. Dinner was okay because it was nice to get out with someone new, but she wasn't with whom she wanted to be with and nothing was nicer than that for her. Terra held her cell to her ear, waiting for him to pick up. All she got was his voicemail for the fifth time straight. She hadn't left any messages, so this time she decided to leave one. "Hey baby, I've been trying to reach you since my flight landed. I'm so ready to see you, so call me." She didn't want to sound whiny or desperate so she kept the message short and sweet. She thought now that she had confirmed that she was in town he would call as soon as he was free as he had promised to always do.

Terra decided to check in at the Pecan Tree Hotel and Suites so that she could take a long hot shower to take her mind off her mother. Her last photo shoot had been in her hometown of Florida, she hadn't been home to in several months and she wanted to surprise her mother. She talked to her mother almost daily but it wasn't the same as feeling her mothers arms wrapped around her.

Her flight was scheduled to leave in five hours, so she decided to spend a couple of hours at her childhood home. She stood outside of the small brick home that she had shared with her mother until she was twelve. It was eight a.m. so she was sure that her mother was still at home. Her car was still parked outside but as she stood outside her bedroom window tapping on it her mother wasn't answering. Terra looked around to see if any of her mothers neighbors were out, maybe she would ask them if they had seen her.

As she looked around she could see people peeping out their blinds and curtains, this pissed her off so she rolled her eyes and decided to call the house. She could hear the phone ringing inside. Pamela Williams still didn't answer.
Terra fought to keep the negative thoughts of her mother being inside sick or hurt and not able to answer the door off her mind. She swallowed the lump in her throat as she listened to her mother's voice on the outdated answering machine. When she heard the beep

signaling for her to leave her message she took a deep breath and spoke to her mother in a sing song voice.

*"Hey Mama, I came by to surprise you this morning. I just knew you were at home this early in the morning and you would cook me some your wonderful apple*

*pancakes. I been knocking for fifteen minutes, you aren't answering so I guess you have stepped out. I really wish you would get a cell phone so I can reach you wherever you are. I'm headed to Virginia now, I love you. I miss you. Call me when you get in."*

Terra sighed, as she pressed end on her cell phone. She reluctantly went back to her rental car. She sat in the driveway for ten more minutes then she started her car and drove away headed to the airport.

Pamela Williams sat inside the house with tears in her eyes wishing she had opened the door for her daughter as she pulled off. She held her grandson in her arms, he was sad she hugged him close.

When Terra got out of the shower, she felt so relaxed, even though her mother still hadn't called. She sighed as she lie down on the bed still wrapped in her towel, as soon as she closed her eyes she heard her phone go off. She had received a text message.

"Hey where are you?" Her heart skipped a beat as she was happy to finally hear from her lover. She messaged him her room number. His response was that she needed to get ready because he was on the road. Terra got up and started searching through her overnight back to find her favorite Vicky's secret body lotion to rub all over her body.

Fifteen minutes later, she was opening the door for her lover. He gave her a kiss that made her knees weak as he pulled the towel from her body, and then he started to take off his own clothes while he stared at her nakedness.

"You have been gone too long girl." Were the only words he said as he took off his boxers, opened his arms to her nodding at his member which was in full salute of her. She glided into his arms. He picked her up then and carried her a few steps to the king sized pillow top bed that the Pecan Tree Hotel and Suites provided them. He sexed her until they fell asleep. She snuggled up close to him listening to the rhythm of his heart while they slept.

# *Back to Reality*
## Malek

It was eleven o'clock at night when he received a call from home to grab some water from the Walgreen's. He had just made love to Cara and couldn't keep his mind on hardly anything else. She had looked so sad when she got out of his car. He wished that he could change things around. Things had gotten complicated so fast; he didn't know what to do.

He found the aisle that had the water and then he reached in the cooler beside the register for a mountain dew. After paying for the items he returned to his truck; as he stepped into the parking lot he thought he saw Cara pull into the parking lot. He needed to know that she was okay and he wanted to assure her that they would discuss everything later.

He started to ride by the car that looked like hers to make sure she was okay if it were her, but his phone vibrated in his pocket. He reached in his pocket pulled out his cell when he looked down at it "home" was displayed on the screen. Malek sighed as he took the call.

"Malek, where are you? I have been waiting for you to bring me some water all day and it doesn't make sense that I have had to wait all day." Sandra fussed at him without even giving him a chance to say hello.

"I will be there in a minute Sandra, do you or the kids need anything else?" He asked with a sigh.

"No, just bring me the water Malek." She griped and then she disconnected the call. He got into his truck and headed home forgetting that he had intended to check on Cara.

Ten minutes later he pulled into the driveway of the home he had shared for the last five years with his wife and kids he just sat in there for a few minutes to get his head together. He kept thinking about how Cara had said she didn't think she could do it anymore. He thought about everything that it meant wondering why it was getting so hard for her when she knew his situation. He wanted to talk some more, but he didn't know what to say. He put his head down on the steering wheel, cursing out loud because he couldn't believe he was in this situation. He opened his mountain dew and took a long gulp, when he glanced at the window he saw the curtain move. His wife was waiting. He took a deep breath and got the water from the passenger seat and then got out of the truck.

The front door opened before his foot touched the first step of the porch. There Sandra Duncan Jones, the woman he had given his last name stood with a pink scarf around her head and a long flowery robe.

"What took you so long?" She frowned as she took the case of water from his hand. She struggled with it but she didn't even stop fussing and he decided that he didn't even care that she was having a hard time with it.

Tonight he decided that he wasn't going to fuss with her. He peeped in on his son and daughter then went to his bedroom. Sandra was in the bathroom with the door shut. He got undressed then he got into bed pulling the covers up to his neck. He turned his back to the bathroom door, and stared at the wall; his mind on Cara and her sudden tears.

He couldn't stop thinking of her skin so soft, her eyes so expressive, her lips, and that smile before he told her why he hadn't been available. He felt himself getting a hard on, so he sat straight up in the bed, swung his long legs over the side to sit up, as Sandra came from the bathroom he was going to the kitchen. He knew Sandra would be upset that he wasn't in the bed beside her. He had come home for his kids and he thought that sleeping in the bed with Sandra would cause problems but his eight year old son asked him why he wasn't sleeping in the bedroom with his mother. He wanted to explain to his son that they were having problems and he wanted to sleep alone. He couldn't find it in his heart to tell that to his child when he had already slept in another house for three months.

He didn't really care that she would get upset tonight because Sandra was always upset about something so that wasn't anything new to him. He had a full workday ahead of him but sleep wouldn't find him until wee hours of the next morning because when he closed his eyes, all he could think about was Cara.

Malek wanted to call her to see if she had made it home safely, he could have kicked himself for letting her drive home after he knew she had been drinking. He sat on the edge of the bed he shared with his wife Sandra and he debated with himself on dialing Cara's cell number. He knew Sandra was possibly watching his every move and his relationship with Cara was something that he wanted to protect. No one would understand it, especially not Sandra. He lay down and looked up at the ceiling until he fell asleep, just as the sun peeped thru the clouds on Thursday morning.

# Cara

She sat in the Walgreen's parking lot, crying some more, the tears that she wouldn't allow to fall in front of him wouldn't stop falling now that she had left his side. She couldn't help thinking about how he didn't even bother to try to stop her when she told him she was ready to leave. It reminded her of the time that he didn't even bother to come to her side after she had lost their baby. Tonight he didn't even try to console her because when Mrs. Jones called he just had to get home.

Cara shook her head at herself because she knew that chances were always that he may go back home to his wife. The separation was only temporary until the man or woman who wanted the separation was able to obtain some papers from a lawyer stating otherwise. During their brief affair, a legal separation from his wife, was something they never discussed. She felt stupid because that should have been the first thing they discussed.

Cara dried her tears and when she looked out the window, she saw Malek leaving Walgreen's. He had his hands full with a case of water. She noticed when he paused at the sight of her car. It was unmistakably her in a black impala tinted up with custom rims.

She knew that he recognized her car, there wasn't one like hers anywhere around but he only paused for a moment in recognition and then he quickly walked into the direction of his truck with his cell phone at his ear. He didn't bother to see if she were okay. After seeing him she sat in the parking lot a little while longer crying until she couldn't cry anymore. She dried her face with a make up wipe from her purse then she left the parking lot, to head back to her apartment.

When she pulled into the apartment complex her cell phone started to ring. Her cell was in the passenger seat. She thought it could be Malek calling to make sure she were okay sadly that thought made her feel better. It wasn't Malek calling it was her cousin Shaia.

It was three a.m. Cara's heart thudded against her chest as she answered. She thought that something had to be wrong if her cousin was calling at this time of morning. She put the car in park and grabbed her phone.

"Hey, what's going on?" Cara held her breath as she waited for Shaia to answer. She even listened hard for background noise.

"Hey, I just needed to talk, what are you doing?" Shaia admitted. She had slipped out of bed to call her cousin. She lay in bed not able to sleep. Her mind was filled with thoughts of her predicament with Bo. Her mind was also boggled with thoughts of Malek and Cara.

"Girl you scared me. I was out. What's going on?" Cara chided as she grabbed her purse from the passenger seat as she got out of her car.

"You were on my mind real heavy. Couldn't stop thinking about you after you left with Malek." Shaia paused long enough to give Cara a chance to respond. She wanted to hear that Cara had only left to discuss a party or something with Malek. She

didn't want to hear that they just left together, just because. When Cara didn't respond she decided to try another approach to find out what was going on.

"I ran into Sandra the other day. You probably don't remember her from school because she moved a lot. She married Malek."

After a long pause, Cara responded.

"I know he's married okay. He just went back to her, he told me tonight." Cara had to say it aloud in order to start accepting it.

Shaia was relieved, that Cara wasn't in the dark about Malek's marriage, but then she wanted to let Cara know as much as she knew, incase Malek hadn't been honest with her about his situation.

"I saw her." Shaia paused to see allow Cara to say something, but she didn't say a word. Shaia continued,

"I saw his wife at the doctor's office. I was there because I missed my period. I needed to make sure the pregnancy test that I took wasn't false. I called Dr. Taylor and she worked me in."

"Okay." Cara listened hard now.

"Are you about to tell me that you are pregnant?" She asked.

Shaia touched her belly, and then she smiled.

"I am. I haven't told anyone. You know how the myth goes, don't go telling anyone until you pass your first trimester. That's not the reason why I am telling you this right now though." She confessed quietly when she heard Bo stirring in the bedroom.


Cara continued to listen as she kicked off her shoes and place her car keys and purse on the counter.

"Okay." She was becoming impatient with her cousin.

"I am not the only one pregnant Cara. Sandra Jones is too."

Cara almost dropped her cell phone. She needed to sit down. She fell back onto the chair.

"Really?" She asked in disbelief.

The tears started to form as she listened.

"Yeah, for sure I don't know if she has told anyone though because she was pretty upset when she left the office. Like she was in tears, and those tears didn't look like happy ones at all."

When Cara didn't say anything else, Shaia asked her if she was okay. When Cara didn't deny her relationship with Malek, Shaia knew something was going on and she didn't want to see her cousin hurt.

All Cara could say was wow. She had to get off the phone. She was glad that Shaia loved her enough to call her at three o'clock in the morning give her a heads up without asking a bunch of questions.

"I love you cuz, I am so sleepy right now. I can barely keep my eyes open." That was the only thing that she could think to say.

"Okay, I love you too. Good night." Shaia was unsure about getting off of the phone with Cara, but she let her get off the phone.

Cara placed her phone on the kitchen counter and then she took a long shower. When she lie down on her waterbed, she felt the effect of the alcohol she had consumed. She felt like she was floating on a river and she was thankful that she had made it home without incident. She was drunk and upset, not a good combination.

She and Malek had a history, but it was over. She had to get over it. She closed her eyes remembering the summer when she got prepared to go to college. She was so excited when she received her acceptance letter that she ran straight to Maleks house.

*She knocked on the door and when his mother opened the door for her, she gave his mother a hug,*

*"Hi Ms. Jones! Is Malek in his room?" She said excitedly.*

*Peggy Jones nodded her head, she was used to his sons girlfriend coming and going. She shook her head as she watched Cara run straight to Malek's bedroom.*

*"Malek guess what! Guess what?"*

*Cara all but jumped into Malek's arms. She shoved her college acceptance letter into his hands and she waited while he read.*

*Malek's older brother Keith had been playing Nintendo with him. He put the controller that he was holding down and then he stood to his feet. He brushed past his brother and Cara as he left the bedroom.*

*Malek swallowed the lump that had formed in his throat after he finished the letter and he gave her a hug. He already knew what the letter said, before she even gave it to him. He was truly happy for her, but he was sad at the same time.*

*Malek listened as she chattered nonstop about her plans and how she was going to spend the summer preparing for her freshman year. She had it all together.*

*"I can't wait. We can get an apartment together so we won't have to live on campus." Cara danced in front of him.*

*"I'm not going with you, Cara." He responded quietly. His response was so quiet, Cara had to ask him to repeat himself. She wasn't sure she had heard him right, but it sounded like he said that he wasn't coming with her.*

*"What do you mean?" She asked for clarity. She folded her arms against her chest and she looked him directly in his eyes.*

*"I missed deadlines Cara. I won't be going with you."*

*For months, she had brought him applications for scholarships and colleges. He had told her that he would fill them out, but they were all blank in his notebook just as blank as they were when she had brought them to him. She stood staring at him in disbelief with tears forming in her eyes.*

*"Don't look at me like that. You are going so you should be happy. I will get everything together so I can start spring semester." He tried to sound enthusiastic but he fell short.*

*"Promise me that you will do what you have to do Malek. We have to do this together." That day she knew that things would change between them and they did.*

*Malek's grandfather became sick and passed away, when it was time to send in his applications for spring entrance. That deadline passed him by again.*

.

The alarm clock went off on Cara's night stand at seven a.m. She was supposed to walk into her office at nine thirty a.m. She looked at ceiling knowing that she had a bad hangover and she wouldn't be able to get herself together to make it to work that morning. She still had so much on her mind. Her past with Malek and what she had allowed to happen in the present with Malek had kept her tossing and turning. For some odd reason A.J. "the boy next door" face kept popping into her head.

She closed her eyes and she asked herself how did she end up a mistress? The things that her mother and aunt had told her rung loudly in her head,

*"every woman deserves a man, who sends her flowers and cards with notes that say I love you, and hugs and kisses just because."*

What had she gained by silently agreeing to be there for Malek whenever he called when he couldn't do the same for her? She had gained nothing but a heart ache, the same kind of ache she endured throughout their relationship. She wanted more than that,

she knew that she deserved more than that. She sent a text to her assistant Margo and she sent the same text to Shaia.

*"I will be there at twelve guys. I don't have any meetings pressing until two. Thanks."*

Cara pulled her covers back up to her neck so that she could sleep for two more hours, and she hoped to sleep the hangover off, as well as the heartache.

### *Alone on a holiday*

*It was New Years Eve, and Cara was bringing it in alone. In a club full of people that she didn't know. Her boyfriend had chosen to spend another holiday with his family instead of her.*

*She was pissed when he didn't invite her to come with him to his moms house; even though his brothers and sisters would gather there with their significant other.*

*Cara had been sure that he would take her.*

*He showered at her apartment and then he dressed, grabbed the bottle of Alize that he had placed in her refrigerator to chill. When he came out of the bathroom, he kissed her on the cheek and left her standing at the door offering no invitation at all.*

*She didn't bother to ask him why he hadn't asked her if she wanted to come this time, she just went into her bathroom, looked in the mirror and she cried, as she looked at herself.*

*From the bathroom she could hear her answering machine answer a call from Shaia asking her what she was doing for the night. She felt like being alone. After two hours of wiping away tears, she sent Shaia a message letting her know she was on her way out. She didn't mention where or with whom. If her cousin knew she would definitely insist that she spend New Years with her. Cara did not feel like being a third wheel between Shaia and her man no matter how cool he was and how far they went back.*

*She dressed in a silver one shoulder blouse with a bow on the shoulder and black skin tight jeans with silver pumps. She wore big silver hoop earrings and silver bracelets.*

*She wore her hair pulled up with pins in the back and Shirley temple curls dangling around her face in the front. Before she walked out of the apartment to the waiting cab, her phone rang it was Terra.*

*"Heyyy, Cuz! Just checking on you. I wanted to see what you were up to tonight. I guess you are out celebrating," Terra paused,*

*"So, Happy New Year cousin! I love you, good night."*

*Cara listened. She thought to herself, no, I'm not out celebrating yet, but I'm on my way.*

*When Cara got to the club called, CLUB CENTER STAGE, she immediately fell in love with the vibe she got when she walked toward the club. Her future brother in law had done a good job on designing the newest club in the city.*

*She had hosted a few events there, since the club had opened, but nothing compared to what you felt when you entered the club on a Saturday night. There was a line wrapped around the building.*

*She was happy that she had brought the pass that one of the owners had given her. He had given her a VIP pass to get into the club whenever she wanted to without having to wait in line. She accepted the pass, thinking she may never get the chance to use it. Tonight ended up being the perfect opportunity.*

*The club heads who stood in line to get in, wondered who she was as she walked past them with the pass in her hand. She loved the attention. The bouncer checked her pass, gave her a brief search and then moved the velvet rope so she could step through. She blew the bouncer a kiss as he watched her walk past him.*

*"Damn you look good Ma." He winked at her.*

*She looked around the club, there were several small stages throughout the clubs perimeter. Each little stage, was surrounded by colorful lights. The walls had mirrors from floor to ceiling. Throughout the night, dancers would be spotlighted and shouted out by the deejay.*

*CLUB CENTER STAGE, had become the hottest spot to be on the weekends. It was also, undoubtedly, the hottest spot to be on this New Years Eve.*

*All eyes seemed to be on her as she went straight to the bar to order her favorite drink. Patron. She only sat at the bar long enough to down one drink, which made her feel good.*

She decided to order a double shot, before she stepped onto the dance floor. She danced, she sipped, and she hadn't thought about her troubled relationship with her boyfriend at all. Nor had she thought about the trouble that seemed to be brewing between her cousin and her fiancé.

Tonight was just what she needed. As she moved to the music, a guy who couldn't have been a day over twenty one, started moving with her. He was keeping up with her, she had to give him props because he could really dance.

She couldn't help but smile as she danced with him. She noticed a few young girls dancing near by start to mean mug her. She didn't care they could have him all to themselves after she danced the New Year in.

He was cute, with a baby face and wavy hair. She whispered in his ear during a slow song,

"So how old are you?"

"I'm twenty four ma." He didn't ask her how old she was. She really didn't care.

She thought she would have to slap him before the night was over because he felt so comfortable grabbing her butt as they danced. No matter how fast or how slow the song he found away to cop a feel. At eleven fifty eight the deejay started a countdown. He grabbed the microphone in front of him and yelled,

"Everybody raise your glasses up and countdown with me as we welcome this New Year right, get them glasses up now, ten, nine," The whole club counted down with him and started screaming and clapping when it was twelve a.m. The young boy hugged her tight and gave her a kiss on her neck, then he whispered in her ear,

" Happy New Year beautiful. I am headed to the bar next drink on me so what you drinking?"

She smiled lightly at him, he was cute, and she didn't want to hurt his feelings. She wouldn't be accepting his drink because she was about to get a cab home.

*"No thank you, I have had enough." He squeezed her hand as if he didn't want to leave her.*

*"I gotta go to the restroom." She said into his ear.*

*He looked at her as if he didn't believe her. She smiled and gave him a kiss on his neck and then she disappeared into the crowd. At four minutes after twelve she was getting into a cab headed home.*

# *Some things never change*

In the cab, was another passenger and she didn't care as long as she got home. The guy talking on his cell phone in the front seat sounded so familiar. She tried to get a better look at him but she couldn't see him. Finally she gave up on trying to see if it were him, she just called his name. When the man in the front seat turned around with his brows furrowed. When he recognized her he smiled. It was who she thought it was.

Malek Jones. Her ex-boyfriend.

She leaned closer to the front seat to get a better look at him. When the light turned green, the cab took off and she fell back against the seat; she hadn't realized that she was drunk, until she started giggling.

Malek told the person he was talking to on his cell that he had to go. He turned around in his seat to get a good look at her and told her to buckle her seatbelt. He asked the cab driver to stop at the next corner so he could get in the back seat, the cab driver didn't seem too happy to stop but he pulled over anyway. Malek slid into the back seat beside her and gave her a hug. As he hugged her, he could smell the alcohol on her breath.

"Wow, what is going on with you? It's been how many years since I seen you five and you drink now?"

"Something like that, and yeah. I'm a big girl." She answered with attitude.

He didn't respond because he wasn't sure how to respond. She studied his face. She noticed that he hadn't changed at all. His dreads had grown out longer, he had let his moustache and goatee get thick but he was still Malek.

Shortly after she came back from college, she had heard that he had gotten married. She had been a little hurt but mostly surprised that he had moved on without her.

She remembered the way they were as she leaned back against the seat looking at the scenery as they headed down the highway in the cab. Malek looked thoughtful as he spoke,

"I am headed back to my car can I go buy you some coffee to help sober you up a little. I don't want to see you riding like this." Cara just looked at him and then he gave him a simple nod. They rode in silence for a few more blocks and through a few more lights. When they stopped, Malek paid the cab driver and helped her from the cab. She still trusted him. He unlocked the doors on his truck and opened the door for her. She slid in. He slid in beside her and started the truck.

She looked at the side of his face, at his strong jaw line, at his dreads that he had started to grow after high school. She thought about how she used to caress the side of his face as he drove places and she was his passenger. She couldn't help reminiscing but now wasn't the time so she looked away. They pulled into Star bucks twenty four hour drive thru and he ordered a white mocha frappacino.

He had remembered her favorite star bucks drink. This made her smile.

They rode around in silence until he started asking questions,
"So, I guess whoever that guy is pissed you off enough that you decided to come out to celebrate alone."

Cara looked at him hard before she answered.
"You think you know me don't you?"

Her soon to be ex-boyfriend had pissed her off by not including her for the last time. Yes, that was the exact reason she had ended up in that club alone.

. "Yeah, Cara Williams I do know you. You haven't changed much."
He observed.

She didn't say another word.  He noticed her shivering, so he turned up the heat and then reached in his backseat for his coat. When he handed it to her, she put it on slowly and kept staring out the window the faint scent of cologne in his coat caressed her nose she inhaled, he smelled so good

"Do you want to talk about it Cara?"
What could she say, it was just as he had said, her boyfriend had hurt her enough that she went out to celebrate the New Year alone.

She was almost embarrassed when she looked at her phone and he
hadn't even called or sent a message to wish her a Happy New Year.
He didn't seem to wonder if she were alone. She started not to
respond but she wasn't mad at Malek, so why was she tripping on
him about to give him the silent treatment?
She looked at him and then answered,
"Not really. So tell me what has been going on with you. Shouldn't
you be at home?"
It was her turn to make him feel uncomfortable, she thought to
herself.

Malek looked at her like she had some nerve asking him that
question. He tapped the steering wheel, opting not to answer. He
didn't want to admit that he should have

been home with his family indeed. Instead he chose to work so that
he didn't have to spend with them.
"Shouldn't you be with your man? You're out here looking all sexy,
alone and drunk tonight, this guy that you call your boyfriend has
got issues if he found something else to do tonight."
Cara agreed, but she didn't agree out loud. She wasn't going to
discuss her boyfriend. She put her drink in his cup holder and turned
up the music. Old school music filled the truck and she wiggled in
her seat. She was moving to the music, but she also had to use the
restroom. Malek knew that wiggle, so he decided to pull up to his
apartment and let her use the restroom.
He and his brother rented a two bedroom townhouse on the
outskirts of town. He would spend time there before he went to his
second job, or just to have some time alone. He had spent a month
there recently. He needed the time away from the place he called
home. His brother did the same. It had turned into a good investment
for them both, even though his brother hardly ever spent time there.
When they got inside he flipped on lights, and told her where to find
the bathroom. She went through a bedroom that she assumed was

*his it had a big waterbed, a big flat screen television, small nightstand, dresser and a lamp. Those were the only pieces of furniture in the room.*

*She used the restroom and then she rinsed her mouth out with the Scope that was on the bathroom counter.*

*She found Malek in the living room sitting on a leather couch flipping thru channels on a huge flat screen television that was mounted on the wall. She looked around the bachelor pad before she sat down on the couch beside him.*

*"I can take you home now if you're ready to go."*

*He offered. He studied her face.*

*Her face hadn't changed since he had last seen her. He looked at her body, and could kick himself for getting turned on observing how she had filled out with luscious curves. She must still be cold, he noticed that her nipples protruded against her shirt and that she had goose pimples on her arms. He tore his eyes away, to listen to her, as she had gotten excited about a picture she saw on an end table.*

*"Oh my goodness, Now you must have hidden this picture from me. You and Keith looked like you could tear up the devil! How is your mom?"*

*"She is fine. She moved to Baltimore with my uncle, a few years ago. How is your family?" Their conversation had shifted to neutral and he was glad.*

*Before she could answer, the door opened. In walked Keith, his older brother holding his girlfriends hand. He did a double take when he saw Cara sitting on the couch beside his brother.*

*"Wow, Cara Williams! I haven't seen you in years. How have you been?"*

*He gave Cara a hug. Over her shoulder, he looked at his brother in question and surprise. Then he stepped back, looked her over quickly observing how much she had grown.*

Even though she had been his brother's girlfriend when they were kids, he noticed that she even more attractive than she had been when she was a teenager. The years had been good to her. He took his girlfriends hand in his again as he introduced her to Cara. "This is Michelle. Michelle this is Cara. You already met my big headed brother. It's good to see you." They disappeared into the second bedroom. Cara glanced at the clock. It was two a.m. Malek looked at his watch, like he had somewhere to go. He asked her again,

"Are you ready to leave?"

Cara shook her head.

"No, not really, but if you are, I'm ready."

He sensed then that she didn't want to go home. He decided it wouldn't hurt to keep her company.

"So what have you been up to?"

They talked two more hours and to him it felt just like the old days. Just like the old days, she fell asleep curled up next to him with her feet on his lap, and he fell asleep with his arm on her thighs listening to the soft sound of her breathing. It wasn't long before the sun came up. It was eight a.m. when his brother tapped his shoulder.

"What's going on bro? Do you have something you need to share?" At first Malek didn't know what his brother was talking about, but then he remembered the sleeping woman with her feet in his lap. He looked at the clock on the wall, and cursed to himself. He felt the need to explain,


"I met her in a cab this morning. She was drunk and I couldn't let her stay out there like that so I took her to my truck, bought her some coffee, she had to use the bathroom so, I stopped here. When she saw that picture she started talking about it asking about moms, that's when you came in."

Malek ran his hand over his dreads. He knew how it must have looked. His brother asked him again,

"So nothing happened?"

Keith looked at his brother in disbelief. He looked at how peacefully Cara was sleeping with her feet on his brothers' lap. He remembered how many times he had seen them in a chair like that when they were growing up. He remembered how much they had loved each other.

"Nothing happened bro; I just couldn't leave her out there alone to get taken advantage of. I swear nothing happened." Malek held up both of his hands like he was being arrested by the police. He felt guilty.

Keith nodded believing his brother.
"Let me know if you need anything."
Keith went back to the room where Michelle was waiting.
He knew about the problems that his brother had been having at home, he had promised his sister in law that he would make sure that Malek came back home to her

soon. Keith knew with Cara back in his brothers' life it would be a challenge, but he welcomed it. His life and relationships depended on his brothers'.

Malek shook Cara gently to wake her. She stretched, covered her mouth as she yawned then she looked around. She looked up into Malek's eyes and realized that she hadn't been having a crazy dream. She had been talking to her boyfriend from high school.

She sat up, the sun was lighting up the room. She covered her mouth to hide her morning breath as she asked him if she could use his bathroom. He nodded and watched her stand up to go. When she was out of the room Malek sat up on the couch and then he covered his face with both of his hands. The whole situation was all innocent, yet he knew he would have to cover it up because of who Cara had been in his life. He hated feeling like he couldn't tell the truth. It was really bothering him now.

When Cara came from the bathroom with a fresh face, he excused himself so he could go in and try to get his head together. When he came out, Cara offered him a smile.

"Thank you so much for looking out for me. I would've been okay but thank you for looking out. You didn't have to do that."

He had to look away to keep his mind off how good she looked to him at that moment. He looked at his feet so he could come up with something to say and all he could come up with was,

"You really don't need to do that again. You were not alright to be riding home in a cab alone. You should tell that guy that you are with goodbye if he makes you feel like that. He should have been with you, but that's all I am going to say about it. I need to

take you home now. If I take you home and he is there waiting for you I am going to have to tell him a little something myself."

She stood up, trying not to make this an awkward morning by asking him who he thought he was after the way he had treated her. She wouldn't be mad at her boyfriend and riding home in a cab alone if he was her man, she thought.

"Thank you Malek." She gave him a timid hug.

He was surprised, but he hugged her back.

He released her and then he took a deep breath as he grabbed his keys.

He really needed to take her home.

"If you ever need an event planned. We are at your service. She offered him a business card as she slid out of his truck when they reached her apartment.

"Every Occasion." He read the business card and then he nodded his head.

"Alright, I might do that."

He watched her unlock the door of her apartment. He realized that he was still sitting in the same parking space with the truck idling even after she had gone inside and closed the door behind her. He *sat there with her business card in his hand tapping it against the steering wheel. He looked at the card, and read it out loud it read. "Every Occasion, Owner and Event planner, Cara Danielle Williams. "We specialize in making sure that every occasion is an occasion no one will soon forget." On the back of the card it listed all the things they offered from photography for the event to catering. He remembered hearing her talk about owning her own business where she*

*would throw parties. He was proud of her because it looked like she had fulfilled her dream and she was successful at it. Malek slipped the card into his wallet and hoped that he ran into her again. Inside her apartment, she decided to take a shower so she took off her clothes and folded them on the bed. It had been an interesting New Years Eve and Day.*

# *Goodbye*
## Cara

Cara's boyfriend, Eric, didn't spend much time with her after New Years. It was early March, and time seemed to be going by fast. Eric claimed that he had been so consumed with his work, and helping his mom it was more convenient for him to stay at his moms; this was supposed to explain why he was never at his own apartment. He claimed that he didn't even have time to stay at his own apartment.

Cara didn't argue. She promised herself that she wouldn't keep stressing over him. She couldn't compete with his mom and whatever else he claimed he had going on in his life. In the back of her mind though she wondered how she went from competing with a mother, to competing with a wife that didn't know that she existed.

Malek had been sending her messages everyday, she messaged him back. He would call sometimes, and she would take a few minutes to speak to him. They were cool, so she didn't see any harm in that.

Cara was surprised one night, as she sat at her computer researching wedding dresses for her client, she received a message from Malek asking what she was doing. She answered that she was working on something for work. She asked him what was up. He asked her if she could come out. She wanted to know for what, and the answer she got in response shocked her, *"I need to see you."*

Cara knew of Sandra Jones he had told her about his children Miles and Mikayla Jones. She knew Malek Jones was the man she had loved since she was a teenager and

she had loved him from the top of his head to his toes. They had a past and she didn't think it was a good idea to see him.

She sat back in her chair after she saved her work on the computer. She thought maybe she was reading more into what was going on than what it was. Before she made up her mind about meeting Malek she called Shaia. She knew that her cousin would probably say that she was dumb for wanting to be in his presence. She would remind her of the miscarriage that she suffered and him not being there for her. She had forgiven him, and it was time to move on, were her feelings.

Cara decided no to mention that she was considering spending time with Malek.

*"Why do you need to see me?"* She sent a message back. As she waited for his response, she tried to reason with herself that it was all right for him to reach out to her.

Her cell phone rang. Shaia sounded like she was on the verge of a breakdown when she answered the phone.

"What's going on Shaia?"

Cara could hear the shakiness in her cousin's voice when she answered the phone.

"Bo was over here acting stupid tonight. He just started throwing all of his stuff around and breaking things he was talking about something that went wrong at the office."

Shaia looked around the living room at the desk that Bo had been designing his next project on; it had been destroyed. She told Cara that when she had come home, he wasn't there, but he had called as soon as she stepped foot inside of the apartment.

"Are you going to be okay do you want me to come over?"

"I'm okay, I just needed someone to talk to." Shaia admitted. Cara talked to her cousin until her voice was normal. She held the phone on her shoulder as she cleaned up the room as best as she could.

"I just gotta figure out how to help him." Shaia sounded confident. She probably sounded more confident than she felt.

"Do you need me to come over?" Cara offered again, she didn't know how she could help either, but she wanted to be there for her cousin if she needed her for anything at all. Shaia sighed as she looked around the room.

"No, you go do what you planned to do, you haven't told me what that is but, I hope you are safe, I love you cuzzo."

Cara disconnected the call after she told her cousin that she loved her too. She looked at her cell phone to see that she had received a message from Malek.

*"I'm stressed out. I need to see your smile."* This message made her smile.

She showered and then smoothed on her favorite Victoria's Secret lotion, she applied lip gloss, and let down her hair. She met Malek at his apartment. When they were face to face, he looked into her eyes and then he kissed her lips. The kiss took her breath away, and scrambled the thoughts in her brain. She couldn't think straight. She felt a stirring in the pit of her stomach, as she looked into his eyes when he pulled back he asked if he could kiss her again. She stepped back, her conscience telling her that she needed to go. They were still standing with their backs to the door. It seemed like they had been standing there forever when it had only been a couple of minutes.

"Are you okay Cara?"

She nodded. She was telling herself that she should have stayed home. Malek looked at his watch.

"Can you stay for a little while?"

She looked at her watch. It was nine p.m. She nodded again. He took her by the hand and began to walk towards one of the bedrooms. For a moment she wondered if Sandra wondered where her husband was at that moment. She wondered if Sandra knew why her husband was with another woman tonight. Malek led her by the hand to the bedroom, with the pretty comforter that she had admired the first time she had come to his apartment. Cara couldn't believe she was there at that moment, she knew she should get right back in her car and go home, but she didn't want to be alone. They sat down on the side of the bed, and he started kissing her. He kissed her face and then her neck. He found the tattoo of their babies name on her shoulder then he kissed it. Her conscience started to bug her, she thought to herself that she had to stop him because if he kept on kissing her there would be no turning back for sure.

She gently placed both of her hands on his chest pushing him back. He looked at her in question with those sex hooded eyes. He asked her in a breath if she were okay. She nodded,
"I think we should chill Malek, I didn't come to make out. I came to hang out. I don't even need to be here right now. Your wife," Cara paused. She wished that she hadn't come.

He didn't argue with her, he kissed her forehead and then he lay back on the bed, he propped up on his elbow and put his thumb to her lips. He just couldn't help himself he had to touch her. He was quiet she was the first to speak.
 "I don't want us to make a mistake that could mess up the rest of our lives you know?" He wanted to tell her that his life was already messed up so it wouldn't matter but he didn't say anything he only nodded. When he didn't answer her verbally she lie down beside him and snuggled up to him closely she looked directly into his eyes.
 "You said you left home, but you didn't tell me if you plan to go back."
He nodded again. He didn't have an answer. He couldn't focus on anything but her lips at that moment. He closed his eyes and then he told himself, that he wouldn't kiss her again. He looked at the ceiling,
 "I understand. You don't want things to get complicated. We both have too much to lose." She nodded in agreement. She could feel his hardness pressed against her side. She scooted away from him a little. When he realized that she had scooted away he leaned over on to her again putting all of his weight on her.
"Where do you think you are going Cara Danielle Williams?"
She faked a scream and told him away from him before her clothes fell off. She begged him to get up and go with her to the living room so that they could talk. He was reluctant, but he rolled away and followed her to the couch in the living room. She leaned against the cushion and put her feet in his lap.

"You want to touch, how about you massage my feet." She suggested with a smile.


He shook his head and started to work his magic on her feet. She was so thankful that she was able to pull away from this man. If they went there, she wouldn't be able to recover.

They spent the rest of the night talking about any and everything. They fell asleep again together on the couch. Keith found them there on the couch in the morning when he walked in.

He had to remind his brother that he was a grown ass married man. He had to remind him that he still had a wife. Maybe, they weren't good right now, but Cara wasn't worth losing the chance to get it right.

Later on that day, Keith paid his sister in law a visit at her job. She was a hotel manager at a middle budget hotel on the outskirts of town. He stood at the front desk while she was paged. He didn't know what he was going to say to her, but he needed to make her think about her marriage, because she would surely lose what she fought so hard to have if Cara stayed in Maleks face.

Sandra Jones came out wearing a simple red blazer and simple black slacks. She had her dull hair pulled up into a bun. She looked very plain, why would anyone want to be with a woman as dull as her he thought.

"What's happening sister in law?" He greeted her with a half smile, which was half genuine.

She rolled her eyes at the sound of his voice and then she looked at the man that stood, before her wearing a shit eating grin that made her want to slap him. She really


didn't see anything to grin about. When she didn't return his greeting and just looked at him like she couldn't stand the ground he walked on became serious.

"I just wanted to come by here to check up on you. I haven't seen you in a while. Is the family okay?"

She frowned at him, her red lipstick too red for her complexion. He had to look away to gather his thoughts.

"What do you want Keith. You know your brother is at that damn apartment the two of you share now and he has been for the last couple of months now. So what family are you asking about?" Her voice was dripping with disgust.

The way she continued to look at him made him wish he had thought a little harder about his approach before he came in to say anything to her.

"I am asking about the kids Sandra. I see my brother at the apartment yes, but I am talking about you and the kids Sandra. Why do you have to make things so difficult? How are my niece and nephew?" This is the reason why Malek had left home. He understood now more than before.

Sandra exhaled before she said another word. She gave the receptionist who seemed to be enjoying listening to her conversation a task to complete. The task required getting up from behind the desk and getting out of earshot.

The young woman obviously knew what she was doing and didn't look too happy about it. Sandra looked at the girls twisted up lips with a frown.

"Is there something wrong dear?"

She asked wishing the girl would say something fly. She would write her up for insubordination if she so much looked at her wrong. Sandra crossed her arms as the girl shook her head no and then walked away from the desk. She wasn't happy.

Keith put his hands in his pockets and pulled out his cell phone, he watched the girl swing her hips extra hard as she walked away. Sandra cleared her throat to get his attention.

"You know I am thinking about giving my mom a party for her fiftieth birthday and I need someone to take charge of it, found this little advertisement and I think that is the way I want to go."
He handed Sandra a neatly folded piece of newspaper. She frowned at him.
"Am I supposed to read this paper because I really don't have time."
Damn this woman is diffucult, he cussed to himself.
He shook his head and pointed to the advertisement that he was talking about,
"Every Occasion."
 Sandra looked at the paper wearing an even deeper frown.
"You know with your business etiquette and all I figure you could meet with them and get the ball rolling."
Sandra handed Keith the newspaper and started back behind the desk.
"You know your mother does not care for me, why don't you get Michelle to do it." She started looking at the computer's moniter, which showed reservations for the day.
Keith hated that she just wouldn't rise to the occasion and say that she would do it. That had to be the reason that his brother couldn't stay in the relationship with her.

"Michelle doesn't have time. I asked her already. I know you are just as busy, but I figure since you deal with business and you know the business side of things you can handle it. At least get the ball rolling for me. I need all the help I can get."
 Keith tried to give her the most pitiful look that he could give and after a few more minutes of convincing, Sandra finally agreed to set up a meeting at,
 "Every Occasion."
Keith gave her a business hug and told her he would come by to visit with the kids later that night. He had accomplished his first goal and he was satisfied with that.
When Cara got back to her apartment her soon to be ex-boyfriend was there as if he had been waiting. He was actually sitting on the

couch playing a video game at seven o'clock in the morning. He hadn't stopped in to see her for two weeks. He only bothered to call twice to check on her. As she set her keys on the kitchen counter she searched the fridge for a bottle of water. Eric was watching her.

"Well hey. Are we not speaking today?"

She wanted to ask him the same question, but she just shook her head. She had grown tired of his game and waved hello. He wasn't satisfied with that. He paused the game and got up to follow her to the bedroom. She thought she should tell him to get out because she was not in the mood for his mess.

"That's all I get a wave? No hug, no kiss? Just a wave? What's going on?"

Cara looked at him. She wanted to tell him he sounded pathetic. She wanted to remind him of all the days that he had walked in and just waved to her, then he was right back out the door. She looked in her drawer for her favorite pajamas.

"What do you want me to do Eric? I am tired of you treating me the way you do and I am tired of feeling like I have to jump through hoops to fit in with your family when I am with you, and I have made up my mind that I am done." She was going to get her locks, and security code changed soon, she knew this for sure.

He looked at her in disbelief when he reached for her hand she pulled away.

"We can't talk about it Cara?"

Cara could feel anger rising in her, she wanted to scream and curse at him from the top of her lungs, she wanted to jump on him and beat him down as if he was an intruder. When she opened her mouth to say something she heard her cell phone alerting her she had a message.

"I don't want to talk. Please leave and leave my key on the counter please and thank you."

She turned her back to him so that she could get her things ready for work. Eric just stood there looking at her like she had lost her mind.

He just couldn't wrap his head around the reason she was dismissing him.

"Is this about my mom stopping by Cara? A year we been together and today you tell me you are done without warning or did your bourgeoisie cousin tell you about that girl at the party, that wasn't nothing."

Cara was surprised with his line of questions especially when he asked her about some girl. She didn't want to tell him she didn't know what he was talking about so she played the role as if she knew. She would deal with her cousin and why she didn't tell her anything later.

"My cousin didn't have to tell me anything. You told on yourself that night. I am tired of playing this game with you, if you don't want to be with me why are you wasting my time? Go be with that woman." She said calmly.

Eric bit his bottom lip, he had feelings for Cara, but at this point in his life he wasn't thinking about settling down with one person. She would make a good wife one day but right now all he could label her as was a good friend.

"I'm wrong I apologize. You're right you don't deserve the way I been treating you."

Cara just stood there debating if she should even remind him of all the reasons she was telling him their relationship was over but doing so would drain so much of energy and after last night she knew she couldn't continue in this relationship, it wasn't going anywhere. She had finally talked to someone about their relationship and when she heard herself talking about it she really didn't need any advice she knew that she didn't belong in that relationship she knew she deserved so much better.

"I have a lot of work to get done today I really don't have the time to sit here and debate with you."

Eric nodded, took her apartment key off of his key ring, laid it on the bed. He didn't say anything as he walked out of the door. He didn't know what to say.

When he walked out the door her heart broke a little, but she decided that she would be okay. She was upset with her cousin for not telling her whatever it was she saw, so she called her up to find out exactly what it was.

"Hey." Shaia answered her cell phone on the first ring.

She was doing some research for a client and had been coming up on dead ends for the last hour and a half. She yawned glad for the break that the ringing cell phone was giving her.

"Hi, I just gave Eric the boot. Now why didn't you tell me about this girl that you saw?" Cara was trying to control her emotions by counting to ten in her head.

"What are you talking about?" Shaia had forgotten about the business party that she and Cara had attended.

"He mentioned that my bourgeoisie cousin told me about some chic. I have no idea what he is talking about but since he brought it up I played along. I want to know why my cousin didn't tell me about this female."

A bell went off in Shaia's head and then she remembered how in plain sight the woman that Eric had been with at the party grabbed his crotch and licked on his ear. Shaia saw it but she didn't say anything to her cousin because she didn't think it was her place. She knew it would sound bad if she said it like that, but it was the truth that's how she felt.

"O, I saw this female grabbing all up on him that night. You told me that you had plans to meet him so I didn't even feel right putting my two cents in."

Now it wasn't often that Shaia Williams didn't put her two cents in Cara didn't understand.

"How did he react? Did he push her away, did it look like he liked it? Where was I when all of this was going on?"

"You had your back to him, and he didn't push her away, he moved her hands. I didn't want to get in it."

Cara couldn't hide her anger any longer so she decided to get off the phone with her cousin before she said something hurtful that she couldn't take back.

"I cried on your shoulder about him not spending time with me, and you don't think I deserved to know that the woman that was standing by his side that night was feeling him up and he didn't do anything about it? Shaia, I really would have liked to know that. I would've felt that I should tell you if that was Bo. I would have made it my business to tell you, because I love you enough to worry about your feelings."

Cara pressed end on her cell phone and then she tossed it to the side. Tears flowed down her cheeks. She wished that she could call Malek right then and pour out her heart, but she didn't know if it was okay to call. She lie down in her bed and cried herself to sleep.

# *Dreams*
## Cara

Saturday morning, she woke up feeling a little better. She had decided that she needed to stay away from Malek especially since she was more vulnerable now that she had broken off her relationship with a man she thought she loved and that she thought he loved him back.

She got up from her bed, and reached for her cell phone which she had plugged up to charge on her night stand. She picked it up to turn it on and when she powered it she received a text from Malek that said good morning. She smiled but she was uncertain about her feelings at that moment. He had married someone else.

It was six a.m. she had a long day ahead of her. She would be directing a wedding that started at two p.m. and then at seven p.m. she would be hosting a retirement party. She and Shaia were going to meet their client at the church to get ready at eleven o'clock. She dressed comfortably in a rose colored coat dress that would match the bridesmaids' dresses. She also wore three inch red bottoms to match.

While she waited for Shaia to pick her up, she ate a piece of toast and an egg. She messaged Malek.

"Hi."

Before she could put the phone down he messaged her back,

"Sleepy head, you must be sleeping in today?"

She told him what her schedule was like and then she answered the door for her cousin. Her feelings were still hurt but they had a business to run so she had to suck it up. Shaia was dressed in a beige suit with a rose color blouse.

"I love those shoes. We need a day off so we can go shopping."

Shaia pointed at Cara's shoes she attempted conversation hoping that Cara hadn't been so upset about breaking up with Eric because he didn't know how to treat her instead of being so upset that she didn't get in her business. She grabbed a bottle of water.

"We should, let's do it soon, are you ready?"

Cara washed her plate, and then she grabbed her phone, Michael Kors bag and her car keys. She was acting so indifferent towards her cousin that before she could make her way to the door, Shaia was in tears.

"I apologize okay? I didn't want to see you hurt anymore than you already were over that asshole Eric okay, so I didn't tell you. Do you forgive me?"

Cara didn't know how to be upset with her cousin anymore upset so, she nodded.

"For the record, I don't care what it is, if you see something that may or may not affect me that has to do with me or someone I deal with, I need to know."

Shaia nodded then she opened her arms so that she could give her cousin a hug.

After the hugged they got into Shaia's truck and headed to Zion Hill Baptist church which was the church they had grown up in. It was where they had spent many a Sunday mornings at Sunday school, and at Wednesday night bible study.

The church had been renovated a few years ago. It was a whole lot bigger than it was when they were young girls. Cara felt like it was going to be the wedding of any bride's dreams. The church was decorated from top to bottom with the colors ivory and rose. It was beautiful, Cara couldn't help wishing that one day it would be her walking down the aisle to give the love of her life her heart forever, it hurt her that the love of her

life had already gotten married and pledged his life to someone else forever. She kept telling herself she wouldn't keep thinking about it as the guests begin to pack the sanctuary.

Cara put on a smile and thought only the duties she had to uphold in representation of "Every Occasion." As she watched the wedding party walk in she saw Malek walking in with one of the bridesmaids that she had met on several occasions when she met with the bride. She felt some type of way watching him with his arm entwined with hers. Malek hadn't told her that he was attending a wedding. She tried to remember the woman's name that stood beside him. She tried to remember if her name was Sandra Jones.

Cara tried her best to focus on the rest of the wedding. She could feel Malek looking in her direction, but she made sure not to look his way.  He looked so good with his dreads pulled back and tied neatly behind his head.  As she sneaked looks at him, she could feel her body reacting as she thought about the way he had made her feel just last night, then she felt dumb because after he left her side he probably went home to Mrs. Jones. The woman he had given his last name.

The bride and groom had decided to use a violinist to play the wedding march. The bride was so beautiful.  She walked on ivory petals and carried a bouquet of rose colored flowers that matched the dresses of her bridesmaid's, her dress ivory lace. Just to see her would bring tears to your eyes.

Cara watched the wedding and she secretly cried wishing that one day she walking down the aisle to meet her groom. She noticed her cousin Terra with the bride's

family. She also noticed Eric's sister sitting next to Terra. They acted like they had known each other forever. Smiling and hugging other family members of the bride that they hadn't seen in a long while, and mingling with the grooms family members.

Suddenly it all seemed to be too much going on, she was so ready for the wedding and the reception to be over, she wanted the whole day to be over. After the nuptials the wedding party took pictures, while Cara and Shaia got ready for the reception which would be held at the Coliseum. Margo and her friend Dana had also decorated the Coliseum from top to bottom, transforming the coliseum into what looked like a ballroom. The bride and groom arrived in a black limousine. The chauffer opened the door and the groom got out first to help his bride out. Love was so beautiful to observe.

The reception went on for nearly three hours. Cara and Shaia congratulated the bride and groom and were on their way to change for their next event when Terra came over to say hello.

"Hey girls, I didn't know that you guys were behind all this nice work. I know you are going to give me a discount on my wedding!" She looked at Eric's sister Nicole, who smiled tightly as she looked at Cara. Cara stared back.

"I'm sorry, Cara and Shaia this is one of my best friends Nicole. Nicole these are my cousins. We grew up in the same house when we were little so you may as well say these are my sisters."

Shaia had never met Nicole so she shook her hand and gave her a friendly smile while Cara just nodded and told Terra she had met Nicole before. Terra seemed a little surprised.

"We should get together soon because I am going out of town for a couple of weeks. I have a catalog to do."

Shaia told her that they were headed to their next event, and they probably wouldn't be done until late. Terra nodded, and then gave both of her cousins hugs. After saying goodbye, Cara had to tell Shaia that Nicole was Eric's sister. Shaia was surprised. She knew that Eric was extremely close to his family, she knew that Cara had spent a lot of time with his family.

"So why did she act like she had never met you?"

Shaia opened her car door.

"That's how his family is. That's what I put up with. I have been with Eric for a whole year now, and that's how his whole family acts."

Cara became frustrated just talking about it. Shaia shook her head.

"You are better than me cousin. I would have read that chick, his brothers and his sisters along time ago. I probably would read his mother too."

Cara just shook her head. She wasn't about to start worrying herself over Eric and his funny acting family again so she just looked in her purse to get out her cell phone. Before she could turn her phone on Cara looked up to see Erica come prancing over to the car.

"I'm sorry I feel so stupid for not saying anything, I didn't know that you and Eric had broken up until he brought some fake looking girl over to Mommy's house for dinner last weekend. Mommy was upset and she wants you to call her." Shaia looked at Cara waiting for her to respond. Cara looked at Erica, and she smiled,
"Really? Your Mommy wants me to call her? I was with your brother for a year, your Mommy never asked me to call her about anything. Your Mommy barely acknowledged me when I sat down at her table for Sunday dinner and I really doubt your Mommy has anything to say.
 "Excuse me, I need to take this."
Erica held her chest like, she was having a some type of problem.
 Cara turned her attention to her cell phone dismissing Erica as she had dismissed her many times before. Cara had two text messages. Shaia was so shocked she hadn't even cranked the car.
"What are we waiting on?"
Her only response was,
 "Damn."
Shaia cranked the car and then she looked in the rearview mirror to back out of the parking space.
Cara scrolled through her new messages. Both were from Malek.
*"What are you going to be doing tonight after work didn't expect to see you today. You looked so good all dressed up. My homeboy got hung over at the bachelor party last*

*night and couldn't come to the wedding so he asked me if I would escort his date for him. I am headed home to get changed."*
*"Maybe we can get together later."*
 She messaged him back.
"Call me after nine. I should be done."

She didn't know what she'd say to him when he called. She didn't know anything at that moment.

Shaia glanced at her cousin,

"Can you believe his sister had the nerve to come at you with that?"

"I believe it Cousin. I'm not surprised the least little bit."

The cousins were quiet the rest of the way to the Hotel.

At the Beltan Hotel, they changed clothes. Cara kicked off her red bottoms and slipped out of her dress, she slipped on a pair of black tights, a green sweater and a pair of sexy boots.

Everyone at the party would be laid back, and they expected Cara and Shaia to handle business, but to be laid back thus they wore laid back attire. Shaia dressed in a blue shirt dress and some boots. They made sure the Deejay was in place, spinning the records that were requested. They made sure that drinks flowed freely at the bar, and that the food was plenty. As they walked around making sure that everything was flowing the way they wanted it to, the evening couldn't get any worse for Cara.

Eric and the woman he was with at the business mingle had just walked in. The room seemed to get smaller. Eric didn't notice her as she floated through the room with a smile, he didn't notice her until the woman on his arm pointed her out.

"I have to go say something to her, this place is beautiful, I have been here before and it didn't look anything like this, wow." She exclaimed, like she was at some celebrity mansion.

He stood back watching as his date walked straight up to his ex girlfriend Cara.

The smile never left Cara's lips as she stood face to face with the woman who shared his bed now. He saw that Cara was a true business woman. Cara shook Stacy's hand, she thanked her and even gave her a business card. He watched Cara at work and he admired her. Stacy came back to his side, he dropped his eyes when Cara looked at him, he was sorry that he came.

Shaia was oblivious to Eric and his new girlfriend being in the room, she asked if Cara minded if she stayed at her apartment for the night. Cara wanted to say no because she wanted to be alone. Instead she told her that it would be fine. Before the evening was over Shaia got a call from Bo asking her if she was coming straight home she decided to go on home. When the event was over Shaia drove her home and then gave her a hug goodnight. As soon as she walked into her apartment her cell phone started vibrating in her hand, she looked and it was Malek calling. Just as she had asked him to call, at nine o'clock she looked at the time it was nine o'clock.

"Hey."

"Hey, can you meet me at my apartment in an hour?"
Cara knew that she shouldn't even give a second thought to spending more time with Malek. They had no future, especially while he had a wife, but she didn't want to be alone. Cara agreed to meet him at his apartment in an hour and a half and she would bring an extra set of clothes to change into.

When she pulled up to the apartment, he was waiting outside, leaning against his truck. She was tired and she wanted to go to sleep, but she greeted him with a smile, because she was sorta glad to see him. He looked into her eyes and saw that she was tired. he told her to take a shower and get comfortable.

"Malek, I didn't come to have a sleepover, I brought jeans and a sweater because I thought we were going out or something."
He reached out, put his hands on her shoulders and began to massage.

"I see that you're tired so why don't you go shower, throw on one of my t-shirts and lay back, lets chill for a little while."

He massaged her shoulders and it felt so good that her common sense seemed to leave her. Her brain was telling her that she could shower and chill at home, but her body wasn't hearing it.

She slowly went up the stairs and went into his bathroom to shower. Silly her, she forgot to ask for the shirt. She called his name, and as if he read her mind he told her that he was going down stairs and that the shirt would be on his bed. She turned off the water in the shower and then when she stepped out of the shower she stood in front of the

bathroom mirror. She sighed and then wrapped the towel that Malek had given her around her body as tight as she could get it.
  She tiptoed from the bathroom to his bed and slipped on his blue t-shirt and then she sat on the side of the bed waiting for him. When he came up to the room he had a blindfold in his hand. Cara looked at him like he was crazy.

  "Cara will you put this on I want to play a game."
He held a pink scarf up so that she could see it. She didn't have an answer, so he asked,
"Do you trust me?"
She nodded and let him tie the silk blind fold over her eyes. He made sure she couldn't see anything. He had to go back downstairs to the kitchen for the tray, so he told her to sit still while he went back downstairs. Cara sat still, with the blindfold covering her eyes. She lie down on his bed and she closed her eyes. Downstairs Malek grabbed the tray and he was headed upstairs to Cara when his cell phone started to ring. He placed the tray on the counter and then he pulled his cell phone from his pocket.
  "Home." was displayed on the screen.
He sighed. His wife had been calling him all day. She had been begging him to come home. When he asked her if the kids were okay, she said that they were. His next question of course was why did she need him to come home so bad then, all she did was say because I think we need to talk. He answered his phone,
"Aren't the kids in bed Sandra?"

Sandra expected that question from him, she wanted to remind him that he had forgot to call them to tell the kids goodnight.

"Ok, put them on the phone." He waited.

Sandra handed the phone first to Mikayla, who kept her father on the phone for ten minutes before she finally said goodnight. Then Miles took the phone from his little sister.

"Daddy when are you coming home?"

Malek hated to hear his son ask that question. He didn't have an answer for his son. He didn't know.

"I told your mama to bring you guys over tomorrow after church so we can play that new Madden."

Miles loved football, and he loved video games. Malek knew mentioning those two things would get his sons mind off of his question. Malek knew he was wrong, but what was really wrong was continuing to live with Sandra.

"O man! I am ready to play that!"

Miles was excited now. He told his mother while he had the phone that his dad was going to play Madden with him, she sighed. Malek hadn't answered the question.

Miles asked more questions about the video game then he told his father goodnight. He was super excited about seeing his father after church. Sandra was tired of Malek avoiding her question.

"Malek, you have been gone for a two months. Don't you think it is time for you to come back home to face your family?"


"Sandra, I keep telling you, I am not ready. I don't know when I will be ready, I don't know if I will ever be ready."

Malek tried not to sound harsh. He knew what her next question was going to be.

"What did I do to make you leave me and these kids?"


Sandra had asked that question every time she talked to him. She just couldn't figure it out. He could tell that she was crying and he didn't want to hear it tonight.

"Look we'll talk tomorrow alright Sandra?"

He disconnected the call before she could say anything else and he didn't even bother to day goodbye or good night. Twenty three minutes and fourteen seconds was how long he was on the phone. He left the phone on the counter and then he picked up the tray. He checked that the doors were locked and then he headed upstairs.

He peeped into the room before he entered. Cara was lying under the covers. He was a little disappointed to discover that she was sound asleep. He placed the tray of fruit on the dresser and then he lay on top of the covers beside her. He sighed, wishing that he hadn't picked up the phone. He closed his eyes. Some time during the night Malek wrapped his arms around Cara as she slept.

At four o'clock in the morning Cara opened her eyes, forgetting for a moment that she hadn't fallen asleep in her own bed but she had spent the night in Maleks bed. She heard unfamiliar voices when she looked beside her, Malek was looking back at her.

"I'm here baby, that's just my noisy brother and his girlfriend."

She closed her eyes and snuggled up even closer to him, he held her even tighter. He thought to himself that it felt so right for her to be there.

He got up at seven to cook her breakfast he was pouring orange juice into two glasses and placing a plate on a tray when his brother Keith came into the kitchen. His brother looked at him long and hard before he said anything. It seemed like he was trying to choose the right words to say. He folded his arms across his chest,

 "Malek what are you doing?"

Malek looked at his brother and then he answered simply,

 "Cooking breakfast. What are you hungry? Cause I didn't cook enough."

 His brother shook his head. "You know what I mean Malek. Is that your wife in there? Or is your wife at home with your kids wondering where you at right now?"

 Malek looked at the closed bedroom door, then he looked at his brother.

"Keith, what's up? You know that's not my wife in there. Are you playing my conscience right now?"

Keith looked offended.

"Do I need to? Who is that in there?"

Keith asked his brother again. When Malek didn't answer his brother sighed.

"Please don't tell me that's Cara in there man. You are messing up big time."

Malek got upset,

"What? I am messing up? Who are you Keith? You told me I messed up when I didn't go off to college and that I messed up when I didn't get married. So I got married

and you keep telling me every chance you get that I'm still messing up. Right now my big brother Keith I really don't want to hear that."

Malek picked up the tray of food and disappeared into the bedroom. He slid back into bed with Cara, to feed her breakfast in bed. Keith stood in the kitchen looking at nothing in particular he was just thinking that he didn't want to see his brother suffer from making bad decisions. In his opinion the relationship that Malek had had with Cara was definitely better left in the past. Malek had a decent family life and he didn't need to jeopardize it by chasing the past. Michelle heard the conversation when she walked in the kitchen she asked,

"Why are you riding your brother so hard?"

She knew it was all wrong, but she knew that Keith wasn't perfect and what was going on with his brother was none of his business.

"If someone was trying to get into our business like that you know you wouldn't have it."

She voiced her opinion, and of course Keith dismissed it and told her in so many words that it was family business and she needed to stay out of it. Since she had known Malek she had never seen him smile as much as he had been smiling since Cara had come back into his life. She had heard a little about Cara and their history, it was a true love story whether it was wrong or right.

While Keith and Michelle were in the kitchen having a quiet but heated debate about what they were doing, Malek carried the food back up to his room. He greeted Cara with a kiss on the forehead. Cara sighed and stretched.

"Its time for breakfast in bed,"

She looked at his sexy smile, and she remembered how she used to love it when she smiled at her.

"I bet you never had it like this."

She got up to wash her face, and hands.

She couldn't help thinking that what he assumed was sadly true. At twenty six she never had a man serve her breakfast in bed. True to his word, when she returned to the bed, he fed her French toast, eggs and turkey sausage. They ate off of the same plate, just like they used to do before he changed.

"I enjoy being around you Cara. You are a breath of fresh air, I feel like I haven't been breathing since we parted."

Cara didn't know what to say, she smiled. She was afraid to ruin the moment, speaking about the truth which was that he still had a family waiting at home for him to return, and that he would still be breathing fresh air if he hadn't switched up when she went to college.

He told her to go get dressed because he had a fun day planned.

"What? You have a day planned?"

She grabbed her tote bag from the side of the bed.

"Yes, I have planned a day for us. You wasting precious time girl."

She threw a pillow at him,

"Will we have to wear blindfolds?"

She said with smile. Malek shook his head no as he watched her gather her clothes and then disappear into his bathroom to take a shower.

He waited to take a shower after her, when he came out he wore just a pair of basketball shorts. Cara looked at his six pack abs and his well toned chest and couldn't tear her eyes away, she didn't notice him trying to hand her a pair of scissors. He grinned at her, she looked away embarrassed. She looked at him in question as he sat down beside her on the bed.
"What are these for?"
He pointed to his locs,
"I want you to cut my locs."
Cara frowned.
"Malek you have been growing these dreads since high school. Why would you just cut them now?"
He looked directly into her eyes,
"its time."
Cara slowly cut his locs. She remembered when he rocked a fade with his baby face. She had missed that face, although that face was in front of her right now. As she cut, she noticed his brows were thicker and his eyelashes were longer than she could remember. Those were features that she had fallen in love with when they met. Ten minutes later his locs lay on the floor at their feet. He gave her a quick kiss on the lips, and then went back into the bathroom.


When he came out she told him how good he looked. He had cut his hair into a fade, he wore blue khakis and a striped grey and blue button up shirt. When they walked out of the bedroom and into the living room, Keith and Michelle were sitting at the table. When Michelle looked up she dropped her spoon and cursed.
"Forgive me Lord. Wow."
Keith was sitting with his back to them, he turned around and almost choked on his orange juice. His brother and Cara looked like a picture they had taken in high school. Keith's conscience started to nag at him, when he saw his brother smile as he walked closely behind Cara.
"Lata ya'll."

Malek opened the front door, he used his clicker to unlock his truck doors. He took drove to the bowling alley in the next town a place where he didn't expect to run into anyone he knew. They had a ball. Laughing, joking and holding hands. They felt like two teenagers again.

As they were leaving Eric and Stacy walked into the bowling alley looking like the happiest couple, one would say the same thing about Cara and Malek, but everything isn't always the way it seems.

Eric had the nerve to speak to her. Stacy even waved.

Cara didn't part her lips to either one of them. Cara counted in her head how many times she and Eric had gone bowling together. She came up with none, because Eric had always acted like it was the most immature and inconvenient thing to do when they were together, but there he was holding hands with Stacy. Cara's feelings were hurt.

Malek noticed her mood change when they got to his truck, he was about to ask her what was the matter when his cell phone rang, it was Sandra Jones. Back to reality.

Mrs. Sandra Jones his wife was calling. His whole demeanor changed as he listened to her talking to him on the other end of the phone. Cara stared out the window, their day together was officially over.

After he ended the conversation with his wife, he asked Cara if she wanted to stop to get something to eat, she told him no. He noticed that she wasn't smiling anymore and she was staring out the window. He didn't know what to say so he just he apologized and squeezed her hand. When he pulled up to her car, they got out and he gave her one last hug,

"Call me later alright?"

Cara nodded then she pulled off, when she got to just down the street, while she was stopped at the stop sign when she reached inside of her purse in search of her cell phone. It wasn't there, then she remembered that she had left it on his night stand. She decided to turn around and go back for her phone, she knew that she was taking a chance going back to his apartment unannounced but it had been less than five minutes that she had pulled off.

When she pulled up to the townhouse she left her car running as she knocked on the door. She didn't intend to go inside she would just have him run in to get it while she waited.

Unexpectedly when he opened the door he pulled her in. He held the sides of her face while he kissed her right there in the front room. When he finally released her she

breathlessly told him that she had come back to get her cell phone. He seemed to be in a better mood then he was when he got off the phone with his wife just a few minutes before.

Malek playfully walked her to the room squeezing her butt thru the back pockets of her jeans and nibbling on her ear. When she got to his room she grabbed her phone, and turned around to tell him goodbye. When she turned around to go back to her car a white Honda Odyssey pull into the parking space directly beside her car and his, there was a woman driving the van. When the van came to a complete stop the vans back doors opened Cara could see the children unbuckling themselves so that they could get out.

Cara put her car in reverse, Malek kept his eyes on her as she backed out of the parking space and drove away. Sandra attempted to follow his eyes but Cara had already turned the corner by the time she looked in her direction.

Malek hugged his kids at the door. They greeted him then they followed him into the apartment with Sandra close behind. She could smell the light scent of perfume lingering in the air.

For a split second, she wondered if Malek had been seeing someone since he had moved out, but Keith came out of his bedroom looking like the cat that had swallowed the canary.

"Sandra you just missed Michelle."

The perfume must have been hers. She dismissed the question that had popped into her head, if there was someone else because Malek had become even more distant lately. He had told her that he needed some space a few months ago but she still hadn't figured out why.

Sandra had asked him what that meant, Malek's only answer was that he had some things he needed to sort out and he needed to do that in his own space. That night she watched her husband pack a rolling suitcase, and a carryon bag a few days later. What could she do? Her husband was leaving his two story four bedroom home with a state of the art gym built in his basement as well as a full basketball court on half of his back yard.

He was leaving all that to stay in a two bedroom townhouse with his brother, her first thought was another woman. She had called his brother Keith at his job the moment Malek put his bags in his truck and pulled out of the driveway. Keith assured her that it was just a phase that all men went through and she needed to respect his space. He promised to make sure her husband didn't stray to anyone else. She wasn't quite satisfied with Keith's promise, but again what could she do? Most women who loved their husbands would fight to make sure his bags never made it to the truck, but it felt like she had been fighting a losing battle for so long she had no more fight left.

### *Regret*

Cara drove home slow thinking how she had never intended to be a mistress, yet here she was allowing Malek to kiss her, and then feed her breakfast in bed. She didn't want to be alone, but she knew she didn't want to be his mistress.

He had told her that he was going to file for a legal separation from his wife. She wanted him to do that, if that is what he had planned to do before she walked back into his life. Cara was sure of that.

When she got to her apartment, she checked her messages. There were two messages from Shaia asking her where in the hell she had disappeared to and then there were messages from her mother. Her mother never left messages. She would always keep calling her until she reached her.

She called her mom, who picked up on the first ring. "Well its about time you called me back. Where in the world have you been?"

Cara sighed.

"Mama why didn't you call my cell phone, you know I always have it on me. Is everything okay?"

Felicia Williams stared out her front door at the kids playing in the street she had lived in the house that had belonged to her parents for almost twenty years and she had to admit she was amazed at how much time had changed that the children were always playing in the street. She shook her head because, her parents never allowed her to play near the street and she and her sister had never allowed their children to play in or near the street.

This day, people didn't seem to notice their kids were playing in the street. She closed her blinds and turned her attention back to her daughter.

"Your Aunt Pam has been trying to reach Terra. Have you heard from her?"

Cara looked in the refrigerator and grabbed her last bottle of water. "Mama, I saw Terra yesterday at the wedding I was directing. I think she said she was going to be going out of town for some catalog. Did Aunt Pam call her cell phone?"

Her cousin was almost thirty. It seemed that her Aunt and Mom would get used to her not calling.

"She did, I did. We can't reach her. Do you think Shaia has seen or talked to her?" It was strange that her mother was calling her to get in contact with Terra.

"I haven't talked to Shaia today either. Is Aunt Pam okay mama?" Cara had been meaning to call to check on her aunt, but she couldn't seem to find the time.

"She is okay as far as I know. You know how your aunt is. You know you girls really worry me, not keeping in contact with each other. Anything could happen. I know you all are grown now, but you need to do better. Call your Aunt Pam and let her know, do you have her number?"

Felicia started the water running in the kitchen sink over the dishes. She was disappointed that the kids she had helped to raise were not closer. She raised them just the way her mother and father had raised she and her sisters to be close. Shaia and Cara were close, but Terra had turned out to be just like her mother. She did her own thing.

"Yes mama. I will see if I can reach Terra. I love you."

After she disconnected the call with her mother she hit her cousin Terra up on speed dial. Her call went straight to voicemail twice. So she messaged her,

*"Hi Terra, Aunt Pam and my mom have been trying to reach you. Call home. I hope you are doing okay. Call me later."*

She tried to keep the message short and sweet. Before she could even speed dial Shaia, Terra had messaged her back.

*"Tell them I am fine. I have been so busy these people have been keeping me on my toes. I will call you all tomorrow."*

Cara called her Aunt Pam as she promised her mother that she would to let her know that Terra had messaged her and that she had responded that she would give her a call when she was free. Aunt Pam thanked her and asked her how she had been doing. Aunt Pam didn't sound as cheery as she always did when she spoke with her.

Cara started to feel guilty because she hadn't called her aunt in a while.

"I've been doing okay auntie. Busy as ever."

Her aunt had a coughing spell which alarmed her. After what seemed like ten minutes Pam stopped coughing and asked Cara about her boyfriend. Cara remembered calling her aunt when she and Eric had first gotten together. She had been so happy. Aunt Pam had warned her of a honey moon period, and sure enough the whole relationship changed in such a short period of time and she couldn't pin point what caused the change.

"I broke up with Eric."

There was silence on the other end of the phone.

"So how are you taking it honey?"

Aunt Pam listened to Cara as she told her how the relationship between her and Eric had changed. When Cara was done sharing her feelings her Aunt gave her advice that she wished she had asked for a long time ago, maybe she wouldn't be going through this right now.

"Well everything happens for a reason honey. You will meet the man for you and just keep in mind that all you went through with that Eric will let you know what you deserve. You deserve a man that will send you flowers, call you to tell you that he loves you. A man that will rub your feet after a long day and you won't even have the chance to ask."

Cara wished she could tell her aunt about Malek. She knew no one would understand that relationship so she quietly listened while thinking of how good it felt to have Malek's attention.

As if her aunt had read her thoughts from over the phone she told her,

"Don't be fooled if a man walks into your life promising to give you all that when he has someone behind him that he has done all that for and she is always waiting for his return. You deserve a man that is yours and only yours. I keep trying to tell that to that daughter of mine but,"

Aunt Pam had another coughing fit and managed to tell her between coughs that she would call to check on her soon.

Cara called her mother back and the first thing she asked her mother was her aunt Pam okay. When Felecia was slow to answer Cara thought the worst.

"Mama is something wrong with Aunt Pam? Please tell me. Is that the reason she is trying to reach Terra?"

Cara's heart began to beat fast against her chest as she pressed the cell phone close to her ear waiting for her mother to respond to her questions.

"Cara to be honest I really don't know. My sister says she is just getting over bronchitis, I haven't heard from her in months and suddenly today she calls having these coughing fits. I am worried about her, but you know how your aunt is, so all I can do is pray that she is okay."

After a few minutes of silence her mother asked,

"Cara, why don't you come to church with me on Sunday?"

Cara hadn't been to the church she had grown up attending with her mother and aunt since she were in college, going to church with her mother on Sunday would probably be good for her.

"Okay Mama, I'll be there, I love you."

Felicia told her only child that she loved her too after she thanked her for reaching out to her cousin. She was happy that her baby was coming to church on Sunday.

Later on that day Cara called Shaia.

"Let's close the office early on Friday so that we can catch up on some shopping and talking."

Cara hardly ever suggested that they take anytime off so Shaia was a little surprised when her cousin made the suggestion, but she agreed thinking that she could use some down time. After they went to the mall Shaia made a suggestion.

"Let's cook. We haven't got down in the kitchen in a while."
 Cara nodded in agreement. They put away their bags into a closet and then they went to the grocery store with their recipe in hand. Cara smiled at her cousin,
"Wow, I didn't know that I would enjoy you so much."
Cara had to admit that she missed spending time with her cousin. They were so occupied with their business, that outside of their little get together's at the bar on Wednesday nights were the only time they did spend together. Even then, most of their conversation was all about the business.

Cara started picking up fruit. Then she paused when she picked up a mango. Cara just stood there looking out the store window with the fruit in her hand. Shaia looked at her cousin with her arms folded. Wondering what she could be thinking.
A little girl no more than three years old came toddling around the corner. She was being chased, and she thought it was funny. Before Shaia could tell Cara to watch out she was knocked to the floor. It happened so fast Cara couldn't believe it, she scrambled to her feet, Malek gave her a hand.
 "Damn, I'm sorry."
He had knocked her down chasing his daughter. They got lost in each others eyes for a moment as he apologized.
 "I am so sorry, that little girl is so quick. Did I hurt you?"


Cara shook her head no, she was at a loss for words because she was surprised to see him. She looked around to see where the little girl had ended up. She was in the arms of a dark skinned woman who had short hair and dark brown eyes. She looked as if she were upset, as she put the little girl in the grocery cart. Malek finally left Cara's side after he nodded hello to Shaia. Shaia recognized the woman and said hello to her the woman waved her hand as if it pained her to do so. She chided the little girl and they walked away.

Shaia was the first to say anything.

"Damn, I didn't know he had married her."

She frowned like she had a bad taste in her mouth. All Cara could say was

"O."

She continued to pick up fruit, and her mood had changed completely after seeing Malek with his wife who now had a face and his children. Shaia noticed her mood change. She tried to lighten it, "You okay, you hit the floor kind of hard."

Shaia meant it as a joke but Cara didn't laugh. She knew something else was on her mind. She decided to leave it alone believing that she and Cara were close enough that Cara would talk to her when and if she wanted to about the Malek situation.

Shaia knew her cousin well so she knew that there was a situation from the moment he took the initiative to take her home from the bar a few months ago.

They continued to pick up everything that was in the recipe list for Jerk Chicken, Jamaican rice and beans and cabbage. When they were done, they ended up in the checkout line beside Malek and his family.

The grocery store couldn't seem any smaller when Bo, got into line behind Cara and Shaia. He had a case of beer and was going back in forth talking about a football game with A.J. a.ka. Ahmad, Margo's brother. Shaia just looked at Bo, he went on and on he hadn't even realized that she was standing behind him. She shook her head as people began to stare at him. He didn't mind that people stared. He kept on with his conversation.

Cara got his attention when she spoke over him,

"Hi Bo."

She smiled and waved also getting the attention of Malek who happened to be standing in the next check out line with his family. Malek tried to watch her discretely as he stood in line with his family.  Bo acknowledged Cara and when he noticed Shaia standing behind her with her arms folded he gave her a hug that made her wish everything were alright because she missed being in his arms. He released her and then he looked at the food in the cart.

"Are you bringing all that home? Your man is hungry. How about we all just go to the house and watch the game, have a bite to eat. Hey A.J. are you down for having dinner with us? What do you say Cara?"

Cara looked at her cousin's fiancée in surprise, from the corner of her eye she could see Malek looking at them and he wasn't being discreet at all as he showed an interest in what he was going on in the next checkout line.

"I don't know about all that Bo, we hadn't planned to go all out." Cara looked at the small bag of leg quarters that they had picked up knowing that that little bit probably wouldn't be enough.  Shaia hadn't said anything yet. The cashier started to ring up the groceries.

 "Come on girl, I picked up some leg quarters myself this morning I was going to throw them on the grill but I think I would like to have what you guys are putting together. I don't think your dude will mind that you having dinner at your cousins house. We all family." Bo looked at A.J. like there was some kind of message he should have gotten from what he said. A.J. looked at Cara shaking his head in amusement at Bo. He had only met Bo a few months before, they had been planning to do a project together, and from what he knew of Bo, he respected. He was a hard working individual and he didn't think he would be disappointed when he worked with him.

Before Cara or Shaia could object to cooking dinner for the two men Bo paid for the food, grabbed the bags and left Cara and A.J. at the check out looking at each other. While Shaia followed close behind him.

Cara looked at A.J. and he hunched his shoulders, and then smiled, "So how have you been Ms. Williams?"

She smiled at him as they shook hands.

"I've been fine, and you?"
They began to walk out of the grocery store side by side. Cara
looked back and caught Malek looking at her. He had a salty look on
his face, what could she say? She should be the one with a salty look
on his face at the moment because the last time they spent time
together he said that he was done with his wife, and a few weeks
later he dropped her off to her car, after telling her that he had gone
home to his wife and kids.
When he dropped her off that night he hadn't even looked back.
Cara acted like she didn't see him looking at her and she just kept
looking at A.J. as they walked out of the grocery store.
When they got to Bo and Shaia's apartment, they laughed and shared
memories of growing up in the neighborhood. Cara remembered
playing truth or dare with him and his best friend Tim.
She remembered her first kiss.
 She remembered the many days that A.J. had walked she and her
cousins to school, and the days when he had kept her company when
everyone else had things to do. When she thought about it A.J. had
always been there.
Dinner didn't turn out that bad. Bo and A.J. watched football while
Cara and Shaia followed the recipe for their dinner. Cara was
thinking of how Malek was looking at her and A.J. as they left the
grocery store, she wondered what he would have to say.
 Over dinner Cara learned that A.J. owned his own engineering
company in Georgia and he was looking to expand with another
company in Virginia. He talked

about putting his baby sister Margo through school. She also learned
that he had just bought his second home on the outskirts of town.
He mentioned that he was looking for someone to share it with.
When he said it his eyes lingered on Cara. She didn't even notice.

After dinner, A.J. sat back in the kitchen chair and rubbed his stomach.

"Ladies, ladies, dinner was wonderful. You should think about opening a restaurant."

Before Shaia could open her mouth to say anything, Bo was all over the comment.

"Yeah my baby can do a little something in the kitchen. She tries to hide it. She may be able to pull a restaurant off though."

A.J. nodded in agreement then he looked at his watch.

"I hate to eat and run but I promised my mom I would go to church with her tomorrow. I need to get home and get my stuff together." Cara looked at Shaia,

"We have to do the same thing. Does your mother still go to Zion Hill Baptist?" He nodded. Cara smiled,

"I guess we will see you there." He gave Shaia a hug and then he gave Cara a hug that lasted a little longer.

"I will have the contract ready for you to have your lawyer take a look at Monday afternoon Bo. I look forward to doing business with you."

He gave Bo a handshake. Then he remembered that he forgot to ask about Terra. "How is she?"

"She is doing well."

They caught him up on Terra and after a few more minutes they all looked at their watches. It was getting late.

Shaia said,

"Cara let me grab my keys so I can take you back to the house." Shaia went to get her keys. Ahmad offered to take her home since he was headed in that direction. Bo asked Cara if it were okay if Ahmad took her home.

He looked at Shaia like they had some making up to do. Shaia looked at her cousin for understanding because she really wanted to make up with her man. Cara told Ahmad that she was good with getting a ride home with him.

"I will see you at church tomorrow. Love you, I enjoyed you this weekend." Shaia gave her cousin a hug and then she followed A.J. out to his car. A.J. was driving a silver mustang. He opened the door for her, saw her in and shut the door. Then he ran around to the driver's side, and slid in the seat beside her.

He cranked up the car, and the sounds of jazz filled the air. He turned the sound down. Cara looked out the window. She gave him her address and when she gave it to him he remembered the side of town that the apartment complex was on because a friend of his used to live there when he was in college he pulled out from Shaia and Bo's apartment complex and then made his way toward Cara's apartment.

"You know my little sister thinks a lot of you and Shaia. I almost believe she wants to change her major so that she can go into business with you guys."

Cara was surprised because it was the first that she had ever heard of Margo wanting to change her major.

"Wow really?"

She looked at A.J. as he maneuvered his car through traffic which was relatively light for a Saturday evening.

"Yeah, I think she is afraid to tell me, I try to encourage her to follow her heart in whatever she chooses to do. If she doesn't want to do what I do then that's fine, I just want her to do something with herself, it's hard out here when you don't have that secondary education you know?"

Cara nodded in agreement, she saw how hard life could be without education could be when she helped her aunt at the Hope House.

"It's good that she has her big brothers' support."

He nodded.

"When our father passed away, Margo was only ten and me being seventeen I had to fill his shoes you know."

Cara nodded with understanding.

"She's a lucky girl."
They conversed a little more, when they pulled up to an ice cream shop just two blocks from Cara's apartment A.J. rubbed his belly while he stopped at a red light.
"You know what would hit the spot right now?"

Cara looked at him with a smile.
"What is that?"
He looked at the ice cream shop. She followed his eyes.
"Ice cream?"
He nodded.
"Yes, some ice cream would definitely complete that wonderful meal."
Cara nodded.
"So do you mind having some ice cream with me before I take you home?"
"No, I don't mind, some strawberry cheesecake ice cream would be good."
When the traffic light turned green, A.J. turned right into the parking lot of the ice cream shop. After he had parked, they both got out of his car and walked side by side to the shops door. A.J. pulled the door open allowing Cara to step in first, she unzipped her purse so that she could pull out her wallet.
"I got this."
A.J. ushered her to the counter and waited for her to order, he ordered a banana split. They sat at a little booth beside the window of the shop.
"It's been a minute since I had a banana split."
 He confessed as he licked his lips before he started to eat the sweet treat.
 "I remember you used to love banana splits, so how is it that you haven't had one in a while?"
 Cara remembered whenever her Aunt Connie made banana splits, she invited A.J. over to have some.

"I honestly haven't had much time to enjoy the things I love."
 The door of the shop opened and in walked two people that Cara thought she recognized from somewhere. The guy had his hands in the pockets of his jeans, he was looking down so Cara couldn't see his face that well. The woman that stood beside him looked directly into Cara's eyes and she put her hands to her mouth.
"Oh my gosh, Clara?"
Cara smiled, recognizing her childhood friend Erica.
"Hi!"
 The woman left the guys side and walked over to the booth where Cara and A.J. sat. Erica smiled,
"Oh my goodness! How have you been?"
 The guy at the counter finally wandered over to the table with his hands still in his pockets. He still looked like he was lost. A.J. put his spoon down.
"Tim?"
The guy looked up, and indeed A.J.'s best friend from elementary school.
"Man what's up!"
The two men gave each other a quick handshake and hug.
 "I lost you when you when you went back to college I heard you doing good right now, congratulations."
A.J. was humble.
"I'm doing alright man. So what's been going on?"


The two men fell into conversation as Cara and Erica did the same. Erica and Tim had planned to get married a month from that Saturday. Erica gave them an invitation that she had in her purse.
"Man, my best man is my brother, he has been complaining about how much money he has spent on his tuxedo, if it wasn't for his bitching you know I would have you as my best man."
 Again A.J. was humble.
"I appreciate that man, I'll be right there either way."

Tim nodded. He looked at Cara for the first time, he wouldn't accept her hand for a handshake, he had to hug her.

"How you doing girl, I'm glad Erica dragged me out the house for her craving tonight."

Erica rubbed her slightly, round stomach. She answered both A.J. and Cara's question by holding up four fingers to represent the number of months she was pregnant.

"Congratulations! Now you know Shaia and I have to throw you a baby shower."

Erica looked doubtful.

"I am sure Tim and I can't afford you guys, this wedding is really taking a lot, and this baby and Jr. they need everything,"

Before Erica could continue Tim answered another question by announcing that they had a three year old son.

"Nothing has gone as planned for us, its been crazy."

Erica tried to explain as if she were embarrassed. Cara didn't want her to feel like she had to explain anything about her life to her.

"Look, I am not one to judge, life happens you know. You have to make the best of it."

Cara offered Erica a warm smile hoping that she would stop explaining her life after high school to her. They sat down at the booth with Cara and A.J., and A.J. signaled for a waitress to come over to take Erica's order.

"Order whatever you like."

Erica didn't hesitate she picked up a menu and ordered her ice cream, A.J. gave the waitress a ten dollar bill and told her to keep the change. It was Tim's turn to be humble; he thanked A.J. The couples sat at the booth until Erica had finished her ice cream and then they said their goodbyes.

Erica gave Cara a long hug,

"It's so good to see you Cara, be sure to tell your cousins that I asked about them. Please call me tomorrow."

Cara nodded.

"Okay I will."
They went back to A.J.'s car.
"Wow."
A.J. looked sad all of a sudden.
"What's wrong?"
He shook his head from side to side,

"When my dad died I took it hard, my mom was able to keep things together but when his dad died everything fell apart for him and his family, and he suffered. I feel bad."
"What happened with Tim wasn't your fault, you shouldn't feel bad." Cara remembered that when he was younger A.J. always had great compassion for others, and as a grown man he still had that quality.
"He was my best friend, I can't help it."
A.J. cranked up his car, and looked in his rearview mirrors so that he could back out of the parking space.
"He still is your best friend, be there for him now."
They drove to her apartment in silence, jazz filled the space between them when he pulled up to her apartment, he parked the car and actually opened the door for her to get out. She smiled, thanked him and told her that she would see him at church in the morning.
He nodded, and stood outside the car while she went to her door, unlocked it and went inside. All she could think was what an interesting day it had been.
Shaia stood in the door until the tail lights of A.J.s car disappeared. When she turned around, Bo was standing behind her. She looked into his soft brown eyes, he opened his arms to give her a hug and she melted right into his strong arms and rested her head against his chest.


"I'm sorry how things have been lately babe. I've been stressed because I want to give you everything. I know you work hard and your business profits a lot but baby as your future husband I want to be the one to provide you with everything."

She had to tell him how she felt. She couldn't hold back because if she held back they may end up in the same situation down the road. She leaned back from his chest so that she could look directly into his eyes,

"Baby when I told you that I would marry you it was because we had talked about doing everything together. I know you want to give me everything. Right now you are giving enough with your love. When we aren't able to do things together, that's when I need you to step up and take care of everything on your own. Until that day comes I want us to continue to do everything together."

He heard everything she was saying he nodded.

"So when we go and pick out our house next week you don't want me to pick it out you want us to pick it out together?"

She nodded not catching onto what he had just said.

"When we sit down with the lawyer next week you want us to sit down together?"

She nodded again as she started to kiss the side of his face, his whiskers tickling her lips making her giggle.

"When we go to the bank to draw up the cashiers check for the closing on our house we going to the bank together?"

She nodded, as he kissed her neck and started to unbutton her silk polka dot shirt. He caressed her breasts and then started unzipping her jeans. It had been so long since he

had touched her like this, he could hardly contain himself as she pressed her now half naked body against his. He picked her up and walked her to the bedroom.

"I missed you baby. I missed you so much."

He began to confess and chant after each kiss and each caress until he was nestled deep inside her sugar walls, with her crying moaning in his ear.

After they lay spent on top of the bed, Shaia thought about what he had said to her about picking out a house and seeing a lawyer and then getting a cashiers' check from the bank.

"Baby, are you saying we are going to pick out our house next week?

He smiled at her and nodded. She squealed and then straddled him so that she could kiss his face. "I love you!" She cried over and over again as he held her close, and soon made love to her again.

## * Back Home*

The sun shone bright on Sunday morning. When Cara got out of bed, she could hear birds chirping outside her window. She stretched then she looked inside her closet. Today she was going to church with her cousin, aunt and mother.

She hadn't been in a while, but she knew nothing had changed. Pastor Williams was still preaching the good word every time he got behind the pulpit. She knew that the choir still sang so heavenly, she knew that everyone would welcome her with open arms. She felt good just thinking about being there.

Cara picked out a grey suit, and then she took a long shower. She put on her favorite lotion after she toweled off, she dressed and then she styled her hair. She messaged Shaia to let her know she wanted to get to church early. Shaia messaged her back that she would meet her at the house.

When Cara pulled up into the driveway, she sat inside her car for a few minutes just staring at the beautiful two story brick home she had grown up in. She remembered when Terra came to live with them, she remembered playing truth or dare in the back yard with her cousins and A.J. and his friend Tim.

She remembered when Malek would walk her home from the bus stop. Cara was in her own little world reminiscing when Shaia pulled her pearl white Mercedes jeep behind her car. She grabbed her purse and then got out.

Cara noticed that Shaia had a big smile on her face. Before she could ask her about her smile both their mothers came outside to greet them. They too, had big smiles on their faces as well.

Felicia looked at the two young women with tears in their eyes. "Just look how beautiful you are. Now if we could just get your cousin here, the Lord will have answered all of our prayers."

Connie nodded in agreement. They all got into Connies mini van and then headed to Zion Hill Baptist Church.

When they entered the Sanctuary of Zion Hill an usher seated them on the second row, they sat with both hands clasped atop their programs and bibles. Those that recognized Cara and Shaia stopped to hug them or kiss them on their cheeks. While some that weren't so sure who they were nodded to them or waved.

When service began, the choir brought the Sunday morning worshippers to their feet. Then Pastor Williams stepped into the pulpit. The man of the cloth hadn't aged a bit that Cara could remember. The only difference in him was the light sprinkling of gray hair atop his head.

 Pastor Williams preached the word and his message was, *"bringing lost sheep home."*

Cara and Shaia noticed the tears streaming down their mothers cheeks. They heard the message in the sermon, and they knew how much it meant that they were right beside their mothers on this Sunday. Cara decided that she would commit to coming to church with her mother and aunt every Sunday from that day forth.

After service, people came over to speak to Cara and Shaia. They all shared brief stories about watching them grow up, and then the conversation would turn to questions

about Terra. A.J. came over with his mother. His mother happened to be Pastor Williams Sister.

A.J. hugged each of the Williams women, as his mother asked how the boarding house and soup kitchen was faring. Connie shared how well she felt her business was doing and that she hoped to expand into a community center for youth by the years end.

Other members of the church who overheard the conversation started asking what they could do to help get the center open because the community really needed it. As they all stood talking about the centers, Pastor Williams came to hug Cara and Shaia.

 He held them both at arms length with Cara on his left and Shaia on his right.

"I haven't seen you ladies since your first semester of college. Your aunt and mother have shared that you ladies are doing very well with your business. You should share with me over a meal how you have been doing and what it is that you do. I have been talking with my nephew about how he has been doing today. I can't believe I haven't seen him since he went away to college either. I am so excited because you young people have really been doing well and I am mighty proud."

Shaia and Cara thanked Pastor Williams.

Felicia asked Pastor Williams if he wanted to come over to have Sunday dinner.

His sister, Sister Loretta Ealy didn't look like she liked the offer at all because she had also prepared Sunday dinner and her brother knew it. She was sure to remind him of how much she had cooked, and most of what she had cooked was food that he liked.

Connie saw the way Loretta was trying to keep her cool. She thought about being ugly about it but she decided to make it fair.

"If its okay with Sister Loretta, she can come over and have dinner with us."

At the mention of having Sister Loretta sitting down at their dinner table, Cara noticed her mothers face flush. If she could have turned red she would have been very red at that moment.

Pastor Williams rubbed his chin and then he said,

"Sister Felicia did you cook that good ole sweet potato pie? Sister Connie did you cook those good ole collard greens that would have the Pastor begging forgiveness for trying to eat the whole pot?"

Everybody couldn't help laughing. Felicia and Connie nodded that they had those items on the menu for Sunday Dinner.

The Pastor turned to his sister,

"Sis, I am going to have to have a seat at the Williams table this evening. It's a rare occasion to get invited and I hate to say that I won't come. I will be there as soon as the last worshippers have left the church." She nodded. A.J. asked if they could take dinner over to the soup kitchen. Everyone, even his mother agreed that it would be a good idea.

Shaia, Cara and A.J. followed his mother to her house. They helped her pack the food up so they could take it to the kitchen. They sat the food out in the dining hall of the building that her grandfather had bought for five dollars. Connie and Felicia had run the kitchen and boarding house for ten years.

To spend time there was very rewarding. Connie made it grow, by getting more support from other businesses in the community she was able to expand the kitchen and expand the boarding house.

As soon as they reached the kitchen Cara took off her suit jacket and slipped on her apron, she grabbed silverware and dinner plates to place at the end of the bar. While Shaia opened up the doors to let the first patrons in.

Back at the house, Pastor Williams was full. He pushed the chair back from the table so that he could stand and told Connie and Felicia that he needed to go for a walk around the neighborhood. "You are welcome to join me. I need to walk this food down." The women declined.

Sister Loretta helped them clear the table and load the dishwasher. She thanked them for inviting her over.

"Next time, you ladies come over to my kitchen and have some of my peach cobbler with my special homemade crust."

Connie nodded and she watched her sister with her tight lips nod as well. When Sister Loretta was out the door and at her car, Connie asked her sister why she had been so tight lipped when Loretta was around, she didn't say anything about it but she had noticed it.

Felicia's eyes filled with tears. She had never told anyone her secret and lately holding it in all these years had been getting the best of her. She was sure Loretta knew

because she was there eavesdropping that night that Felicia had never talked about. It was the night that had changed her whole life. She shook her head not wanting to talk about it, but Connie wouldn't let it go. She followed her sister to the living room.

"Felicia, we are almost fifty years old and so beyond secrets. Please tell me."

Felicia broke down in tears she sat in the recliner with her back to the door. Connie handed her sister some tissues.

"When mom and dad got sick I came home. The night I came home, I went to visit a friend. She wasn't at home, but her brother was there. He told me that I could wait for her, that she would be home soon. So I waited, for thirty minutes. I left her a note. I went to leave and her brother told me that I should wait, he was sure that his sister was on her way. I really wanted to see her because I hadn't seen her since high school."

Tears were falling so freely from Felicia's eyes that she couldn't see. She closed her eyes, as she continued.

"He started asking me questions, like where I was from, he told me that I looked so familiar. That I looked like this pretty girl that he used to date. We started conversing, and before I knew it, two more hours had passed. His sister hadn't shown up. I decided that I was just going to leave. Before I could leave, he touched my arm. I looked at him.

He had the most beautiful eyes. I got lost for a second before I knew it he was kissing me, and touching me and I didn't tell him to get off of me. My body betrayed me, the things he was doing to me felt so good. I had never just slept with a guy that I had just met. It happened, so fast."

Connie looked at her sister wondering what was so bad about that night that had her in tears.

"Okay Felicia, how did that night change your life? I don't understand why you are so upset."

Felicia looked at her sister wishing that she had been able to keep the secret a little while longer. She took a deep breath before she continued,

"He kissed me and we had sex. When it was over he told me. I wish I knew where I remembered you from."

Connie was quiet. She wasn't sure what Felicia was saying.

"I got dressed, and while I was getting dressed, Loretta started knocking on the door. She was mad, she was telling him that she knew that he had someone in there. He tried to make me go out the back door. I wouldn't. I put on my clothes, and I walked out the front door. Loretta frowned at me, she acted like she wanted to fight me. I wasn't going to fight her. But I wasn't going to let her beat me either, she called me all kinds of names. She told me that I was a hoe for sleeping with her man just like my sister."

Connie looked away. She thought about the guy that she had loved with all of her heart, who had the most beautiful eyes and had done things to her that made her lose her self control. Then she thought about how soon after she had become pregnant, with a little girl that had beautiful eyes. Like her father.

"Felicia, what is Cara's fathers name?"

Felicia shook her head that she didn't know while the tears fell from her eyes. Connie was upset and crying now.

"Why don't you know sis?"

When Felicia answered, they didn't hear the front door open.

"I found out that I was  pregnant a month after that. I figure that it had to be him. I tried to contact him. I tried to get Loretta to help me, but she swore she broke up with him that night and she didn't know how to reach him. I also, found out that the friend that I had ended up at the house to see that night had moved to California and she had moved almost a year before I came to look for her. He didn't even know how to reach her."

Connie shook her head from side to side.

"Felicia, do you know what this means?"

Felicia shook her head yes, she had tried to look at it differently over the years but it didn't change what truly was. Felicia dried her eyes and listened to what her sister thought was logical.

"Felicia, I think we ended up pregnant by the same man. I think Cara and Shaia are sisters."

Felicia fainted. A.J. was coming into the house, he saw her fall and without a second thought he rushed to her side.

"Cara, hurry get me some water or something."

Cara could barely move, she had overheard the conversation. Her feet felt like lead. She went to the kitchen, running past her aunt. She didn't know how to feel. Like a zombie she gave A.J. water for her mother, who was now in his arms.

Shaia was right behind them as they walked in the house, she had to have heard what Connie had said. Felicia came to, and promised A.J. that she was okay. Cara stared at her mother she remembered all the times she had asked where her father was and her mother telling her that she didn't know where he was.

"Mama, you really meant it when you said you didn't know where my father was. You don't know who he is?"

Everyone was quiet. They looked up when Shaia walked into the room with her arms crossed. She was upset.

"This is too much."

Tears fell from her eyes now. A.J. wanted to offer his words of encouragement, but he didn't know if he should open his mouth. After ten minutes of silence he broke it and said,

"I will ask my mother if she knows where he is. She may remember."

Everyone just looked at him. Cara was still in a daze as she walked to the door; she looked at the flowers that hung in baskets over the porch. A.J. followed her to the door and then touched her elbow to get her attention.

"Will you be okay?"

She nodded.

He tried to think of something to say that would change her mood. He hoped to get a small smile from her.

"Nothing much changes if you think about it, you are still family."

She simply nodded in agreement. A.J. looked at her sad eyes, and then he looked at his watch. He had an early meeting at work tomorrow it was important for him to be in attendance so he had to leave but when he looked at Cara standing there looking like she had lost her best friend, he didn't feel that he could leave just yet.

"I always wondered about my dad, I only asked my Mommy once or twice, and every time I asked it seemed to stress her out so I didn't ask anymore. Now I know why it stressed her out."
A.J. noticed tears streaming down Cara's cheeks as she admitted her thoughts to him. He didn't know what he could say that could help the hurt that Cara must have been feeling so he lightly rubbed her back.
"It's going to be alright Cara."
Cara nodded and then she looked at her mother who sat on the couch staring at the wall. Cara decided to sit down on the couch beside her. There was nothing else that he could say or do at that moment so he decided to go ahead and leave. Before leaving he said to Cara.
"Call me if you need me okay? Here take my number, if you just need to talk, you have my ear. I promise you I will ask my mother what she knows tonight."
She nodded. While handing him her cell phone so that he could put in his number into her contacts. Then he left.

Cara looked at her mother. She studied the gray baby hair at her temples, her small nose and her smooth brown skin. She remembered asking her mother time and time again about her father. Her mothers answer was always the same,
"I'm not sure where he is."
Now, Cara knew that her mother wasn't sure who her father was either. Felicia looked at her daughter. She looked directly into her

hazel eyes. "I'm sorry I never told you that I really didn't know who your father was Cara.

"I was ashamed to have gotten pregnant by a man that I knew nothing about. You know when you're young you don't give too much thought to the consequences of your actions, I am so guilty of just doing what I felt."

Felicia sighed, allowing warm tears to fall down her cheeks.

"I could have ended up in much worse shape than being pregnant. I could have gotten some disease that I couldn't get rid of, he could have been some crazy man that bashed my head in when we were done. That's why I tried so hard to get you to think differently. I wanted you to always be aware of consequences, because there are those after every action."

Cara nodded.

She gave her mother a hug, and told her that she loved her. She wanted to get home so that she could think because her thoughts were all over the place.

Shaia was upset because the man who was her father had never taken the time to see how she was doing in all of her twenty seven years, she was upset because her mother

had to raise her on her own all because her father was a coward and wouldn't own up to his responsibility to her.

Connie just went to her room and she shut her door. How could the man she had loved with all of her heart sleep with her sister and father her child. The news just wasn't easy to swallow.

When Cara got to her apartment, she wished that she had someone to talk to. It had been almost two months since she and Eric had been over. She couldn't call Malek, and her cousin Terra couldn't even be reached. She took a long hot shower and went straight to bed.

The next morning she went to work with everything that had happened on Sunday fresh on her mind. She handled her meetings with potential clients better than she thought she would considering everything that had been on her mind.

Two days later it was Wednesday and the office was only open for a half of a day, so that she could run errands for clients. It was twelve o'clock and Cara decided she needed to get some fresh air before she could start anything else.

Before she could go out of the office to get some fresh air, A.J. came waltzing in. He kissed his sister Margo on the cheek and then he handed Cara fresh flowers.

"Just the lady I wanted to see."

She accepted the flowers. She sniffed them and smiled.

"You didn't have to."

He straightened his tie.

"I wanted to. I got some news for you and your folks. Can we go out for lunch?"

She wasn't sure if she was ready to hear what he had to say, but she nodded and told Margo she would be back shortly. She had a meeting with a caterer at three p.m. Margo nodded okay, and watched her brother open the door for Cara, and then place his hand at the small of her back to lead her to his car.

Today, he drove his black Yukon Denali. When he opened the truck door the smell of new leather rushed to greet her. Cara inhaled as she sunk back into the passenger seat. He closed her door, and then got in on the drivers side. When he cranked up the truck, the smooth sounds of jazz filled the truck. Cara closed her eyes. She felt so at ease she was ready to relax her mind.

After hearing that she and the female she had grown up with, and had known as her first cousin all these years turned out to be her sister had been messing with her head.

She wasn't only bothered because she didn't know her father because he didn't care to know that she existed and the same pain fell on the shoulders of her closest friend, her cousin and now her sister.

Even though Shaia had taken two days off to get her head together she felt that her head was still spinning. She got out of her bed, showered, dressed and headed straight to her child home to see her mother.

Connie hadn't been able to rest since her sister shared her news either. She couldn't believe that Felicia had kept something like that from her for so long. When Felicia was pregnant, Connie would ask her who and how. Felicia would tell her that she didn't want to talk about it or him and she would change the subject or leave the room.

Now she knew why the secrecy. She believed her sister but for the last two nights a thought had been nagging her that she couldn't shake.

Maybe Felicia didn't know that she had had a one night stand with her nieces father, but then again after it happened, after she found out that his name was Deon Fletcher maybe she kept the secret all these years, because she found out who Deon Fletcher had been to Connie.

Those thoughts worried her so bad that she decided to confront her sister. She had to know what her sisters' truth was.

Connie looked at the clock on her night stand, she knew her sister would be on her way to work in an hour so she called her and asked her if she could come by on her way.

Connie dressed in black slacks and a sweater and then she went down stairs to start a pot of coffee while she waited for her younger sister to come over. Connie sat down at the kitchen table, drumming her fingers against it and looking at the clock on the wall. Twenty minutes later she heard the front door open, and she heard her sister calling to her from the living room.

"I'm in here."

Felicia came through the kitchen door dressed in bright pink printed scrubs; the beautiful colors boasted spring as it was indeed early spring, and everything was coming to life after a relatively cold winter.

The flowers that they had planted along the sidewalk that led to their front steps and the rose bushes that their father had planted for their mother were pretty and green. Soon they knew the roses would be ready to bloom.

Felicia looked in the refrigerator for apple juice. She reached into the cabinet for a glass, and while she poured her juice she looked at her sister sitting at the table with an empty coffee mug in front of her.

"Good Morning Connie, what did you have on your mind early this morning?"

It was a little after six a.m.

Connie didn't know where to begin, just last night she had it all together in her mind, but she didn't know what to say now that her sister was standing in front of her.

Connie sighed,

"I have had a lot on my mind since Sunday."

Felicia knew that soon there would be more questions about that night that she'd have to answer. She had thought about it non stop since she had gone home on Sunday night.

She waited for Connie's next statement or question. She leaned against the counter waiting.

"So did you know that Deon Fletcher was my ex?"

Connie couldn't hide the tears that had begun to form in her eyes. It hurt her to say his name.

Felicia had wanted to talk about this situation with someone for years. Her sister Pam was the only one who knew some of the story.

"I didn't know until Sunday. You know when you were with him, you never introduced him to us. I was off at school, I had never met him. You never talked about the ex that you got pregnant by. Do you remember how you used to act when someone asked you a question about him? You would go off like, you had lost your mind after you had Shaia. I promise, I didn't know that that man was your ex."

"Sis, you said that Loretta said something to you about being a ho, like your sister because she had walked in on the two of you. You didn't know then?"

Felicia shook her head, she put the glass of juice that she had poured down on the counter without taking a sip.

"No, how could I know? Loretta was always saying something negative about us because she couldn't stand us back then remember? I wasn't even paying attention to her when she said that. I just remember that she said it."

The coffee that Connie had poured in her mug had gotten cold. No more steam was rising from the mug as it sat untouched on the table in front of her. She remembered very well that she had kept Deon a secret from her family.

Her father didn't like him, and she didn't believe that he had given Deon a fair chance to represent himself. Her father had gone as far as forbidding her from seeing him. Connie was in college, she was over eighteen and she didn't believe her father had the right to do that. She crept around with Deon, going to the movies, out to eat and even to visit his family. Then she found out she was pregnant when she was in her last year of college.


She couldn't hide a baby from her father, because she still lived at home. When he found out that Deon was the father of her unborn child her father made it hard for her.

He took the keys to her car, he gave her a curfew, and he once again forbade her to see Deon Fletcher. She remembered when her father looked at her round belly when she was six months pregnant like he was disgusted as she helped her mother prepare Sunday dinner after church.

"Has that punk even bothered to ask you to marry him? Has he even offered to give you and his child a place to stay?"

She hated the way her father talked down about Deon, she wanted to get married to Deon just so that her father would stop putting him down. She knew Deon wasn't perfect. He wasn't in college and he still lived at home with his mother even though he was twenty one. Deon had had a few run-ins with the law; she didn't doubt that her father had gone as far as to have him investigated by some of his buddies.

Deon never had a chance to prove himself to her or her family. Connie didn't care about proof, all she knew is that he loved her and that she felt the same about him. Her heart was broken when she asked him if when she graduated, if they could move away together and he had told her that he couldn't. She didn't see that he was afraid, but she started to believe that he was a punk just like her father had said.

While Connie sat at the kitchen table reflecting, Felicia looked at her watch, her shift started at seven and she only had twenty minutes to get to work.

"Look, I gotta get going. I will talk to you more about this later but, please know that I wouldn't lie to you about Deon. I have no reason to lie." Felicia poured the apple

juice that she never drank into the sink and then she left the kitchen, a little aggravated by her sisters questions. She wondered if her sister thought she was so scandalous that she would sleep with someone knowing that he had lain down with her own sister.

Felicia hadn't been as close to Connie as she had been with Pam. Connie seemed to always be upset about something that no one else could understand, just as she seemed to be upset at that very moment.

A few minutes after Felicia had left, Shaia pulled up to her childhood home and let herself in with the key that each family member had a copy of.

"Mommy?"

She called as soon as she pushed the door open, she walked through the living room and the kitchen, Connie wasn't there so she went up the stairs. When she was outside of her mothers' room she peeped inside.

Her mother was standing in front of the dresser mirror fixing her hair. Shaia didn't waste anytime with her apology she pushed open the half closed door to step in her mother didn't stop grooming her hair as she looked at her daughters reflection in the mirror,

"Mama, I am so sorry I yelled in here the other day. I was just so hurt and confused that I didn't realize I was screaming until after I had but to know find out that my cousin all these years is actually my sister after all these years?"

Shaia looked at her mother, she couldn't hold back what she really had a problem with,

"Mommy what bothers me the most tho, is that you could have found out where my dad was all this time, and you didn't even bother."

Connie took a deep breath, everything about her relationship with Shaia's father had been complicated. She was ashamed because she hadn't tried a little harder to find Deon Fletcher, regardless of what anyone had to say, he was the father of her child and her child deserved to know her father.

Shaia sat down on the side of her mothers queen sized bed. The bed was as soft as she had remembered. She wanted to curl up and close her eyes but it was time to face the day.

"Shaia I'm sorry. I could have handled the situation a lot better than I did. I was so hurt and confused back then, I let my hurt feelings get in the way of making the best decisions for you, please forgive me." Connie sat down on the bed beside her only child.

"He was my boyfriend. I thought that he loved me. When I got pregnant with you it seemed like everything changed. After I had you even more changed and I was so hurt." Tears flowed freely from both of the womens' eyes.

Shaia had never seen her cry so she didn't know what to do. She reached for her mother's hand.

"I'm sorry."


Her mothers hand was soft in hers. They sat at the side of the bed holding each others hand for what seemed like hours before they moved to start the day. They finally went down the stairs.

Downstairs, Connie looked at her daughter and asked her why she hadn't gone to work that day.

"I need some time to myself. I was wondering if I could go to the kitchen with you take a little time to get my head together."

Shaia bit into an apple, and she played with her cell phone. Connie looked into the hazel eyes of her only child.

"So this is how you are going to deal with finding your father Shaia?"

Connie placed her hands on her shapely hips as she waited for her to answer. She looked at her daughter and wished that she had talked to her about men and relationships when she was younger, but she hadn't.

"What do you mean mama?"

Shaia looked at her mother. She wasn't sure how she wanted to deal with finding her father. That was the question she kept mulling over and over in her brain.

"He is your father, no matter what he did or didn't do. He made a mistake and he will be judged for that on judgment day. You shouldn't turn your back to him. I am mad with him I won't sit here and act like I'm not, but you know what I know I will be okay."

Shaia called Bo. Just as she thought he was upset because she hadn't called to let him know that she was okay and that she was visiting her mother. Sunday night he had held her tight when she needed to be held and listened to her as she needed someone to listen to her. She loved him for that.

"I am going to the boarding house and kitchen to help my mom today. I will see you as soon as I get home. I love you." Her heart melted when he told her that he loved her back. She got into her mothers jeep and they went to the kitchen.

By the end of the day, Shaia had done four more hairdos, and had four more hairdos scheduled at the end of the week, when she promised to come back. The residents were pleased with Miss Connie's daughter.

Cara couldn't help smiling as A.J. pulled a now and later form his pocket and gave it to her. He had just told her that his mother Loretta had revealed to him that the man that could be her father was locked up in a jail in Georgia. He had been there for ten years.

She wanted to tell her mother and aunt that she wanted to go to him. She wanted to have her lawyer set up DNA testing. She wanted to know the man who never knew she existed.

"Are you going to be okay?"

Cara looked at the now and later and at the sheet of paper that held the location of the man that could possibly be her father.

"I am. I want to thank you so much. You didn't have to go thru the trouble. We would have gotten something."

He nodded,

"Yeah, I know. I just wanted to make this part easy for you."

He pulled back up in front of the building of, "Every Occasion,"

He got out and opened Cara's door. He walked her back into her office, he squeezed her arm and told her that he would see her later.

Margo smiled at Cara like she knew a secret.

"Did I miss something?"

Cara asked her, as she picked up her memos and started toward the elevator.

"I didn't know you were the girl that my brother used to talk to and about when he was in high school."

Cara was surprised.

"I didn't know either."

She laughed, sniffing the watermelon now and later that A.J. had given her. Margo shook her head, with a smile. It was two thirty and Cara had thirty minutes before her next client. She looked at her phone when she got up to her office. She hadn't received any new messages. She called her mother at work; she worked as a part time charge nurse at the hospital.

"Hi mama, I found out where he is today."

## *Better late than never*

Felicia had to sit down, she very seldom sat down on her job unless she were talking to a patient and didn't want to overwhelm them by standing over them. She didn't know what to say.

"Where is he?"

She held her breath waiting for her daughter to tell her that maybe the man who had impregnated her sister wasn't the same man whom she had slept with. She could feel the palms of her hands sweating as she held the phone tight waiting for her daughter to say something else.

"His name is Deon Fletcher. He is serving a fifteen year sentence for aiding and abetting armed robbery. I am going to see him this weekend mama. I have to look him in the eyes."

Felicia covered her mouth with one hand as she listened to her daughter tell her how she had contacted her lawyer to draw up paternity papers that would force the man to take a DNA test in his cell.

Felicia had to get herself together, she was on the job and she still had four hours to go. She told Cara that she would speak with her about it when she got home. She took a deep breath to calm herself and then she went back to her job duties.

Saturday came quick for Cara. She had so many things on her mind that she didn't know if she were coming or going but she knew she had to get herself together.

A.J. checked on her everyday. Today he was coming to the prison with her for support. She needed it. Shaia couldn't come she had to host a retirement party. So, Cara

called her mother and her Aunt Connie. They were both nervous but they agreed that they needed to get it all over with.

The ride to the prison was long but A.J. drove unselfishly. When they pulled up the prison and got out of his truck A.J. stood behind the women as they went into the dreary looking prison to confront the man who had changed all of their lives.

They went through metal detectors and strip search and then they waited for almost two hours for visitation hours to begin. The buzzer wrung and they got in line to go beyond a huge grey metal door. Beyond the grey metal door were several tables and chairs. They were told to sit down as the inmates were led in. Cara watched each man as they came in and each inmate knew who was visiting them because they went straight to the table where the visitor was seated. The last inmate that was led in stood at the grey door looking around trying to find a face that he recognized, and when he looked in their direction, Connie covered her mouth to stifle her cry.

A.J. rubbed her shoulder.

Cara stood.

The man dressed in the royal blue jumpsuit stared in her direction. The guard said something to him and he slowly walked over. Cara didn't say anything as she handed him papers from her lawyer.


Connie looked at him; he was still ruggedly handsome with piercing hazel eyes, those hazel eyes that she had fallen in love with and the hazel eyes that her daughter and niece had inherited.

 Deon read the papers and he sat down with out a word. Everyone was quiet, waiting for someone to break the silence. Felicia looked at the man who had fathered her child, who was also the man that had fathered her sisters' child. He looked just as he did the night she had met him with more muscles and less hair.

He looked up from the papers. Then he sat back in the metal chair with his hands clasped on the table top. The two older women that stood on the opposite side of the table were indeed sisters. He couldn't believe that the story he had been told was that he was the father of two children by these women, but at the same time he knew that it was true.

 He had slept with both of the women, only one of them he had known and loved, while the other he had met briefly and by chance. Felicia wore her long hair in a single french braid while Connie had cut and colored her hair a light shade of brown. The younger woman who had yet to say anything after giving them the papers looked at him with piercing hazel eyes. He dropped his head.

"Look I did a lot of things I wasn't proud of years ago. I am sorry for any problems you are dealing with because of me. I am so sorry." Connie wanted to laugh then she wanted to cry or even get something to bash his head in. She had loved him, no matter all the negative things that the people in town had to say about him. She loved him and was willing to sacrifice everything she had for him.

He didn't give a damn about her or her feelings and he let her raise a child, his child on her own.

She was bitter. Connie was a few seconds from losing it she couldn't believe all he had to say was that he was sorry. She had her hands balled up into fists. A.J. didn't want her to get kicked out of the prison after coming all that way to see him. He rubbed her shoulder to get her to calm down and he asked her if she were okay.

"I'm sorry."

Those were the only words that he said, he started to say them over and over again as tears began to fall from his eyes and he began to ask the Lord for forgiveness.

Connie got up from the table and she went to the guard to ask him if she could please be let out. The door opened to let her out and it clanged as it shut. The whole scene had turned out to be too much for her.

Felicia looked at the man in front of her. She studied his face.

"I know it was many years ago and you were so young and foolish. Do you know you screwed over countless people with your actions and people are still affected by the foolish things you did. I know I didn't have to let you touch me. I was foolish for that and I don't know why I needed to come here to ask you if you remember me because it doesn't even matter. I just needed to look you in your eyes and I wanted to be here to support my daughter."

Felicia exhaled and kept her head held high.

"So will you take the test?"

Cara felt bad for the man. She felt bad for her mother because she literally got screwed but she felt bad for the man that could be her father because he was truly sorry for the things he had done and there was nothing he could do to change any of it, and no matter how strong he looked on the outside it was eating him up on the inside. He looked into her eyes, not even bothering to wipe away his tears, and he nodded.

"Yes I will. It mentions another person, are you Nashaia?"

He looked at A.J. He shook his head no and explained that he was a friend of the family.

"Shaia, had to work today."

Cara explained as she slid the folder across the table in front of her, she flipped through some papers and she pulled out Shaia's pictures. She had put in their baby pictures and recent pictures.

The grown man started bawling all over again. Over the chatters in the visitation room, you could hear his choked up sobs.

"I have to go. I need to go get on my knees right now. I am so sorry. Please tell her I am sorry. I am ashamed, because I stand here apologizing to you, having wronged you and I never knew your name."

He looked at Felicia, whose eyes were filled with tears now.

"My name is Felicia."

The hour and fifteen minutes for visitation went by fast, the buzzer went off to signal that it was over. The inmates were rounded up after they gave their loved ones one

last hug and goodbye and then when the doors clanged shut shutting the inmates in. The visitors got in line to go out a door that slid open to the outside.

The ride back to Virginia seemed much shorter than the ride to Georgia. The ride back was silent except for the soft sounds of jazz coming from the Bose speakers in the truck.

When A.J. pulled up to the house Connie and Felicia thanked him for the ride as he opened the door for them to get out. After they had gotten out of the truck Cara stayed behind.

She didn't know what to say or how to feel. She hadn't known who her dad was all twenty six years of her life, and now she was finding out that the man that is her cousins father is also hers. She just didn't know how to feel.

"Are you going to be alright?"

A.J. asked her. He knew she was sad, who wouldn't be after seeing the person who was supposed to always be there to guide and nurture her for life sitting in a prison cut off from the world. Cara nodded in response.

"Thank you so much for all of your help. Thank you I'm okay."

She smiled at him, and he nodded. He opened her door. When she slid out he had to hug her. When he hugged her he hugged her tight because he knew she needed it.

"Call me if you need me Cara."

He released her and watched her walk up the sidewalk and he watched her step up the three steps to the front door of her childhood home. He remembered watching her

take that same walk so many times before when they were kids. Who would have thought they would still be here right now almost fifteen years later.

He cranked up his truck to head home. Hoping that he could continue to help the Williams family some how.

Three weeks later it was Tim and Erica's wedding day. Cara was looking at herself in the mirror, she and Erica had gone to a boutique so that Cara could choose a dress that matched the colors of their wedding. While Cara tried on dresses, Erica sat outside the dressing room waiting.

"You know Cara, you and A.J. keep telling us you aren't a couple, but you sure act like a couple. Y'all are so cute together."

Cara just shook her head, she wasn't thinking about a relationship with anybody right now, although nothing was wrong with having A.J. as her man. She felt that she needed to guard her heart.
She ignored Erica's comment, she held the dress together as she stepped from behind the dressing room curtain,
"Can you zip me up please, thank you."
Cara stood in front of the mirror with a lavender gown that touched the top of her feet. She loved the way it hugged her curves.
"So what do you think?"
She asked Erica.
"I think its pretty, all the dresses you have tried on have been pretty and they have fit well so it all depends on you."

Cara shook her head from side to side,
"You are really, no help at all." They both laughed. Cara decided to get that dress and a matching pair of strappy heels. She decided to get a shawl too because although it was mid April, it was still cool outside.
"A.J. really is a good guy Cara."
Cara sighed as she and Erica walked back to her car.
"I know he is, but I'm just not ready for another relationship. I've dealt with a lot of mess this last year. I think I should chill out."
Erica noticed that Cara had begun to look aggravated, so she didn't say anything else about A.J.
Saturday just before the wedding, A.J. buzzed Cara outside of her apartment building, she looked at her monitor and then buzzed him in. When she opened the door for him he stood there with a single white rose;
"A rose for you, beautiful."
She smiled as she accepted the rose.
"Thank you handsome."
She grabbed her clutch from the end table beside the door and then she followed him out the door. When they got to the wedding the parking lot was already full, Cara saw a lot of faces that she

remembered from her old neighborhood and from school. This would be like a class reunion for them both.

As soon as they got out of the truck, people recognized A.J. and they came over to shake his hand, Cara stood close to him, as it would have been rude to walk away.

When they stepped into the church, A.J. placed his hand at the small of her back, and they walked in together. Tim stood at the alter; beside his brother and the preacher, he looked fairly, nervous.
He happened to look up as she and A.J. slid into their seats. A.J. nodded to his friend, Tim nodded back. The ceremony was beautiful. When it was time for the reception, Erica urged Cara to stand with the other single women who wanted to catch her bouquet, Cara didn't want to catch a bouquet but she didn't want to seem like she was sour so she stood there among the other women.
Erica purposely threw the bouquet right at Cara, who had no choice but to reach out and catch it to keep it from hitting her in the face. Some of the women congratulated her while others walked away from her not saying a word. Ironically A.J. ended up with the garter. Erica made it her business to grab Cara's hand and pull her over to A.J.,
"I want to be sure you dance, this first dance together."

She winked at them and then she seemed to glide into her husbands arms. A.J. shook his head, and then he looked down at Cara as they begun to dance to Keith Sweats,
"Make it last forever."
He whispered close to her ear,
"Thanks for coming out here with me."
She smiled up at him, and touched his neatly trimmed goatee and mustache with her fingertips as if noticing how clean cut he was for the first time.

"I was glad I could come." She admitted.

The D.J. played lots of old school joints taking everyone back to a place or a time in their lives when what they remembered was great, at least that is what kind of memories A.J. and Cara shared. As they danced together until the reception was over they noticed that they were among the only two couples left on the floor. The bride and groom sat at a table feeding each other cake.

A.J. loosened his grip on Cara's waist and he led her to where the newlywed couple sat and then he reached inside his tuxedo coat, he pulled out an envelope and handed it to them. Tim finished chewing before he asked what it was.

"Look in there man."

Tim opened the envelope slowly, and then he reached inside and pulled out two tickets. The tickets were for a honeymoon in the Bahamas, there was also a check for one thousand dollars. Tim almost dropped the envelope.

"I can't, we can't accept this."

He looked at Erica, she nodded in agreement.

"You are insulting us if you don't take it."

A.J. looked at Cara for help, she had booked the tickets and had contributed half of the thousand dollars. Tim shook his head,

"We can't pay you back man."

He looked sad.

"This is a gift from the both of us, gifts you don't have to pay back and you guys need this time together anyhow because I'm quite sure you won't have much time to enjoy each other once you have two little ones to care for."

Erica looked like she was considering it. Tim asked her to get up from his lap so that he could stand to his feet, he made a motion to embrace A.J.

"Thanks man. You don't know what this means to us."

He let A.J. go and then he hugged Cara.

"I need for y'all to go ahead and get married so that we can attend your wedding and then start welcoming some little ones."

A.J. just shook his head because he had told Tim time and time again over the last couple of weeks that he and Cara weren't together, it seemed like he had spent a lot of time telling him that he didn't like Cara as a girlfriend back when they were kids too.

Even though he kept saying that, Cara seemed to keep invading his thoughts. Cara smiled at both Erica and Tim not bothering to respond to what Tim had just said.

"Well you two newlyweds have a goodnight, we will be leaving you alone now."

A.J. gave Tim a handshake, and Erica hug, then they left the reception hall. Once in A.J.'s truck Cara thought out loud.

"I think they make a great couple."

She hoped that they're union would be blessed. A.J. agreed,

"They have always been good together."

It was five o'clock in the afternoon and she didn't have anything else planned for the day because she had taken the weekend off to attend the wedding. It wasn't often that she didn't have an event to host and as she thought about going home to her apartment and doing absolutely nothing she got excited.

"So what are you smiling about over there?"

"Going home and doing absolutely nothing is what I am smiling about."

A.J. nodded.

"Everybody needs that down time. I am heading back to Georgia, so I can get a head start on some projects."

"Well, I wish you had some down time this weekend. It seems like whenever I see you, you just got off of a job, taking a break from a job, or on your way to a job. You made time to attend your friends wedding and you made time to help me out with my dad I just want to say thank you."

"I would do it all again if I needed to and you have thanked me enough already Cara."

They rode the rest of the way to her apartment in silence. When they pulled up to her apartment he got out to open her door, and when she got out she gave him a hug, thank you was on the tip of her tongue and somehow he knew it because he put his index finger to his lips, kissed her forehead and told her to have a good night.

He watched her enter the building and when he was satisfied that she was safely inside of her apartment, he pulled out of the complex, content with the way his day had gone.

## *A change has come*

After the paternity test came back 99.9999% positive that he was both her father and Shaia's; Cara went to visit him every week. The ride was long but A.J. always volunteered to keep her company by riding with her. So, they rode.

They made a weekend of it, after visiting hours at the prison they would get a hotel room with double beds and they would sit up and eat pizza while playing cards until they fell asleep. Like the good ole days.

Shaia wasn't sure how she felt about having a father in prison that never took the time to check on her mother while she was pregnant. She wasn't ready to let go, of the fact that he had never been there for her or her mother. She hadn't visited him in prison once.

Cara had begged her to go him once or twice, but she was dead set against going to see him. She and Bo sat down to have dinner one night and he just asked her out of the sky blue, if he had gone to prison would she push their child to come visit. The question caught her off guard.

She looked at her fiancé like he had slapped her in the face.

"Bo, I have a relationship with you. You are right here with me right now when I go through my pregnancy I know you want leave me alone. This man didn't even check on my mom. When I was born he didn't even check on me."

Shaia was bitter. Bo didn't want to press the issue too much, but he thought about it and he felt that if he were in Deon Fletchers shoes he would want his child to sit down

in front of him once so that she could hear his side of the story. Bo reached across the table for Shaia's hand. She was fiddling.

"Baby there are two sides to every story and you have heard your mothers side, I think you should listen to your fathers side. It may make a difference in your feelings."

Shaia nodded just to get Bo to let the subject go. The rest of dinner they were quiet. Bo told her that she should go get out of her clothes, because he was going to run her a bath. He knew that a soak in the tub and a nice massage would ease her mind, and that is what that bath did. She kissed him and thanked him for being so wonderful. Earlier that week she and Bo had picked out a beautiful two story house that had five bedrooms and two and half baths. It was a lot of house Bo admitted but he was ready to fill it up. She couldn't wait to tell him that they would be turning one of those rooms into a nursery soon, while she was meeting with an interior decorator for the house she picked out things for a nursery.

Since she had found out she was pregnant she spent more and more time at the Hope House and kitchen with her mother. Being at the kitchen was rewarding and it made her so thankful everything that she had.

One afternoon Bo came to pick her up. He wanted to surprise her with a beautiful bracelet because he had landed another project and he was so excited that business had picked up so much. He took her to the restaurant where he had begun his proposal. They ordered the same dish and he ordered a bottle of champagne. Shaia looked at the champagne that he had poured into a flute for her. He lifted his glass for a toast and she lifted her glass of water.

Bo looked at her with his brows raised,
 "What's wrong babe. Want you toast with me."
She smiled.
 "I am toasting with you babe. I just can't drink that alcoholic beverage."
 He looked at her blankly for a moment. She just smiled.
"What you telling me Shaia?"
He sat straight up in his chair.
"Bo, I went to the doctor and I found out I am pregnant."
She smiled as she saw what she had she had just said begin to register in his brain what she had just said.  Bo leaned back and then he stood to his tall 6'2" height. He took Shaia by the hand and asked her to say that again.
"I'm pregnant baby."

He picked her up off of her feet and hugged her so tight. He yelled at the top of his lungs.

"Yes! Yes! My baby is having our baby."

He kissed her all over her face in the middle of the restaurant. People at nearby tables smiled at them, some clapped in congratulations. As Bo said over and over, I am going to be a daddy. Shaia had to pull back from his embrace to breathe, but she couldn't stop smiling because he was happy.

They sat back down, and Bo told her that he was the happiest man living.

"I can't wait to make you my wife and move into our home so we can make some more pretty babies."

It took a while for him to calm down. They left the restaurant and went home. When he sat down on the couch he pulled her gently onto his lap and then began to talk to her stomach, as if the baby inside could hear him. He rubbed her stomach and laughed to himself.

"Thank you Lord. I am going to take the best care of you. I love you."

She led him to their bedroom and to their bed. She missed him and she wanted to show him how much. She would share with him about how she had enjoyed working at the kitchen with her mother.

Bo helped her out of her clothes. When she was just in her panties and bra, he kissed her stomach that was slightly rounded with a hint of being full. He massaged her feet and caressed her calves and thighs.

He took a little extra time touching her, a little extra time kissing her just to show her how much she meant to him. When he finally made love to her he cradled her in his arms as he delivered each stroke with love. Shaia sighed and held on, glad that she had listened to Cara about fixing her relationship with her fiancé.

# *A name with the face*

It is a sunny afternoon at, "Every Occasion."

Margo has the afternoon off because they had expected the rest of the day to be fairly slow. Shaia sat at her desk flipping through a file while Cara talked on the phone with a potential client who wanted to come by to see where they were located.

Shaia ran to the door to let a delivery guy in with a bouquet of beautiful tropical flowers. She started grinning as she signed for the flowers.

"They are so pretty."

Cara nodded in agreement, as she talked with the client on the phone. Shaia sniffed the flowers then she looked at the card. The name that was written beautifully across the front of the card wasn't hers. She placed the flowers on the desk in front of Cara. Cara was surprised when she saw her name. She pulled the card off the arrangement so that she could read it and it simply read,

"Smile, you are beautiful,"

It was signed, by A.J.

Cara smiled as she sniffed the scent of the flowers as she walked the woman on the other end of the phone straight to the front door.

The woman wore a simple grey suit with a blue blouse; she also wore her hair in a loose bun atop of her head. Cara tried to remember where she had seen the woman before as she looked so familiar.

She asked the woman to have a seat at the desk so that they could begin the process of deciding what type of party to plan. The woman commented on how beautiful the flowers were, Cara thanked her and then she began asking her questions about the party.

"So Ms. Jones what type of party will we be helping you plan?"

The woman clasped her hands in her lap and looked at the wall like she was disinterested.

"It's a birthday party for my mother in law. She will be fifty."

Cara nodded, while jotting down the information.

"Do you know how many people you want to have come to her event and what type of décor interests you?"

The woman sighed, and shook her head as if she had done something all wrong. "I'm sorry. I don't know any of that. My brother in law just dumped this in my lap with no information. I am sorry to come in here wasting your time. I will make an appointment to come back when I know more. Thank you so much."

Cara looked up at the woman in confusion then she picked up a clipboard and a business card.

"What's your name ma am. I can set you up for an appointment whenever you are ready we have time to get it together so don't worry."

The woman smiled blankly and then she began to write her name at the top of the questionnaire. Cara looked at the woman's name and absentmindedly dropped her pen. She swallowed and then picked up the pen slowly.

"Sandra Jones."

The woman repeated her name with a smile.

"Fiftieth birthday party right?"

Cara tried to keep a smile as she continued to write.

"Yes, for my mother in law. Peggy Jones. She has two sons and two and a half grandchildren. She is really loved by her family and this is such a big deal I don't know if I am the one that should be putting this together."

Cara nodded and grabbed a bottle of water from Margo's stash in her desk.

"Two and a half grandkids huh?"

Cara remembered that Shaia had told her that she had seen Sandra Jones at the gynecologist office. The woman placed her hand on her stomach.

"Yes. I haven't told anyone yet."

Cara casually drank almost the whole bottle of water before she gave the woman an appointment card.

"Well I tell you what Mrs. Jones I will help you make this a very nice event for your mother in law."

Sandra Jones thanked her as she put the card in her wallet and then walked out the door.

Shaia had been watching her cousin from her desk. When the woman walked out the door she went over to where Cara stood to as if she were okay.

"Yeah, I guess I am alright."

Cara answered as she watched the woman drive away in a White Honda Odyssey. Cara had to sit down. She fanned herself.

"Cara what is going on?"

She looked at Shaia and she decided to tell her the whole truth and leave nothing out. When she was done she put her head down on Margo's desk.

"I am so embarrassed that I fell for that. How did she get pregnant if they were separated?"

Cara looked at Shaia like she expected her to have the answer to that question.

Shaia was a little surprised to hear that her cousin had fallen back into Malek's arms especially after all that had happened between them. After all that had happened he had ended up marrying someone else. Shaia sighed as she looked at the regret in her sister's eyes.

"Wow, sis."

Shaia laughed out loud as she listened to herself say sis, referring to a woman she had known as her cousin since they were kids.

"You haven't seen or heard from him in months. He told you the last time you saw him that he had gone home right? So bury all that, and move on."

As she sat at the desk getting a headache she had to admit what Shaia was saying to her made so much sense. She thought about how she hadn't been worried about Malek since he hadn't called.

She looked at the flowers sitting in front of her on the desk and she began to think to herself damn I really shouldn't be bothered about his wife coming into her business. They were done, and nothing else mattered. Cara nodded her head and exhaled, because the book of Malek and Cara had been closed.

"I guess I just have a hard time accepting the fact that we didn't get the chance to get anywhere together and all the attention he started to give me was the kind of attention I had always wanted from him and from Eric."

Shaia smiled as she stood too her feet and smelled the bouquet of fresh flowers on the desk.

"Now you must allow the man that is trying to shower you with all that love and attention that you yearned for a man to give you, give you that attention and forget about the ones that let you go."

Cara smiled, fingered the card with A.J.s signature on it.

"Thanks, Sis."

"Cara you should remember this too, you and Malek went as far as you were supposed to go, I believe the season came for you two and it went. The time you had was all it was supposed to be. You can't make it more than that, it's done."

Cara nodded as she looked into her sisters eyes. Cara took a deep breath to settle her case of nerves and then she started to gather her notes and the client folder that she had been working on before Sandra Jones had walked in.

"So, sis I am going for a visit tomorrow."

Cara didn't look up from the papers that she was gathering. Shaia nodded, she knew that Cara and A.J. had been visiting her father for the last month and a half. "Okay. Is he doing okay?"

She asked of the man that has been identified as her father. She still hadn't been to face him yet.

"He's okay. He asks about you every time I go. He wants to get to know you Shaia."

Shaia had been thinking about forging a relationship with the man who was her father. She hated that she had missed the time with him as a little girl. The piggy back rides, the first date talks and always feeling like, "daddy's little girl".

She had missed a lot. She rubbed her slightly swollen belly and vowed that she wouldn't allow her son or daughter to go without knowing what it was like to have a father in his or her life.

"I think I am ready to get to know him to."

Cara jumped up from the seat behind the desk to hug her sister. Shaia hugged her back. She had made up her mind that it was time to face him. She thought about what Bo had said to her, that there were two sides to every story, she was being unfair by not hearing Deon Fletchers side.

The next day was Saturday and Cara, A.J., Shaia and Bo were on their way to the grey and dismal prison in Georgia. Bo took the wheel while A.J. sat next Cara in the back seat. She had told him that he didn't have to come. He told her that he didn't mind accompanying her to see her father and to give his support to her and she was glad he was there.

She hadn't figured why he was always there, but she thanked him. He nodded that he heard her and he bit his tongue while he nodded because he wanted to tell her that he was right there for her as long as she needed him and he wasn't going anywhere. He wasn't sure that she was ready to hear that yet.

When they arrived at the prison, they went through search and security and then they waited until the heavy metal doors slid open, releasing Deon Fletcher into their presence for an hour and fifteen minutes.

Deon Fletcher looked just like the other inmates in his navy blue pants and shirt.

When he looked up, he wasn't just like the other inmates he was their father.

When the guard released him from the hand cuffs so that he could embrace his daughter he stretched and wrapped his big arms around Cara. He had only glanced Shaia, he wasn't expecting her to come to see him since she hadn't been yet.

All he had were her letters of question and hurt because he had been absent from her life. Cara embraced her father and she whispered into his ear as they embraced.

"She finally came."

He looked up and into Shaia's hazel eyes. Both of their eyes filled with tears and he opened his arms to embrace her. Cara tried to move but he wouldn't let her go. He hugged them both. He hugged them tight, and Shaia didn't want him to let her go. He kissed her on the top of her head. He whispered to himself with his eyes turned toward the heavens.

"Thank You Lord. Both of my girls are here."

When they all settled down at the picnic like table, Shaia introduced her future husband. Bo stood and he shook Mr. Fletcher's hand. He thought to himself that there was definitely no denying that the three of them were from the same family as there was a strong resemblance between them.


Shaia spoke to her father for the first time, he held her hand and didn't flinch when she asked why he had stayed away even after she was born. She had never understood because she felt like nothing in this world could keep her from her child except death.

Deon Fletcher had prayed about it again and again whether or not he should tell his daughter and her mother that he had stayed away because he had been threatened by someone they loved dearly.

"Lord forgive me if I am wrong for telling you this right now. I understand that your grandfather has passed away and he isn't here to defend himself. I don't know if he ever intended to say anything even if word ever got out about his role in my time in prison,"

"He told me that he was owed a favor by the D.A. who had been assigned to my case. He told me he would make sure I spent the rest of my life in prison if I ever came near his daughter again. Connie begged me to come to a Drs. Appointment with her, and I didn't have it in my heart to tell her no,"

He paused as he pulled an old piece of paper from his shirt pocket. He passed it to Shaia.

She slowly opened the piece of paper and then she saw that it was an ultrasound photo. It was dated a couple of months before she was born and it also had her mothers name and medical record number on the side She had no doubt that the photo was real as she held it close to her heart, she listened intently to her father.

"I went to that appointment with your mother and I listened to your heart beat and I saw your little body on that screen. That day changed my life. I don't know how but your grandfather found out. I got picked up a few days later, and I was extradited to Florida. I couldn't understand why because I had never been to Florida. So how would someone have anything on me in Florida? I stayed locked up in Florida for two months, they brought me back to Virginia, and they couldn't hold me on those bogus charges."
He looked hurt as she continued his recollection of everything that had happened. He never stopped looking into his daughters' eyes.
"When I came back to Virginia and tried to see you because you were born a week before I was brought back, your mother threatened to press charges against me if I came near her or you and I was already in enough trouble so I stayed away. I sent pampers, money and clothes. Your grand dad sent all of it back.  I kept doing it though, and I did this for a year,"
 "Your mother wouldn't have anything to do with me and it hurt, so bad but I couldn't do anything about it. My family told me that I could take your mother to court, and at the time I just didn't have it in me to do more battling before a judge. That was stupid of me, but hey I was still young, I didn't realize it could make a difference. I started getting into trouble again. When I was near your grandparents place I would watch your mother taking you out for walks and to the parks. I ran into your aunt a lot and I thought she was beautiful. I had no idea that she was your mother's sister. I am ashamed of how I took advantage of her she didn't deserve that."
His words caught in his throat.

He looked at Shaia searching the eyes that mirrored his to see if she understood and believed him. Shaia sighed.

"So you had no idea that Felicia was my mother's sister. And you weren't just doing it to get back at my grandpa for keeping you away from me?"

Deon Fletcher looked into both of his daughters eyes.

"I loved Connie with all my heart, and I would never do anything like that to hurt her. Felicia was just another pretty face."

He reached for their hands, when their hands were in his he brought their hands up to his lips and he kissed them.

"I have made so many mistakes and I have missed out on spending so much valuable time with you. I am so sorry. I know I can't make it up, but as long as you will have me until the day you bury me, I am going to be apart of your lives. I have a hearing scheduled in three months and my lawyer tells me that I may be able to get out on good behavior."

Hearing that was definitely good news to both of the young women. They wanted to get to know their father. Their meeting was overdue. Before he went back behind the sliding metal doors he hugged them tight and through tears he thanked them for coming.

The visit ended too soon as always.

Shaia promised her father that every weekend she would come to visit, and when her belly got too big to travel.

She hoped that her father, will have been released so that he could be in Virginia on parole. When they left the prison they decided to spend the rest of the afternoon

sightseeing and tasting the tastes of Georgia. They even decided that they would get a hotel for the night and then drive back to Virginia in the A.M.

A.J. paid for a suite with double beds for Cara and himself. When they got to the room he handed Cara the remote while he laid down on one of the beds. He put his hands behind his head and looked up at the ceiling. She handed him back the remote.

"I am going to take a shower. It has been a long day. Could you see if a good movie is on?"

A.J. nodded, and then he turned the television on and began to flip thru the channels. He thought about how he and Cara had ended up conversing on the night of his senior prom. The boy that she had been in love with stood her up, and she was crushed. It showed in her beautiful eyes when he saw her at the store that night.

*When he saw the unshed tears glistening in her eyes he didn't want to see her alone so he tried to strike up a conversation about anything he could to get her to stay by his side and it worked.*

*When she left home, she took off her beautiful silver prom dress and threw on a t-shirt and a pair of shorts, her pretty face was still made up. The hint of silver eye shadow brought out her hazel eyes, and her cherry lipgloss made her beautiful lips shine.*

*He hadn't spoken with her in almost two years. He was a senior and a popular football player while she was a shy sophomore. He noticed that she had grown up a lot.*

*He called her name as she placed an apple juice, a Tahiti treat and a bag of sun flower seeds onto the counter.*

*"Hey, Miss Cara Williams."*

*She looked up to see him standing behind her and he could tell that she started to blush.*

*"Hi A.J."*

*She handed the old man behind the counter a five dollar bill. When she got her change she started walking towards the door. He put his bag of chips down so that he could catch up with her.*

*"Are you just coming from the prom?"*

*He thought about his stupid question after it left his mouth. She didn't answer at first, she looked down at her plain t-shirt and shorts and he could tell she was thinking about giving him a sarcastic answer but he knew that it wasn't in her character.*

*She kept the comment that she was thinking to herself and she simply answered him no. She kept walking out the door and to a Honda Accord parked in front of the store. He followed her.*

"I didn't either. I don't think I missed anything. My boys were bugging me about going, and when I told them really didn't want to go, they left without me."

She looked up into his eyes, he didn't know what she was going to say, when she smiled it didn't matter.

"I remember when you and Tim made a bet that he would be the first to grow his goatee, I see you have yours now, I haven't seen him so who won?"

He laughed because he was surprised that she remembered that bet. He stroked the hairs on his chin.

"Tim won that one. I got my mustache first though. You have a good memory girl."

Cara smiled as she opened the car door. He didn't want to see her leave yet. His mind raced with all the things that he wanted to say to her, all he could think of at the moment was to comment on how her mother still loved her Honda. The Honda that Cara was driving had been thru many beatings.

He remembered when he and Tim were racing their bikes and Tim ran right into the side of the passenger door of the Honda putting a big dent in the door. He also remembered a time when the neighborhood kids were playing baseball and a loose ball hit her back window cracking it. She fixed what she could with no fuss. Everyone loved Miss Felicia.

Cara nodded. She had inherited the Honda that had been battered, by the neighborhood kids, and she knew where just about every dent came from.

A.J. rubbed his head trying to think of other things to say. He was getting frustrated because he was at a loss for words in her presence.

"So what are you getting into tonight, since you obviously aren't going to any after parties."

"Nothing, I need to take my mom back her drink, and I really should park this car."

*She admitted as she looked at the time on the dash.*
*She had been away at the store for thirty minutes. A.J. took a deep breath then he asked,*

*"Well I'm not doing anything, I'm bored so can I ride with you?"*
*Cara looked at A.J. then she looked at her pager, zero pages.*
*"Sure. I would like some company."*
*She unlocked the doors and A.J. slid into the passenger seat. She drove around the corner to her house.*
*When she pulled in the drive way her mother was standing on the porch. Felicia was relieved when she saw her only child pull into the driveway unharmed. She watched as her daughter got of the car, and then she saw the person on the passenger side. She assumed it was Malek.*
*The young man stepped onto the porch behind her daughter and he held out his hand to her.*
*"Hi, how are you Miss Felicia?"*
*His voice was a deep baritone now, she remembered the young boy from two doors down that always had a lot of candy in his pocket.*
*"O my, you have grown."*
*She gave him a hug. She asked about his future plans, and he told her that he had gotten a scholarship to college. He was going to study to be an engineer, and play football. She told him that she was proud of him and that it was good to see him and then she kissed her daughters cheek before she went inside the house.*
*"Mama I will be outside for a little while."*
*Her mother nodded and closed the door behind her.*

*A.J. thought about the picnic table where they would sit and talk when they were younger.*
*"Do you guys still have the picnic table in the back yard?"*
*Cara nodded that the picnic table was still there. He suggested that they go have a seat on the picnic table.*

They sat and talked for hours just like they used to do when they were kids. They reminisced and ended up talking about the day they decided to play truth or dare.  Cara blushed.

"I can't believe we did that."

Cara admitted, she remembered how nervous she had been and how big of a crush she actually had on A.J.

"Man Tim would not let that go. We played ball and I thought he would get it off of his mind, this dude started talking about it soon as we walked off the court."

A.J. thought about his childhood best friend and how much trouble they would get into all because he wouldn't be quiet.

"Didn't Tim have a crush on Shaia? Every time I turned around they were fussing about something."

A.J. agreed.

"Yeah he had a crush on her but she fussed with everybody."

They both laughed.

"Is she still that hard to get along with?"

Cara couldn't help but to laugh because Shaia still could be a little hard to get along with..

She and A.J. started to talk about the plans they had for the future as they talked he noticed how she would check her clear pink pager frequently. Her pager didn't go off once as they talked until three o clock in the morning.

When A.J. looked at the time on his own pager he told her that he had to get going.

"I have to work at ten this morning. I need to get a little sleep in."

Cara nodded in understanding as she stood from the picnic bench to stretch.

"Thank you for keeping me company here you are spending time with me while my own boyfriend stood me up tonight and hasn't even bothered to call."

*A.J. stood to his feet. He wanted to give her a hug because if he were her boyfriend he would never stand her up. He was nervous about hugging her but he thought to himself "you only get one shot." He reached for her hand and then he pulled her gently into his arms for a hug. She hugged him back. The hug lasted longer than your friendly twenty-second hug, but they didn't speak about it. He released her and then he walked her back to her front door he leaned down and kissed her on the corner of her mouth and then watched her go inside, before she shut the door he called to her not sure if he would get the chance to see her again.*
*"Take my number down."*

*She nodded okay and then disappeared for a few minutes to get a pen and paper. He called out his number and then he walked home hoping that she would call. He sat in the hotel room thinking about how much he thought a lot of her when they were kids.*

He looked up when Cara came from the bathroom, wearing a simple pair of polka dotted sleep shorts and a simple pink tank top. Even though what she wore was simple and not considered sexy he was turned on by the sight of her skin and of her toned arms and thighs, he was turned on because it was her.

He cleared his throat and then handed her the remote, sat up on the side of the bed and asked her jokingly if there was any hot water left. He wasn't prepared when she hit him with the pillow.

She wasn't prepared when he grabbed a pillow to hit her back. They hit each other with pillows for almost fifteen minutes and the only thing that stopped them was the ringing of the hotels phone asking if they needed a wake up call in the morning.

"Thank you again A.J. for being here. It means a lot. I don't know why you have been here for us, but I really appreciate it because you could be doing a whole lot of other things and thank you so much for those beautiful flowers you sent yesterday. They did make me smile."

Cara gave him a quick hug before she lie down on the bed, she covered her mouth as she yawned. A.J. looked at her. He had to let her know what he was feeling.

"I care about you. And if I can help you in anyway then expect that I will."

He could tell that she was surprised to hear what he had just said and she simply nodded. He pulled the comforter over her and she watched him disappear into the bathroom.

Twenty minutes later when he came from the bathroom Cara was sound asleep. He smiled, and then lay down on his bed and closed his eyes knowing dreams of Cara would come as the dreams of her always did when he closed his eyes.

The next morning they checked out of the hotel and went to eat at the famous Roscoe's Chicken and Waffles referenced in some songs and talked about as one of the places you want to visit when you get to Georgia.

Shaia and Cara fell in love with the restaurant as soon as they took the first bite. They made plans to visit every time they came back to visit their father.

"I am going to gain about ten pounds every time."

Shaia joked. Bo nodded his head thinking about his son or daughter resting in Shaia's womb. He was still overjoyed that she was carrying their child and he thought about all the mistakes that Deon Fletcher had made, and he promised himself that he wouldn't make the same mistakes. He would always be there for the woman he loved and his child only death would keep him away.

He and A.J. went outside while the two sisters finished their meals. Bo looked at A.J., whom he had met in business several years ago and had become a good friend.

"So tell me about your attraction to Cara. I can see it."

A.J looked through the window of the restaurant at Cara and Shaia. He looked at Bo and he shook his head.

"She has always been that one that I wanted to be around, I wanted to do things for, I wanted to see her smile. I went away to college and when I came back she had gone away, I had girlfriends but that one right there was not far from my thoughts. Now that we have crossed paths again I don't think it's coincidental. I think this time I need to make sure that she is in my life to stay."

He chuckled to himself as he thought about how his father used to say she would grow up to be one of the good girls. His father had called her a keeper and from what he saw and he knew his father had judged right. Bo nodded from what he knew of his soon to be sister in law and the family that she came from she was a good girl. He and Bo went back inside of the restaurant and the waitress was clearing their table so A.J. pulled out his wallet and gave the waitress a twenty dollar bill.

"Sir do you need change?"

They had paid for their meals before they sat down. A.J. shook his head no. "That's your tip, keep smiling."

The young waitress, couldn't hide her blush. The man that was standing in front of her was as fine as Dwayne Wade was to her, she had to remind herself that this man was there with his woman so she had to play it cool and not blush too much in front of them.

"Thank you, thank you so much."


Cara and Nashaia looked at Bo and A.J. they shook their heads at them as they opened up their purses and put ten dollar bills underneath their glasses for the waitress.

Cara and Shaia had jobs as waitresses when they were in high school, they both knew that a waitress made more money off of her tips than she did from her paycheck so wherever they went if they got served well then they tipped the waitress well.

"You know you just made her day."
Cara commented as she stood up from the table looking into A.J.'s eyes. He placed his hand at the small of her back and they walked out of the restaurant side by side.

"Yeah, I like making people smile. You know that."
She nodded, remembering how he walked around with a pocket full of candy when they were kids. Bo opened up his wallet, pulled out a ten dollar bill handed it to Shaia. She placed it underneath her glass and then she took her fiancé s hand they waved the waitress over to the table and then they walked out behind A.J. and Cara. Back to Virginia they were headed.

### *Due Time*

Aunt Pam was sitting at the kitchen table when Cara came in to get a bottle of water from the refrigerator. She was dressed in a beautiful blue blouse and slacks, and she was reading the daily newspaper, and sipping coffee. Pam had come for two reasons, one to visit her childhood home and two, to make things right.

"So who is this nice young man I see coming by to keep you company and check up on you all the time?"

Cara couldn't help but smile, because only her Aunt Pam would ask her a question so straight forward like that.

"A.J. used to live two houses down when we were kids."

Pam looked at her niece waiting for more details and when Cara didn't offer anymore details she went on with her observation.

"Okay you all grown up now, and he don't look like he still at home with his momma two doors down so why is he hanging around so tough right now?" Cara looked at her aunt to see if she was serious with her questioning. Aunt Pam looked her directly in the eyes.

"I think he thinks a lot of you. Am I wrong?"

Cara reached into the fridge for her water then she sat down at the kitchen table with her aunt. She had been thinking a lot about A.J, lately.

"I think he does think something of me. I just can't figure out what, I won't complain about it because I like him being around."

There she had admitted it.


"Does he know it?"

Her Aunt Pamela just wouldn't quit, but that's why she was so easy to love.

"I don't know Aunt Pam. I haven't asked him."

They both shared a laugh. They hadn't laughed together in a while.

"I think you should let him know that you do."

Cara closed her eyes and she thought about the men she had allowed in her life and how they had hurt her. She wasn't so sure about opening up to another one even if she had known him over half of her life.

"Aunt Pam, I don't know, I don't want to get hurt again."
"He won't hurt you. He cares about you too much. I can see it in his eyes when he looks at you. I didn't get to meet those other ones so I can only speak of this one. He's the one."
Pam didn't say anything else she just let her niece think and Cara did just that.
"So, Aunt Pam tell me about Terra's dad. I was surprised to see him here."

Pam got a far away look in her eyes.
"You mean the relationship that I have with him? He is good to me. I have been foolish, I admit that I was foolish over this man. I didn't know what to do with the things he was showing me, when he showed me. I almost lost him, and I am glad that I opened my eyes and I accepted the love he was trying to give me."
Pam smiled at her niece. She reached across the table to pat her hand.


Cara thought about A.J. and when he had come to the office to pick his sister up, he had given her a pack of watermelon now and later just like he used to do when they were kids.
He had remembered that they were her favorite. He had also been sending her flowers and cards with no occasion, he called her and he made himself available to her without her asking. He showed that he cared. That's the type of man any woman would dream of having in her life. She smiled to herself when she heard a light tap on the front door.
 Her Aunt Pam leaned in her chair to peep into the living room. It was A.J.
Cara stood to her feet and then she leaned down to kiss her Aunts cheek.
"I love you Aunt Pam."
Pam smiled at her niece, very proud of the woman she had become.
"Love you too sweetheart."

Cara bounced to the door with a smile on her face. She opened the door to let A.J. in. He smelled of Izzy Miake cologne, she inhaled with her eyes closed.

"Hey."

She spoke to him, when she opened her eyes he had this silly grin on his face. "Hey yourself. What have you been up to?"

"I've been working hard on this fiftieth birthday party at work, trying to make it come together nicely and just helping out around here. I haven't been to my apartment in weeks, how about you, is business falling the way you want it to so that you can expand?"

He sighed like the question bothered him.

"I don't know if it will work out with expanding this way. I am having some issues with my team in Georgia. I don't think they will be able to handle the things if I move out here to oversee this expansion getting off the ground."

Cara was a little disappointed, because that most likely meant that he would have to leave soon. She didn't want him to go.

"So does that mean you would have to go back to Georgia for a while?"

He noticed the sadness in her voice and in her eyes. He wondered what was on her mind. This time she would tell him after all she thought, what would she have to lose by telling him that she liked him being around?

He sat down on the couch and she sat across from him in the recliner. She felt like a little teenager telling a little boy that she liked him after school.

"A.J., I would miss you if you go. I know you need to do what you have to do for your business. I guess I got so used to having you around."

He couldn't believe his ears because he had been wishing that she would say that to him for so long. He took his time trying to think of the right words to say to her without being too forward. He stood to his feet, and she looked at him like she was afraid he was going to leave, but he held out his hand to her and when she put her hands in his he pulled her to her feet.

"I would miss you too."

He looked at her lips, and he melted into those hazel pools of her eyes. She asked as he put his arms around her waist.

"What does that mean?"

He smiled as he tried to think of the words to say, they should have come easy because he had been waiting for the right moment to say them.

"It means that I think about you when I wake up, I think about you all day until I see you or talk to you, and when I lay down at night you are on my mind. It means that I want you to be apart of my everyday, I need you to be apart of my everyday."

She blushed, then she wrapped her arms around his neck.

"I think I can be apart of your everyday."

He looked deep into her eyes as he thought about the last few months. When she walked into that check out line with Shaia, he hadn't been able to get her off of his mind since.

He leaned down to kiss her and before he could touch her lips with his her cell phone started to ring. Her intentions were to ignore it but the house phone started to ring as well, and her Aunt Connie came jogging down the stairs. "I am expecting an important call about the building across the street from Hope House."

She announced when she reached the bottom of the stairs. She was so excited that she hadn't even noticed how close Cara and A.J. were standing. She hadn't even noticed that she had interrupted their kiss. A.J. caressed her waist as they watched her aunt pick up the phone and listen to whoever the caller was on the other end. It was good news because she started to smile big.

When she got off of the phone she told them that the realtor has accepted her offer, and had also made some suggestions about grant writing for funding of the building.

"Everything is coming together and I am so excited. You two I am going to need lots of help soon."

She ran back up the stairs. A.J. smiled down at Cara.

"Now where was I, yes about to claim those lips."

Cara smiled as he tilted his head to kiss her. She met him half way standing on her tip toes. The kiss was soft, the kiss was sweet. She thought that maybe she was ready to try love again, after the kiss she leaned back to look in his eyes.

"I have to be honest, I'm afraid, but I want to trust you so bad with my heart. Kissing is easy, sex is easy. I want what isn't as easy, I want love."

A.J. had been in a couple of dead end relationships himself so he understood her completely.

"I'm going to do my best to give you all the love you can stand and more, and I promise we'll take it day by day."

He hugged her, and she rested her head against his chest, and it felt right. This kiss opened the book of them and it was due time for that book to be written.

Cara wondered if something were wrong with her cell phone because it hadn't rung all day. She pulled it from her purse when they were in A.J.'s truck headed back to her childhood home. She didn't have any missed calls but she had received a message.

## *Surprises*

Another couple of weeks had passed, it was now the first of May, and the temperature had warmed up nicely. With the help of her father, Terra had bought a three bedroom house for she and her son, Josh.

She begged her mother to come to stay so that she could help take care of her needs but of course Pamela Williams was so stubborn she told her daughter that she would have every thing she needed right there at her childhood home with her sisters until she decided to go back home to Florida.

Pam didn't want her daughter to make her life about taking care of her because she wanted her daughter to have a life of her own. She didn't know when she was going back to Florida or if she were ever going back. Since she had been home in Virginia, she didn't think of Florida as much of a home.

Terra's father could tell that Pam didn't want to go back to Florida. He had decided that he would stay right by her side until she decided what she wanted to do. His mother would have wanted him to do that, he thought as he looked at his grandson play with the neighborhood kids.

It was a sunny Saturday morning and Cara had gotten up early to go to her cousin Terra's new home to help her decorate. She had started hanging curtains just as she had learned from her grandmother. She had her cousins' windows looking like the windows that you see in the Southern Living magazines.

After finishing the whole living room she and Terra sat back to admire her work. Terra looked around the room and loved how all

the beautiful colors melded together to make for an eye catching room. "Aunt Pam taught you well cousin."
Terra stood back and looked at her work.

"Well my mom gets some credit, but most of the credit goes to my grandmother Mrs. Ruby Baxter. My dad had taken me to spend a few weekends with her one summer at her summer home and she happened to be decorating. She taught me a little bit of what she knew, I didn't get to spend much time with her, but I do miss her." She fingered a picture, which was framed of her when she was about ten years old. She was standing beside a frail lady that could have passed for Betty White's sister.

Terra placed that picture back on the mantle and she looked at the other pictures that she and Cara had placed there. There were pictures of her cousins, pictures of her mother and her aunts and lots of pictures of Josh. There were no pictures of her and the man that she loved. She had albums full of pictures of the work that she had done as a model.

None of those pictures were of her and her significant other.

"My mama stressed that I should be independent and make sure that a man would know that he didn't have to take care of me, or I didn't need anything from him. She taught me that it was okay to be alone. At first I was okay with that it didn't matter. Now I am so lonely Cara. I don't think I know how to love."


Cara looked at her cousin. She wanted to ask her cousin at one time had she been in love with the man that had fathered Josh, but she didn't know how to begin asking.
She admitted,
"Aunt Pam, would always tell me that a man should call me just because, he should open my doors, he should be there for me without me having to call. At first I suppose I was just settling with Eric and even Malek because I was afraid to see if anyone else would do all that you know?"

She paused to see if her cousin were going to ask her what she meant by settling with Malek because only Shaia knew about their brief affair. Terra was too wrapped up in her own thoughts to pay any mind to the mention of Malek's name.

She only looked at her cousin before she admitted,

"Mama used to tell me that too, I guess that's how I fell for the first man that ever opened the door for me, the first man that ever called me just because. That's how I ended up pregnant with Josh."

Terra looked hurt as she finally admitted it to herself.

"So what is the deal with Josh's father?"

Cara finally asked, she saw the hurt in her cousins eyes and she wanted to help her if she could.

"He is a no show. I chased him and I chased him until I finally learned why he was running from me. He doesn't know that I know, but he is someone else's man. What rule in love applies to falling in love with a man that goes home at night and sleeps with someone else? I didn't know, and when I found out I couldn't just turn the love off. My

son has to suffer because I made that bad choice, and I hate myself for it. He deserves so much more than I can give him."

Terra started to cry, silent tears streamed down her cheeks. Cara didn't know how to answer, because she had recently been caught up with someone elses man. She knew that she would never be happy because she only could have some of his love, some of his time, some of his attention. She wanted it all, she deserved it all. Terra took a deep a deep breath, she admitted what she said next just as much to herself as she were admitting it to her cousin.

"I'm not even worried about me now. I am worried about my son."

Cara wrapped her arms around her cousin, she didn't know how she could help her but she would do whatever she could to help.

"Just let me know what you need help with and I will help you. Just because his father isn't here doesn't mean that you are alone in this T."

That nickname she hadn't called her cousin in years. Terra gave her a weak smile.

"Thanks Cara, I needed that. I know I haven't been the best cousin, but I love you Cara."

The two women hugged, and decided that they wanted to give Shaia a wedding shower. Terra was interested in becoming a partner in the business of "Every Occasion" so Cara thought it would be fitting to let her help organize the event for Shaia and Bo.

Cara gave Terra some tasks to handle while she worked on the fiftieth birthday party for Malek's mother. Everything was coming together nicely, the party would be

held at Club Center Stage, and she had invited sixty guests and had pulled together a nice dinner menu for the guests.

The Monday before the party Sandra Jones came into Cara's office to sign the final contract and to pay her balance. As she waited at Margos' desk for Cara to come down stairs to get her, she admired the flowers that had just been delivered. She commented,

"Wow someone gets some beautiful flowers every time I come in here. They are beautiful."

Margo smiled.

"Yeah, Ms. Williams is so loved."

She didn't have to wonder how her brother felt about Cara. He was always showing her. Cara hadn't seen the latest arrangement sitting on Margo's desk, but Margo was sure that she would receive them today as if it were her first time receiving flowers that week. He had been sending them everyday, for the last two weeks. He had to go back to Georgia on business so he decided that he would send her flowers and gifts everyday until he came back..

Cara came down, dressed in a tan wrap around skirt and a beautiful peach wrap around blouse, she wore three inch heels and her hair flowed down her back in beautiful curls, she always dressed to impress but today she looked so good Margo had to comment.

"Boss lady, you are so pretty. I had to tell you that. These were just delivered for you and Mrs. Jones is here. I apologize for being all out of order. I should have mentioned her presence first."

Cara wanted to bend down and sniff her flowers, she wanted to snatch the card from the little holder to see what A.J had to say today. He had promised to send flowers everyday that he was away until he returned. She hadn't seen him since she admitted her feelings.

It had been a couple of weeks and she missed his presence, even though he messaged her every morning before going into the office and she called him every night before she went to bed, it wasn't the same as having him near. She had to keep chanting to herself to handle her business first. She smiled as she greeted Sandra Jones. She hadn't seen her in a month, her belly was a little bit rounder and you could tell now that she was with child.

Today, she wore her hair pulled back into a loose ponytail and she wore a plain white blouse, and simple black skirt, no make up, no smile. What in the world had Malek seen when he got with her? Cara pushed those thoughts to the side,

"Come on up Mrs. Jones, it is almost time to pull this party off, are you excited?"

Cara climbed the stairs with Sandra a few steps behind her. She held her hand out to have her sit in the chair and she noticed how sullen she looked.

"I am just so ready for this to be over."

Cara wanted to ask her what was wrong, just because that was the type of person she was. She cared about people. She had to remind herself that she and Mrs. Jones were not friends. She had been the other woman that this poor woman had no clue about.

A wave of guilt washed across her that changed her happy mood. She was also ashamed. She could hear her cousin Shaia telling her that she needed to put her game face on, because if she knew that Malek was still sleeping with his wife, nothing would have ever happened between them.

Cara sat down at her desk, with her back straight she opened up the file with Sandra Jones' name on it and she began to conduct business.

"This is the guest list, this is the complete menu and seating chart. There will be a sign in book at the door for each guest and the still video is complete. The party will begin at seven p.m. The D.J. will be in place at six p.m. everything looks great Mrs. Jones."

Mrs. Jones looked over the papers in front of her and then she signed by the x on the final page.

"I want to thank you so much for all of your help. I still don't know why my brother in law put this on me knowing that I wasn't welcome to the family in the first place especially by his mother." She shook her head from side to side as she looked in her purse, she retrieved a check and placed it into Cara's hand. Cara wasn't sure how she should respond, so she just said,

"In four more days it will be all over."

Sandra stood from the chair and she nodded as she walked out of the office. Normally Cara walked her clients out, but today she didn't feel like walking this client.

Her thoughts were on Malek and wondering what had happened that he ended up with someone like Sandra Jones. Her office phone rang, she peeped at the caller I.D. display. It was A.J.

Her smile returned as she picked up the phone and sang into the receiver,

"Hello!"

His deep voice made her melt as he greeted her back.

"Hello you. How is everything going?"

She wanted to tell him that everything was going wonderful since he had called but she kept those feelings to herself and told him that everything was okay and that she loved the flowers.

"I am glad. You will get them everyday until I get back there now, make sure you read the cards."

She smiled and nodded like he was standing in front of her.

"Okay. Is everything going okay for you?"

A.J. looked around his office, he peered at the employees shuffling past his window.

"Busy, but that's to be expected. I embrace being busy, and I look forward to a busy week, especially if I get to see you at the end of it."

Cara blushed, as she looked around her office at all the flower arrangements that she had received. She decided that she would take some home and to her mothers house.

"Aww you are too sweet. I look forward to seeing you too."

She chatted with A.J. for a few more minutes. As soon as she hung up the phone Margo buzzed her to let her know that her next client was downstairs. She took a deep breath, looked at herself in the mirror on her desk and then she stood to her feet. She put

her smile on and then she headed down stairs to get her next client, there was money to be made.

The week went by fast, as promised each day Cara received a flower arrangement and a card. Each card came with a different instruction. He had sent her a blank check to purchase a whole new outfit for Friday night. He told her to get dressed at the office and to be ready by six. She worked hard to have all of her work complete for the day and the week.

Margo laughed at her on Friday as she locked the front door and ran upstairs to her office. She lay out her new dress, a crème color fitted dress that stopped just above her knees.

It was rouched, at the sides to accentuate her curves. She had tried on the dress at least five times after she had purchased it. She knew when she put on that dress all eyes would be on her wherever they were headed for the night. She took a shower in the small bathroom in her office and she applied fresh gloss and eyeliner. She had learned along time ago that she didn't need a whole lot of makeup. Her beauty was all natural.

 Fully dressed she looked at the full length mirror on her wall and she was satisfied that she looked beautiful. When she got down the stairs A.J. had just stepped into the office. He was holding a single red rose. He looked good enough to eat wearing black slacks and a shirt that hugged every muscle in his upper body. She told herself, "damn I didn't know he was so cut."


When she was within arms reach of him, he handed her the rose and then he lifted her chin to give her a kiss. Margo was standing at her desk with a big smile on her face.

"I am so happy for you two."

She hugged her brother then she hugged Cara.

"I will see you at three tomorrow Boss lady."

 Margo smiled as she held the door open for them both. Cara locked the doors to Every Occasion and then A.J. led her to his truck. He opened the door for her, when she tugged on her seat belt he gently closed the trucks door. Margo stood at the curb watching. She could hear her tell her brother,

"You better do that!"

 He told her to have a good night, and then he slid into the truck beside Cara. "You look beautiful." He leaned over to kiss her again.

"Thank you."

 He turned the keys in the ignition to start the truck and then he eased the truck into traffic. The sounds of jazz filled the car, as did the soft musky smell of his cologne. Cara leaned back against the seat and closed her eyes. She was thinking to herself that it felt good to have someone shower her with so much attention and affection and she didn't have to tell him that she wanted it.

"Are you okay over there?"

His deep voice caressed her ears.

"I am fine. Thank you for asking."

She studied his features, strong cheekbones, his smooth chocolate skin, and his razor cut was sharp. The man looked so damn good she couldn't stop staring at him. He paid attention to the road but to acknowledge her he reached over and held her hand. She felt like a teenager.

When they finally made it to where they were going he opened the door for her and held her hand as she stepped out of the truck. He kissed her cheek, and then he wrapped his arm around her waist and they walked together to the entrance of the restaurant. He gave the maitre'd the name of his reservation, and then a hostess led them to a little booth near the window.

There was a little stage, and on the stage was a man sitting on a stool playing a saxophone. She noticed other instruments in chairs behind him. He was playing solo and the sounds coming from the saxophone sounded so good. She smiled in appreciation, as did the other patrons.

After their meal, A.J. stood and offered her his hand. He wanted to dance. Cara looked around there wasn't anyone else dancing, but she didn't mind because she wanted to be in his arms. He held her close and she closed her eyes as she placed her head on his chest. She felt like she belonged there in his arms. Two hours later they were back in his truck.

He asked,

"So did you enjoy that?"

She nodded yes.


"I really enjoyed that, thank you so much for sharing something that you enjoy with me. I knew you were into jazz because every time I get in your car or your truck it's caressing my ear. I didn't really appreciate jazz until I met you."

He nodded.

"I am glad you liked it."

Thirty minutes later they were pulling into a neighborhood with houses that looked like mansions. Cara wondered where they were headed but she didn't ask she just sat back and enjoyed being his company. He pulled into a long drive way which led to a big two story house.

The house was bright white against the dark of the sky. The driveway turned off to a circle that led to the front steps of the house. A.J. put the truck in park and then he out slid of the truck and walked around it to open her door. He took her hand as they walked up the steps to the front door.

When he paused she thought that he would knock, but instead he pulled out a key. After he unlocked the door he led her inside.  She hadn't been into to too many houses with foyers.

This one had a foyer that had two large high back chairs with a table between them. There was a coat rack in a corner, beside a beautiful painting of a man playing a saxophone. He led her up two steps from the foyer and into a large room, with a fireplace.

There was no furniture in the room, just a blanket, some pillows and a basket in the middle of the floor where a couch should be.

"Let's get comfortable."

 He suggested as he stepped out of his shoes. She removed her shoes in awe as she looked around the large room. She couldn't help thinking about how she would decorate it, if it were her space to decorate.

 A.J. stepped away so that he could turn the chandelier on dim, he reached in his pocket and he pulled out a little remote. He pressed one button and the smooth sound of jazz filled the room. Cara smiled wondering where the speakers were hidden.

"Wow. This is nice."

 He placed the little remote next to him as he sat down on the pillows next to her.

"Yeah, my dream was to have a place like this, where I could incorporate my love for jazz into every room."

He had a dreamy look in his eyes.

"So this is your place? It's so beautiful."

He looked into her eyes as he answered.

"Not yet. The person who had this house built lost the love of his life before it was finished. He told me he wanted to sell it and he thought he wanted to sell it to me. I asked him what he thought I would do with this entire house; he told me that I was young enough to do something with it. So I have been thinking about it especially if I expand my company this way."

He really wanted to tell her that he knew that he would buy it when he found the one to move in with him to make it a home. He felt like he had found her but he didn't want to scare her away.

"That would be so nice if you could do that."

He watched her as she mentally took note of all the features of the house. He opened the wicker basket which held grapes, strawberries, peaches, and mangos. He took out a small cutting board so that he could cut the peaches and the mango, he also pulled out two wine glasses and a glass of wine. She looked surprised as he held a grape to her lips. She smiled shyly and bit a piece of the grape. He popped the remaining piece into his mouth.

She quietly reached for a strawberry and then put it to his lips. He looked into her eyes as he took a bite of the sweet berry. His bite wasn't small so there wasn't a piece left to feed her, so he picked up a strawberry and put it to her lips. She bit a small piece again, and then took a sip of wine before she finished the piece that was left. She thought to herself a man is feeding her fruit, and this time she wasn't dreaming of someone else's man.

They fed each other fruit, drank wine and talked well into the early morning hours. He wanted to hold her in his arms, so he moved the empty basket to the side and opened his arms. She went into his arms, where she felt she belonged. They leaned back on the pillows and just listened to the sounds of jazz. He rubbed her bare arms, and she kneaded his chest as she listened to him breathing.

"I can't believe I am finally spending time with you."

He admitted, she admitted that she felt the same.
"See its different for me, because ever since the night of my senior prom, I knew that you or someone like you was who I wanted to spend my time, my life with."

She looked up at him quizzically.
"Even though I was crying over someone else?"
He nodded.
"I knew that dude wasn't the one for you. How in the hell could you find any excuse to stand a girl like you up for a prom that he invited you to? I wanted to say something to him so bad after that night. Before, the prom all he was doing was walking around bragging about who he was taking and where he planned on taking you after the prom. Then he stood you up? What kind of mess is that?"
He could feel himself getting upset as if it had happened yesterday instead of ten years before.
"I knew that you thought a lot of that guy, so I just kept quiet. When you came home from college that summer, the last summer that I saw you I watched you. I saw something different, when you came to church and I could look directly into your eyes I could tell that something was missing. He hurt you."
He remembered seeing her helping her mother and aunt in the dining hall at their church. She was the same girl he used to give watermelon now and laters to but at the same time she wasn't the same. It was the summer before his senior year in college, and he had just got finished playing ball at the gym with some friends he was walking past her house when he saw her sitting on the picnic table in the back yard. He decided to say something to her. She remembered it too.

*When he came around the corner singing to himself, she was looking up at him as he came into view. She remembered his muscled arms and his chest and she remembered the song he had been singing.*

*"Ask of you." by Raphael Saadiq.*
*A.J. sat down on the picnic table beside her as if he had been invited to sit down.*

*"What's up stranger?"*
*He smiled at her and she gave him half smile back,*
*"Nothings up with me, what's up with you?"*
*He looked at his watch,*
*"I just got finished balling, I been on the court for the last hour and a half. I hope my mom has cooked something good, cause this dude is ready to eat."*
*He rubbed his stomach as she shook her head at him.*
*"I hate to break the news to you like this but your mom said she was going to help my aunt at the boarding house tonight. She hasn't been home since four."*
*It was almost eight o'clock, A.J. looked at his watch again.*
*"I think you are going to be very disappointed." He knew that what Cara had said was probably right.*
*"So you want to go get some pizza with me?"*
*She started to say no thank you but she looked at her watch and looked the empty house; she decided that she didn't want to be alone. Shaia had a date, and of course, Terra was on a shoot.*

*Her mother was working at the hospital and her Aunt Connie was at the boarding house.*
*"Yeah, can you give me a few minutes?"*
*He nodded and told her that he would be back in fifteen minutes. He ran to his house to take a shower. He hadn't planned to go eat pizza, but since he was*
*going with her he didn't want to go with her stinking.*
*When he came back to her house*
*to pick her up driving his little black Honda Accord, his member jumped at the sight of*
*her. She had changed into a pair of red shorts that showed off her thighs and a halter*

*top that hugged her breasts.*
*He could hardly keep his eyes off of her, as he ran around to*
*open the door for her and watch her slide into the passenger seat.*
*He could barely keep*
*his eyes off her thighs as he drove to, "The Pizza Den" which was a*
*few blocks from*
*their neighborhood.*
*She didn't seem to notice as she was quietly staring out the window*
*as they drove along. He had no idea how much, her life had changed*
*in just her second*
*semester of college. He pulled up and ran around to open her door*
*and she looked at him*
*like he was crazy.*
*"I can open my own door you know."*
*He simply stated,*
*"I know you*
*can, but something my father always taught me, a man should never*
*allow a lady to*

*open her own door and a man that allows a lady to open her own*
*door isn't a man and*
*he has no respect for that lady."*
*She didn't know what to say to that. He had a system*
*in his car, and he was pumping some Guy, "Lets chill." She couldn't*
*help checking him*
*out, he had changed into a money green Nautica tshirt and black*
*jean shorts. He smelled*
*so fresh, she inhaled the scent of him as they rode the few blocks to*
*the restaurant.*
*When he pulled into the parking space in front of the pizza joint, he*
*ran put the car in*
*park and then he ran around to open the door for Cara. She shook*
*her head from side to*
*side with a smile she wasn't used to a guy opening doors for her, the*
*only guy she had*

*ever gone out on dates with was Malek, and she always opened her own doors. A.J.*

*paid for two buffets and two drinks and they filled their plates and cups and they sat down in a window booth. He was so hungry that before she could*

*even finish her second slice of pizza he was up to fill his plate again. She shook her head*

*at him as he started on slice number five.*

*"Wow, man you eat like that?" They laughed*

*as he explained that he hadn't eaten more than a protein bar all day. He asked*

*her about school and how everything was going and she told him that she was at the*

*top of her class.*

*He told her that he was at the top of his and he already had a job lined*

*up when he was done. He loved that they could always talk no matter how long it had*

*been since they had seen each other, they could always pick up wherever they had left*

*off. As they talked he noticed that the sadness that he had noticed in her eyes before*

*gone away. After an hour they were back in his car headed home. There was no one*

*home at either house.*

*He didn't want to say goodnight just yet so he asked her if she wanted to watch a movie at his house. She agreed. He led her to his room and then*

*popped in House Party.*

*They acted out every scene. He knew that Cara was that girl that his dad had always told him about. She was everything he knew he wanted in a companion, he looked at her as she sat beside him on his bed. Cara was engrossed in the movie, but she also felt him as he watched her and what she felt she had always tried to hide.*

*During the part of the movie when Kid and Gina were kissing after he got*
*out of jail, somehow her legs got tangled up with his and she ended up on his lap and*
*his hands were kneading her soft breasts while he was kissing on her neck. The movie*
*was forgotten as they found each others lips and began to kiss so deep that all you could*
*hear was the kissing sound.*
*They had tuned out the t.v., he slipped out of his t-shirt and she had made it out of hers they were upper body skin to skin. He picked her up and lay*
*her on the bed, he got down on his knees and kissed her thighs, he worked his way up to*
*her belly and then to her breasts. Her bra went in the pile where there shirts were. She*
*cradled the back of his head as he nibbled and suckled on her breasts, Cara felt like she*
*could cry. He reached down into her shorts and when he touched her she let out a little*
*moan that turned him on so much he couldn't hold his own moan of pleasure.*
*He kissed*
*her and she began grinding against him, he reached into his night stand to retrieve his*

*wallet which held some protection. She rubbed his chest as he tore the packet open with*
*his teeth, he looked at her and he noticed the tears streaming down her cheeks. "Are you*
*okay Cara? Are you sure you want to do this?" She wiped her tears away while she*

nodded her head hard.

"Yes, I'm sure, please don't stop."

He cupped her chin so that he
could look directly into her eyes.

"I am going to ask you again, are you sure?" She didn't
answer, she kissed his lips and reached down and began to massage
his member which
had softened at the sight of her tears. He broke the kiss long enough
to roll the condom
on and then help her out of her panties and shorts. They kissed more,
he wanted to take
his time, even though he didn't know when his mother would come
home. A.J. kissed
her shoulders, he kissed her breasts, then he kissed her stomach and
he buried his
head between her legs. She cried out so softly as she came over and
over again with each
stroke of his tongue he whispered in her ear if she was ready as he
got ready to enter her
wetness with his manhood.

Cara was a little bit in a daze because she had just experienced her
first orgasms.

When she recovered, she kissed his lips and answered yes to his
question. He slowly pushed forward to enter her and then he almost
lost it as, he was greeted by her tight warmth around him.

He savored the feeling as she did. Cara was so special to him, he
took his time and he kissed her deeply as he moved in and out of her.
She moaned so softly in his ear he had trouble concentrating on
making himself last. Time seemed to stand still until they

both heard a car door slam outside. They looked into each others
eyes, knowing that it was his mother returning from the Hope House.
Cara wrapped her legs around his back and urged him on. He
prayed that he had locked his

bedroom door, as he made love to the girl he had had a crush on since middle school. She,
held on to him as he moved in and out of her in a quick but full rhythm she didn't mean
to bite his lip when she climaxed. She had never felt the sensation that was coursing thru her, she knew that she had her first orgasm. When she caught her breath she apologized over and over kissing his lip. Her voice was enough to send him over the edge as he climaxed he could hear his mother calling from down stairs, he could hear her feet as she
began to climb the stairs. He gave Cara one last kiss, as he scrambled to get up from
between her legs.
"yeah, ma."
He answered to keep his mother from knocking on his door.
"Did you eat honey?"
 She asked from the hallway. He told her that he had stopped to get pizza after he played

ball, he told her that he thought he had to go back out because they were out of soda.
She told him that she was going to take a bath. By the time his mother started her bath. Cara was dressed and standing behind his bedroom door. She wanted to laugh because she didn't know how in the world she had ended up there knowing that his mother would undoubtedly be coming home soon. He opened his bedroom door and peeped out to see if his mother was in the bathroom yet.
 When he was satisfied that she was in the bathroom, he led Cara out of his room and down the stairs. They tiptoed until they made out onto the porch and when they were down the sidewalk, they couldn't contain their laughter about almost getting caught. They walked side by side quietly after their laughter, subsided neither one of them knowing what to say.
"So, what are you doing the rest of this summer?"

*He wanted to spend more time with her, he wanted to get to know her now. They were no longer twelve and fourteen years old, nor were they sixteen and eighteen years old in high school. She was twenty now and he was six months away from his twenty second birthday. He and Cara were all grown up.*

*"I will start my externship in a couple of weeks what about you?"*

*He told her that he had to start his externship as well at the company that wanted to hire him upon his graduation. They were going their separate ways again.*

*"I know we're not a couple or anything, I would like to hear from you more than I do."*

*A.J. hoped that she felt the same.*

*"I don't know A.J, so much is going on in my life right now, I don't know what the future holds."*

*He wasn't surprised by her answer, he had hoped that her answer would be different.*

*"Call me okay?"*

*Cara nodded her head when they reached her house. He watched her go inside wishing that things were different.*

*He waited for her to call that summer, but she never called. He often wondered why. As he held her hand presently and they stared up at the ceiling,*

*"So even when we saw each other at the grocery recently and when we had dinner at your sisters house, you didn't even act like you remembered the time that we spent together."*

*Cara was quiet, she didn't revisit their past because she was afraid. She wanted to start off with him being honest so she admitted that she had been afraid.*

As they lie together in this big house he knew that he couldn't let that happen again. He leaned up on his elbow so that he could look into her eyes.

"Cara, I need to be honest with you, I'm afraid if I fall back this time I may not get the chance to have you in my life the way I want to again."

"A.J. I have been hurt. I am not the same innocent girl that you used to like back in middle school. So much has happened. I know I am not the same person." He shook his head from side to side.

"I won't hurt you Cara."

"I don't think you will hurt me A.J., that's not what I meant."

She wasn't sure of what she meant by telling him that she had been hurt because she was sure he knew.

"I have made some mistakes that I am so not proud of."

His answer,

"Who hasn't made mistakes?"

Cara told him about getting pregnant when she was in college, she told him about how Malek had turned his back on her and she had no closure until recently. She told him about the brief affair and she told him about Eric. If he wanted to be with her then she felt that he needed to know it all so nothing could come back to bite her. He listened to her pour out her heart.

She didn't know the rules about love because no one had taught her. She felt like honesty and trust meant a lot in a relationship. She knew that she wanted to have both of those things going into this relationship.

"I hate that you went through all that Cara. Believe that there is a reason for going thru the things that you go thru in life, most of the time its to make you stronger, I really believe that."

They talked until two c'clock that next morning, Cara knew she needed to get some rest for the party the next day, but to be up talking with A.J. just felt right. He moved a piece of stray hair from her eyes as he asked,

"Do you want to go home tonight?"

He asked her as he looked at his watch.

"I want to be right here with you."

She admitted. He kissed the corner of her mouth. He hated that he didn't have a blanket to wrap up with. He hadn't planned for them to sleep in their clothes.

"Let me take you home tonight and tomorrow we can camp out here when we make sure we have everything we need."

Cara nodded.

She stood to her feet and when he stood he grabbed her up into his arms, then he kissed her with so much passion she felt a stirring in the pit of her stomach. She remembered all those years ago wrapping her legs around him, and letting him make love to her. She knew she could have that tonight, but she wanted their relationship to be different. She wanted that fairy tale that she used to read about. No one had ever told her that she *could have* the fairy tale life, nor had anyone told her that she couldn't.

A.J. turned off the chandelier and the music and then he grabbed the basket. He and Cara held hands as he locked the doors to the house and opened the truck door for her.

She settled back in the seat and looked out the window as he drove her to her apartment. When they got there, they stripped down to their underclothes and held each other under the covers in Cara's bed.

The next morning while Cara slept, A.J. got up to cook her breakfast. He tapped her nose to wake her and then he served her breakfast in bed. She smiled, again this was *her man* feeding her breakfast in bed.


At twelve p.m. she finally got up to take a shower and A.J. waited while she got dressed and ready to go to Club Center Stage to begin transforming the space for the fiftieth party.

"Good luck to you sweetheart and I will see you tonight."

He kissed her forehead and closed her car door. Cara felt good about her new relationship with A.J. she walked into the club with a smile on her face. Margo was waiting for her inside. She had picked up the file and had begun to lay things out.

"Hi there."

Cara called to her as she put her bag down and began to pick up the seating chart.

Margo smiled at her and gave her a quick hug. In an hour and a half they had transformed the space they needed in Club Center Stage to a fiftieth birthday party for Ms. Jones.

At six thirty the guests started to arrive, Malek and Sandra Jones walked in with the guest of honor at exactly seven p.m., the fifty guests who had come clapped for her. She covered her mouth in surprise as she saw all her friends and family gathered around to wish her a happy birthday.

Malek stepped over to Cara to thank her so much for putting it all together. He acted as if he wanted to hug her, but she made sure to keep everything all professional.

"Your wife had a vision and we made it happen. Thank you for the business."

As she talked to Malek, she noticed his brother Keith sneaking peeks at her. She decided to wave at him.


"You know your brother should really calm himself down, why is he eyeballing me right now?"

Malek looked behind him at his brother who was sitting next to Michelle and his niece and nephew.

"He'll be okay. Are you doing okay though? You look good."

Before she would have been all over herself about his compliment, but today what he said didn't matter.

Before she could politely dismiss him she saw her cousin Terra walk in. Terra held the hand of her son Josh. Cara stepped to the door to speak to her cousin before she could open her mouth Terra was already apologizing.

"I'm so sorry cousin, but I sat up all night trying to make up my mind about doing this, I gotta do it. I can't sleep another night without letting my son know who his father is."

Cara didn't get a chance to ask who or what she was talking about, Terra had stepped past her with Josh in tow. She stopped at the table that Keith, Michelle and Maleks children were sitting at. She didn't hear her cousin when she told Keith that he needed to meet his other son.

Terra saw that the little boy sitting at the table looked just like her son just a little bit older. She didn't know that the little boy was Malek's son.

"I tried to call you, I tried to come see you at work so I could talk to you in private, but you keep avoiding me. I am so sorry to embarrass you or bring this to your attention this way but I owe it to my son. You owe it to your son."

Keith looked at Terra like she had lost her mind. Michelle stood up she didn't know what was going on so she introduced herself to Terra. She reached out to shake her hand. Terra shook her hand and managed to smile at the woman whom she felt had taken her place.
"What's your name sweetheart?"
Michelle kneeled down so that she could be eye to eye with the little boy,
"My name is Josh."
Michelle nodded with tears in her eyes. She swiped them away quickly and then she stood to her feet. She looked at Keith and then she walked away. Keith couldn't follow her, he didn't want to draw any attention away from his mother.
He spoke as calmly as he could he couldn't believe that Terra had come to him like this,
"Terra can we speak outside?"
Terra shook her head no.
"The only thing we need to speak about is you visiting and helping to take care of your son. We can do all that later, please acknowledge him."
Terra held her head high and she dared Keith to challenge her and say that Josh wasn't his son. She knew that he carried around a picture of the little boy in his wallet,

Michelle had also seen the picture. She had been going through Keith's wallet to get cash for dinner one night and she saw it.
 Terra also knew that Keith's mother knew about Josh. She would always send money and cards on his birthday and for Christmas. Terra knew that if his mother

acknowledged that Josh was her grandson then Keith knew that he had fathered the child. Peggy Jones came over and she gave Josh a big hug.
"I finally get to meet you. You are the greatest gift I have gotten for my birthday today do you know that?"
 Josh gave his grandmother a shy smile. She hugged Terra and told her thank you with tears in her eyes. The day had been so full of surprises she didn't know what she should do next. Keith still stood there looking stupid. The longer he stood there the angrier Terra became. Peggy walked over to her oldest son Keith and she introduced him to his son. No one could have done it better. He got on his knees in front of his son,
 "Hey man. Nice to meet you."
Josh looked back at his mother then he shyly smiled at the man in front of him. He quietly asked,
 "So are you my dad?"
Peggy covered her mouth as she looked at her son with tears in her eyes. Peggy knew that Keith had been so bitter since his father left them behind when he was only twelve he was upset because she had struggled hard to raise her two sons to be good men.
She felt she had done the best she could and she hoped that he would finally do the right thing by his son and not follow in his fathers footsteps. Keith nodded as he took the little boy into his arms and hugged him tight.
"Yes, little man. You are my son and I am your dad. I am so sorry I missed so many years with you. I'm here now."

Keith couldn't explain how he was feeling. Terra had called him over the years, begging him to come see about his son, and when he did acknowledge her he didn't want to talk about him, he just wanted to sleep with her. He had never seen more than a picture of his son, he had never sent him a birthday card or a gift, nor had he played Santa Clause putting gifts up under the tree.

Terra was ashamed of carrying on a sexual relationship with the man who wouldn't talk to her about their son. She had lain with him hoping that one day he might change his mind about raising a son with her. She could only see him behind closed doors, and now she knew why. She wanted to ask him what was so hard about taking care of his responsibility to his son but she didn't even see the point of asking when she had never held him accountable.

Terra had only asked for him to come see him. She was guilty of thinking if she slept with him, and didn't pressure him he would one day come see about his son.

When Keith stood up to his full six foot one height, he picked the little boy up in his arms and placed him on his left hip and then, he looked into Terra's eyes, she had tears streaming down her cheeks. All he could do at that moment was apologize.

He reached out for her and she slowly came to his side. He hugged her with his free arm and kissed her forehead.

"Thank you, thank you for bringing him here and I apologize for avoiding you and avoiding the conversations you tried to have with me about our son."


Terra's anger with Keith subsided. She knew when she laid down the night before she couldn't go another day without confronting Keith and whomever else needed to be confronted. She wasn't sorry.

Cara was busy making sure that all the guests were okay. She didn't know exactly what was going on, she would ask her cousin later.

Margo had stepped to the side to take a phone call, whomever she was speaking with she was giving them directions to the club.

Margo gave her a goofy smile as she breezed past her and went to the entrance. She opened the door, and her brother walked in. He was dressed in a pair of khaki slacks, a coral shirt and sperrys. He looked so good Cara had to remind herself of where she was because she wanted to walk right into his arms and give him a kiss.
"Hello."
She greeted him with a wave as he handed her the rose.
"Hello beautiful."
He kissed her on the corner of her mouth and then stepped to the side.
"The decorations are nice."
Cara mouthed thank you. She was so happy that A.J. had come to see her at work she didn't even notice that Malek hadn't taken his eyes off of her since A.J. walked through the door.
When the party was over and everyone was leaving as she gathered her things she looked at her cell phone and noticed that she had received a message. She didn't even take the time to look at it. The man that she had been waiting to hear from was standing beside her right now and she wasn't worried about anything else.

"I didn't know you were coming by."
She stood beside him outside the club.
"I hadn't planned to, but since you were on my mind I wanted to see you. How about I take you to the movies?"
She nodded okay and then she thought about her car parked around the back of the club.
"I need to take my car back home and maybe change my shoes."
She looked down at her six-inch stiletto heels knowing that she wanted to be more comfortable at the movie theatre.
"Okay. I will follow you to the apartment then."
A.J. walked her to her car, he opened her door, waited for her to get in and out on her seatbelt. Then he closed the car door and went to his own car.

While en route to her apartment her phone was going off with messages. She decided to sync her car speakers with her phone so that she could call her family to make sure everything was okay.

She had a feeling the messages were from Malek and she definitely didn't have anything more to say him than what she had already said which was thanks for the business.

His mother was so happy with the way her party had turned out. She hadn't spoken to Ms. Peggy who had been there for her after her miscarriage. She thought a lot of Ms. Peggy but she had decided to plan the party just like she would any other party and keep everything professional.

"Dial Shaia."

She told the system to call her sister. Shaia answered on the first ring. "Hey Sis how'd the party go?" She asked while soaking her feet and ankles. She was now seven months pregnant and she could barely see her feet. Bo had been so caring during her pregnancy that every night she sat between his legs so that he could massage her neck and her back.

"The party went well. Ms. Peggy looked very happy, and oh we need to meet up with our cousin soon."

Shaia raised a brow.

"What's going on with Terra? Is she okay?"

Cara hunched her shoulders as if Shaia were there in the car beside her.

"I think she is okay but she may need someone to talk to soon about some of the changes that are going on in her life."

Shaia couldn't imagine what else her cousin needed to talk about. She and her mother had managed to hide a child from her family for five years she couldn't imagine what else could be going on in her cousin's life right now.

"Okay, so what are you doing?"

Cara looked in her rearview mirror and smiled as the silver mustang followed her.

"I am going to the movies."

She hadn't told her sister that she and A.J. had finally had a date and this would be their second. She hadn't told her sister that the man who had always been there to open her door, make her smile when she really felt like crying and had sent her flowers

almost everyday for the last two months had told her that he would always be by her side if she would let him, and she decided to let him. Shaia looked at her phone as if she didn't know who the person was on the other end.

"With who?"

"With A.J. so I will give you a call tomorrow, love you."

Shaia told her that she loved her too and then disconnected the call. She looked at Bo with a look of amazement in her eyes.

"What's up?"

He looked at her with surprise because she had turned her whole body around to look him in the eyes.

"My sister is going to the movies with A.J."

Bo nodded.

"It's about time."

Bo resumed rubbing Shaia's back.

"What do you mean it's about time? What do you know about it?"

Bo just shook his head from side to side knowing that he had started a debate and his fiancée was ready.

"All I know is he has been talking about how he felt about Cara for a while now. I told him that she had been in a messed up relationship and she deserved someone that was going to love and respect her to the utmost, he said he was ready to give her that and more, and that he was waiting on the right time, I guess the time came."

Shaia looked at her man, she gave him a long kiss, which required her to take her feet out of the water to turn completely around.

"I love you man. Good looking out."

He noticed that her feet had made a puddle on the floor next to the couch. He threw a towel down there and kissed his fiancée some more. Cara was a good person and so was A.J. He was glad that they were spending time together. He knew now that he would ask him to be his best man.

He also knew that as long as Cara was happy, then Shaia would be happy and that is the way he wanted to live his life. His happiness would always depend on hers.

 Bo's grandfather and grandmother had been the picture that he had of love growing up. His grandfather worked hard to make sure that his wife was happy and that his children were taken care of. He rubbed Shaia's belly and knew that whoever came out to greet him in two months he would do everything to make sure that him or her had everything they needed from the first minute of their life outside of the womb and that he would provide the picture of happiness for his child.

A week and a half later Malek Jones sat in his truck staring out at the lake. He had decided to take a short drive away from home just to clear his mind. So much had been going on with him and around him he felt like he was about to lose his mind.

Sandra now seven months pregnant waddled around like everyone owed her the world. He thought that it was because of her hormones so he let it go, and was there whenever she called and gave her as much space as she needed at the same time.

Today, he just couldn't stand being around her, his brother had come by to let his son play with his cousins. Malek was proud of his brother because he had seen him do a complete one eighty since the little boy came into his life. He was happy for his brother, at the same time he felt bad for Michelle who had stuck by him through his mess.

After his mothers party Keith had told Michelle that he couldn't be with her because his son needed him. She told him that she could be there for him and his son. He sent her packing when he told her that he didn't think it would work out even thought they had been a couple for three years. Michelle didn't shed any tears in front of him, she went into the bedroom that she had shared with him off and on for almost two years and she packed up her things. She placed her key to the apartment on the kitchen table, turned her back and walked out the door. Malek couldn't believe that he would let her go just like that and he told him so.

"Keith, was it necessary for you to let her go like that?"
Keith didn't answer his brother because he didn't feel he needed to. Malek got upset when Keith didn't answer he just turned his back and began to straighten up things in the kitchen that didn't need to be straightened up.
"She was a good person man so how is she not good enough to be around your son?"
Keith still didn't answer.
He grabbed the key off of the counter and put it on his own keychain. He could feel his brother staring at him and he didn't like it so he decided to bait him for an argument.

"Why you worried about it? You want to mend her broken heart too? She doesn't drink so you will have some problems with that."
Malek felt a raging in him that made him want to punch his brother for saying that. He thought maybe he was just hurt or angry and it was coming out on him since he was there. He let his brothers' comment go, but he wanted to be sure that his brother knew that he was letting it go.
"I know you're upset Keith man and you just saying stuff right now, but you should really call Michelle up and apologize to her for the way things went down I know you don't mean to hurt her."
Keith looked at his brother long and hard. He couldn't believe he was even still talking to him after he had insulted him.
"Malek, little brother you can't tell me anything about relationships. You can't tell me anything at all."
"Keith for years I listened to your advice about my relationships. I listened to your advice about Cara and I listened to your advice about Sandra. I even listened to every thing you had to say about every woman I have been with since I was old enough to deal with

women and you sitting here telling me that I can't say anything to you about your relationship when I see the mistake you making?"

Malek reached into his pocket to retrieve his truck keys. He had to leave his brothers presence. As soon as he got ready to walk out the door Keith told him to worry about what mistakes he was making because he was good. That had happened almost a

week ago and it was still bothering him as he sat in his truck trying to get his head together.

He had been sending Cara messages since the party and she hadn't responded. He knew it had been a few months since he had contacted her and she probably felt like he had left her hanging but it wasn't like that, he had to handle home first. He saw this familiar looking guy approach her on the night of his mothers party, he had also seen the guy pick her up from her business. He still worked at the bar around the corner from her spot.

Ever so often he would take a break, and he would walk around the corner at five fifteen to see if she happened to be coming out the office. Some days she and the younger girl would come out together, sometimes she would come out and the guy would be waiting for her. He never knew the best time to catch her alone. He realized that he missed her despite how they reconnected, he missed her. He thought about the night he had dropped her off at her car, he remembered the tears she shed, he wished he could turn back time to when they were teenagers, he would have joined her in college, instead of listening to his brother tell him he should work and go to a community college close to home.

When he found out from his mother that Cara was carrying his baby he shouldn't have listened to his brother tell him that she was trying to trap him into a relationship. He shouldn't have listened to his brother when Cara miscarried that she was trying to guilt trip him. He shouldn't have listened to his brother when he told him that Cara was bad for him.

Everything that his brother had said negative about Cara she stood for the opposite. His brother didn't know Cara, so he didn't know why he had listened to him.

He watched a couple and a child feeding the ducks in the lake. He thought about his unborn child with Cara. Tears started streaming down his cheeks. His brother told him that he needed to worry about the mistakes he had made, things had gone so far he couldn't do anything but worry because he didn't know how to fix it.

He had been away from home for two hours when his cell phone started to ring. He looked at the caller I.D. and "home" was displayed on the screen. He ignored the first call, if she called back he would answer because it may have been important. He got off the truck and he left his phone on the seat. He needed some fresh air so he decided to walk the trail around the lake.

Twenty minutes later he came back to his truck, his phone beeped. The display showed ten missed calls from home and four missed calls from his brother. Something was wrong, and instead of calling back he turned his key in the ignition and headed home.

Sandra paced the emergency room in tears as she waited to hear how her son was doing. He had been outside playing when all of a sudden Josh and her daughter Mikayla came running inside, because Miles wouldn't stop screaming. Miles wasn't a screamer so she knew something was wrong.

When she got outside Miles was on the ground and she couldn't get him up, nor could she calm him down as he was screaming at the top of his lungs. Her next door neighbor heard the commotion she grabbed her cordless phone and then dialed 911.

When the ambulance came her neighbor offered to watch Makayla and Josh while she rode in the ambulance with her son.

Keith asked her if she would sit down. She looked at him like he had lost his mind. She said through her teeth,

"That's not your son in there. That's my son in there. You can't tell me what to do or how to feel. I am not your brother."

She said it through clenched teeth, but she was loud enough for other people to hear.

"I have been listening to you since I met you, and nothing has gone right for me since I met you. I am so done listening to you when you keep telling me things are going to get better between Malek and I. It's all good Malek will get over it you say. It has been almost nine years and Malek hasn't gotten over anything. You don't know your brother as well as you think you know him."

Tears flowed like a river down her cheeks, and Keith felt bad. He remembered when he came back home from the basic training and he had over heard Cara telling his mother that she was pregnant with Malek's child. His brother was only twenty. He didn't need to be tied down with a baby. He took his brother out that night and got him pissy drunk.

When his mother called to tell him that Cara was waiting for him, Malek was so drunk he couldn't even speak audibly. Almost a month later his mother received a call that Cara had miscarried, he was happy about it.

His brother was devastated but he couldn't let him stop what he was doing. He had to keep pushing him to move forward. He told his brother that it was a blessing for he and Cara.

They were both too young to support a child. Malek worked during the day and went to the community college at night. He finished school at the same time Cara did. Keith had managed to intercept every letter and every call that he could until Cara finally gave up, she stopped calling and she stopped writing.

Keith introduced his brother to Sandra Phillips. She was a woman that had become infatuated with Keith after a one night stand. He bluntly told her that he couldn't be with her but he knew someone that was just like him that could. That person happened to be his brother.

Sandra fell into bed with Malek and soon found out that she was pregnant, she gave birth to a baby boy that she and Keith hoped would help Malek forget about Cara. Sandra was convinced that she had won Malek completely over when he asked her to marry him, after they were married she got pregnant with Makayla. Something had always been missing in their relationship.

She figured out early that she just couldn't compete with Cara Williams, a few months ago she had never seen her or she had never heard of Cara Williams. She had never heard the woman's name come from her husbands lips, but she began to understand what this woman had on her when she met her, and it was Keith that had set up the meeting and here he was in her face right now telling her to give Malek a minute to get his head together.

"When is he going to get his head together? I have called my husband at least ten times and he hasn't answered my calls. It isn't the first time that he has ignored my calls Keith. Although he doesn't answer my every call, he has been an upstanding man, he's been right here with me to support these kids and watch them grow, but you and I know that I am not the woman he wants in his life."
She looked hard at Keith.
Keith called his brothers cell phone again. Malek happened to be pulling up into the driveway at his home. He had been sitting there for at least five minutes, debating on sending Cara yet another message telling her how much he had been missing her. Before he could press send his cell phone began to ring in his hand. It was Keith.
"Yo, Malek where you been? We need you to come to the hospital quick. Something is wrong with Miles and we have been here at the hospital for the last hour now."
Maleks heart dropped at the mention of his sons name. He sped out of the driveway with his hazard lights on. When he reached the hospital he saw his brother, his mother-in-law and Michelle. They were all gathered around Sandra, and he couldn't help thinking the worst had happened.

Sandra couldn't speak, because she was crying uncontrollably. He asked what was going on Michelle took the phone away from Sandra and she begin to tell Malek what was going on.

"The doctors are running tests now."

She explained what had happened. As he listened to her he couldn't sit down. His heart was racing and his mind was everywhere. Keith tried several times to get him to sit down. Malek just shoved his brother away from him each time.

He knew it wasn't the time or the place to handle his brother but he couldn't control his emotions at that moment. After what seemed like hours the doctor came out to give them an update on Miles' condition. He explained that blood testing showed that he had sickle cell anemia.

"I have our hematologist on his way up to explain what having sickle cell anemia means and how it will affect this young man and you."

Sandra's mother asked the doctor if she could see her grandson and if he was in much pain, while Sandra sat there in a daze. Michelle patted her back worried that she was in shock.

"He is stabilized we have given him some morphine to help with his pain. You may go in, try to keep it three family members at a time. Our hematologist will be here soon."

The doctor nodded and waited a moment to see if anyone had any questions. When he was satisfied that no one had any questions he left the room which was reserved for families. Sandra's mom stood to her feet and she looked at her daughter to see why she hadn't moved or said anything. She stood there looking at the floor.

"Are you alright Sandra? I am going in here with Miles now, I know he is scared."

Michelle noticed that Malek was staring hard at Sandra. Before she could say anything Keith was offering her a hand to get up from her chair.

"Come on in there and go see your son. He's okay."

Sandra didn't take the hand that Keith had offered she struggled to get up from the seat on her own. Malek watched her, and he decided to go in to kiss Miles on his forehead so that he would know that he was there. Before he went inside he told Sandra that he wanted to speak with her real quick before she went inside.

Her mother went in, and Sandra stood there looking at Malek like, he was a piece of trash.

"You and I need to figure this out Sandra. My son has gotten the trait from both of his parents. I remember this from high school like it was yesterday, the only way that little boy in there could have sickle cell anemia is if he got the trait from you and I. I am not a carrier. Where did the other trait come from if he's my son San?"

Michelle looked at Sandra in surprise. Sandra noticed that everyone was looking at her, Michelle, Keith and Malek were looking directly at her. She couldn't stand the pressure she broke completely down. Keith had to open his mouth and he couldn't have opened his mouth at a worse time.

"Man, you can figure all of that out later, what you need to be concerned about is that little boy in there."

Keith didn't see it coming when his brother closed his fist and threw a punch to his right jaw that sent him sailing into the wall. He hit the wall with a thud, and slid to the

floor. Michelle and Sandra shrieked in shock, a security guard that happened to be walking the halls went rushing into the waiting room. He started to call for back up with his walkie, but Keith scrambled to his feet while he was telling the guard that he was okay and that he need not worry about any problems. The security guard looked from Keith to Malek,

"I am going to need one of you to leave."

Keith wiped the blood from his mouth with his shirt and he volunteered to leave.

"I'll go, no problem this is my brother and that's his son in there so I will go. We good bro right?"

Malek just looked at his brother,

"Nah, don't go just yet I want you to take a paternity test with me." Before Keith could object to it, Malek was up at the desk asking the nurse what was required to obtain a paternity test.

"You don't need a paternity test to tell you that that is your son in there. You have taken care of him since the day he was born, don't matter what a test show because that's your son." Michelle was a little disturbed as the scene unfolded in front of her. Sandra still hadn't moved from where she stood. Malek said,

"We need to know so that if he needs a blood transfusion because of this disease, a family member will be a good donor for blood that's one reason this needs to be obtained."

The nurse at the desk agreed, she asked the hematologist who had just come to see Miles, if he could sign an order for a paternity test. Within minutes, she had a kit out and

she swabbed Malek's cheek first. She put on the proper label, opened another test and then swabbed Keith's cheek.

Sandra followed the nurse into Miles' room and she listened as the nurse explained what she wanted to do with the q-tip. Keith looked at Sandra thinking that she would say something, but Sandra was done. She had no more fight left. She knew how the test was going to come back. She didn't need a test to tell her that Miles didn't belong to Malek.

She felt ashamed as Michelle looked on. She had called Michelle because while everything was going on she needed a friend. Even though Keith had dumped her she had expressed that she was there if Sandra ever needed her. When Sandra called, Michele came to her side as a friend.

Right now, Michelle had a look on her face like she no longer belonged. She quietly told her that she had to go, and to tell Miles that she would visit him tomorrow. Michelle looked at Malek and felt sorry that he had to go thru that situation. She especially felt bad for the little boy in that hospital bed.

Michelle didn't even bother to look at Keith as she left the waiting room and went home. She believed that he deserved everything that was coming to him. Malek asked the nurse how soon the test would come back and she told him he would be notified of the results in forty eight hours. He gave her his cell phone number just incase he wasn't at the hospital when the results came down. Then he left Sandra standing there so that he could go sit at Miles' bed side.

He stayed there all night. Only leaving the little boys side to check on his daughter at the neighbor's house. He didn't know what he would do if there were anymore surprises sprung on him that night. He called his mother to let her know that her grandson was in the hospital. He was sure to tell her that he was okay. She promised to be on the next flight out of Baltimore within the next couple of hours. He needed his mother by his side. Cara still wasn't answering his messages, she had even turned off her phone since he started calling.

## *A day for a queen*

It was a beautiful warm fall morning when the Williams family gathered to watch Bo and Shaia exchange vows in their backyard. Cara and Terra had gone all out making sure that the backyard was decorated in a way that the couple would not forget the first time they exchanged vows, because when their child turned a year old they planned to have another ceremony.

This ceremony would be small and quaint but nothing short of spectacular. Connie, Pam and Felicia made sure Shaia had the most beautiful cake that she had ever laid eyes on. Everything was white. White lilies were her flower. They had white chairs for the few guests that they had invited. Her dress was hanging up, it was all white with the most beautiful bodice that she had ever seen. Cara had picked that dress out among three other dresses. Each dress was catching to Shaia's eye but the first dress was the one that caught her heart.

Shaia had been in tears all morning as Terra did her makeup. "Look girl you are going to have to stop it with these tears because you are going to destroy your make up." Terra blotted away her cousin's tears with a smile.

"I'm sorry I am just so happy, thank you for all of your help."
Cara and Terra gave her a group hug and told her that they wouldn't have it any other way. Soon it was an hour before the ceremony and everything had been in place for at least thirty minutes. Everyone was dressed from head to toe in white.

Bo stood at the make shift alter just near a silver arch which was decorated with white taffeta, the unity candelabra stood tall just beyond that with tall stark white candles for the newly married couple to light after they had said their vows.

Bo was nervous and he couldn't figure out why.
"This woman and I have been together since college and I feel like I should've done this along time ago, so why am I so nervous right now."

His palms were sweaty and he was sweating like it would be the first time he had ever met Shaia.

"Calm down dude."

A.J. laughed then he turned to his uncle hoping that he could give his friend some encouraging words to calm him. A.J. kept his eyes on the back door hoping that his surprise would work out as planned, he looked at his watch and it was fifteen minutes to two o'clock it was almost time for the lady to walk down the aisle.

He took a deep breath as he looked at the family members that were seated already and then back at his watch. The clock was ticking away.

The photographer that worked all of Every Occasions event that needed a photographer was getting ready to take her position in the back yard so that she could capture each moment of the ceremony with her camera. Her husband would make the video.

She congratulated the beautiful glowing bride as she and her husband left the room. It was now one fifty five. Shaia said a silent prayer as she stood up in front of the mirror. Terra smiled at her cousin,

"You look beautiful Shai, are you ready?"

*Shai* had been her childhood nickname.

Shaia sighed with a big smile,

"I been ready!"

Promptly the ceremony began. Six year old Josh dressed in a white tuxedo opened the back door as the music begin. Everyone watched as first Terra walked slowly down the porch steps and down the white runway to the arch where the groom, the best man and the Pastor stood.

Cara followed her, she looked as beautiful as ever, she smiled at her family, she smiled at the groom, the best man and the Pastor. She could feel tears threatening to fall as she looked at each of her family members and she noticed her father sitting in the second row of seats. She wanted to run to him, and give him a big hug, but she had to keep it together until after her sister said her vows. She knew that her man was behind her fathers presence, and she loved him for that. She would tell him that today she thought.

Everyone stood as Nashaia appeared at the door. You could hear everyone whispering how beautiful she was as she began to walk towards her groom. Her father Deon Fletcher, dressed in all white moved to help his daughter walk down the steps. He held her hand, and then he kissed her cheek after she had stepped down. He whispered in her ear that he loved her, then he stepped to the side, and watched his daughter walk down the little aisle to the man that she was about to promise to love and be there for, for the rest of her life.

When she made it to the alter Bo grabbed her hand. He had tears in his eyes, because he loved the woman standing before him so much. She was definitely his queen, and he would spend the rest of his life working hard to make her happy.


By the time the Pastor pronounced the couple man and wife Mr. And Mrs. Bryan Oden there wasn't a dry eye in that backyard.

After the ceremony the photographer took photos of the bride and groom, and pictures of the family. Deon Fletcher stood off to the side, while the cameras flashed. He was so thankful to be there watching his two beautiful daughters all grown up, smart and strong he gave the Lord thanks as he stood there. Cara noticed that he was standing off so she excused herself from everyone else and she touched his hand.

"Come on, you're family too."

He wanted to tell her that he didn't feel like he belonged; he remembered only a short time ago asking both of his daughters forgiveness for not being present in their lives. Cara would tell him with a smile,

"It's not all your fault what happened in the past you're in our lives now."

Those words kept him going they just didn't understand. He would say to himself, yes I'm here now so I want to make every second count. He held his baby girls hand and allowed her to lead him to the front of the cameras, where he would stand with his oldest daughter Shaia. He couldn't be more happy as he stood there holding them both in his arms. He looked up to see Connie watching him. He had so much to say to her, there were so many things that he never got a chance to say. He had written it in letters that she had never received; he had called only to receive the dial tone in his ear. It had been years since he had loved her and since she had loved him, time hadn't erase what still needed to be said.

He was able to move away from the flashing camera. He stepped over to where Connie stood. She looked one way, not acknowledging him. He still expected that reaction from her. She was always guarded.

"You know I need to tell you that I am so sorry for everything that happened. I keep playing it over and over it my mind how I could've done so many things differently, it doesn't change the outcome but, I just want you to know that I am so remorseful. I am so sorry Connie. I wanted to be there."

Connie nodded. Shaia had told her everything that he had said when she visited him the very first time. Pam had tried to tell her but she refused to listen to her. If she had listened to her sister, tell her what was going on maybe she could have changed the outcome.

Maybe she could have stopped her father from sending the only man she had ever loved away from her and his child. Maybe they would have had a chance to make it as a couple, raising their daughter together if her father had just given them a chance. She looked into his eyes and told him that she forgave him. He looked at her like he couldn't believe that she had finally forgiven him.

 "I forgive you. Please forgive me for not believing in you."

 She took his hand and gave it a squeeze. He nodded acknowledging that he did forgive her. His prayers had been answered. They stood together and watched their daughter smiling on her wedding day.

Shaia looked back at her parents with a smile on her face. She had married the love of her life, they were expecting their first child and the man that had been absent

from her life since she was born was now standing with her mother watching her, all she could do was smile. She thanked her family for pulling the ceremony off in such a short period of time. She and her new husband prepared to get ready for their honey moon in South Carolina.

It wasn't Cancun or the Virgin Islands like she had dreamed because she couldn't go far while she was seven months pregnant but she was still happy.

A.J. and Cara stood at the curb waving goodbye to the newly wed couple as they rode off in the white stretch limo that had been waiting for them while they exchanged vows. A.J. wrapped his arms around Cara's shoulders and kissed her forehead.

"You look so beautiful dressed in white."

She missed his meaning behind his words. She smiled up at him, thanking him for the compliment.

They went to his apartment which he had just moved into in the last month because spending all the time at his childhood home with his mom while he was in town was getting old. He needed a place of his own to entertain Cara in. Once they got to his apartment she decided she wanted to take a shower. She hung her white dress up with care and disappeared to the bathroom with a kiss.

## *Letting go*

Malek still hadn't gotten a response from all the messages that he had sent to Cara. It had been months since his life had been turned upside down. He still couldn't get over the betrayal of his brother and his wife. He had ended up in a triangle that he would never have imagined being caught up in.

He had raised his wife and brother's child as his own since the little boy baby took his first breath, and it destroyed something in him to find out that way. He had named that child, held that child, heard that child say his first word and even watch that child take his first steps. His world was all messed up. When the smoke settled the person he thought he'd always be able to call wasn't there.

It was five thirty on a Thursday afternoon when he decided to take the chance of stopping by Cara's job to see her. He needed to look her in the eyes to ask her what was wrong that she hadn't returned his messages or his calls. As he walked across the street, Cara was coming out of the office and locking the doors. He stood back so she wouldn't be surprised to see him when she turned around he wanted to stay within her view.

As she locked the doors, and set the security codes he couldn't help getting aroused as he looked at her from head to toe, the red suit that she wore tastefully caressed her every curve, her hair was pulled up into a sexy bun, and her perfume wafted in the air around her. He was so turned on he had to take a deep breath to calm himself down. As she set the codes on the door she could feel someone standing there and when she cut her eyes in that direction she could tell that it was a man. When she turned to face

that person who was obviously waiting for her she was surprised to see Malek Jones standing there with his hands in his pockets.

"What's going on stranger?"

He greeted her.

She smiled at him promising herself that she wouldn't get aggravated with him because she knew he was going to ask her why she hadn't returned his messages or his calls.

"I've been so busy. I am rushing to meet my family now."

He could see that she didn't feel like being bothered, so he backed up a little bit because the last thing he intended to do was to upset her.

"I am not trying to hold you up. I just wanted to see that you were okay. I haven't heard from you in a while."

The fact remained that he hadn't heard from her by accident. She looked him over missing the feelings that she used to feel when she was near him.

"I'm fine. I hope you are."

He wanted to tell her what had been going on in his life. He took her smile as an invitation to pour out his heart.

"Man I have been through a lot these last few months."

She nodded,

"Yeah it's been a tough few months for me too. Shaia got married, she is having her baby any day now, and I finally met my dad. It has been a lot going on these last couple of months."

Just as he began to tell her about all his issues, the silver mustang that he had often seen come to pick her up pulled up to the curb. She waved hello to the driver and then she signaled for him to give her five minutes.

Malek was immediately offended, because that meant that five minutes was the only time she had for him.

"I'm sorry to hear that you are having a hard time, you're strong,"

Before she could finish her sentence he interrupted her.

"But you don't know."

She stopped him by holding up her hand.

"You're wrong. I know a lot. Keith talks a lot, did you forget he's my nephew's father? All of that that went on I think it was extremely grimy. I can't imagine how you feel but I know you are handling it because you are so strong."

The wind blew a stray piece of hair into her face, and when she raised her hand to push it back away from her eye, he saw the diamond twinkling on her finger. He had known her for a while, he knew that she wasn't a flashy person at all and he also knew that she didn't wear much jewelry at all.

He had to ask,

"So you're got engaged?"

She looked at her hand and then she blushed.

"I am so happy right now Malek."

She looked at the pink ice princess cut ring on her finger. It wasn't an engagement ring but a promise ring given to her by A.J.

She didn't bother to correct Malek, all he needed to know was that she was finally happy.

Malek looked at the ground, his heart hurting because he remembered being able to make her smile the way that she was smiling right at that moment. He was a little embarrassed so he started staring at his feet. He couldn't even offer congratulations. He was so wrapped up in everything that had been going on in his life that he didn't even take the time to notice her.

He wanted to tell her about the pending divorce from his wife. He wanted to tell her about his new business venture. He wanted to tell her that he was finally ready to pursue a relationship with her. All he could say was,

"Wow, I got papers going for my divorce and you're getting married."

She noticed that he had set his jaw which she knew meant that he was upset. She didn't know what for, but instead of getting in her feelings with him she told him how his soon to be ex-wife had come to her with a business card of hers that she had gotten from his wallet.

"She wanted to sling accusations, but I quickly let her know she had no ground to stand on so she needed to let it go. Can't believe she apologized and stalked back out my office door like she had lost her best friend." Cara remembered feeling sorry for the woman. All she wanted was the man that she had married to love her, and because she wasn't honest from the beginning she lost him.

As Cara looked at the good looking man in front of her that she thought she loved since Jr. High and she admitted to him,

"I've always waited on you Malek. I waited to see what you were going to do before I did anything even way back when we were teenagers. I didn't allow myself to truly be happy without you. I waited for months for you to call. All you had to do was say hey and you never called. I waited for you. It wasn't fair. I deserved more than you could give me. I had to let go."

He looked at the hurt in her eyes and he felt bad. He wanted to apologize for not making his own decisions way back when it mattered the most what direction they would go. He knew their lives would be so much different if only he had stood up to his brother the day Cara came to tell him she was pregnant. Before he could say another word, the dude in the mustang was walking around the front of the car so that he could open the passenger door for Cara.

Malek heard Cara telling him to take care as she got in the car, and as the dude closed the door for her, the dude nodded to him as he went back around to the drivers side of the car.

He felt like he had lost his best friend as he watched the mustang pull into traffic and then disappear up the street. At that moment he vowed to always be there for his children and to make sure they knew about love, and not taking those you love for granted.

Inside the car A.J. asked Cara if she were okay because as soon as he pulled up to the curb he recognized Malek. Cara smiled at him and reassured him that she was okay. She leaned over the center console of the car to give him a kiss on the cheek. He didn't

know if the kiss was for reassurance that Malek standing there didn't bother her, or maybe she was kissing him as a greeting.

He decided he wouldn't read into it because, she had told him how she felt about Malek and he was sure that his presence in front her business that afternoon or at anytime didn't affect her.

## *Six months later, Finally*

Cara and A.J. had spent almost every weekend together from November to May. Together they watched the leaves turn from gold to green, and their friendship had gotten stronger with each passing day. It seemed to get stronger each season.

Cara had been in the office all day, making calls and finishing up paperwork on upcoming events. Since she had been in the office she had been getting a lot of calls on her business phone, someone would call and not say a word. It aggravated her, so much that the last time she received a call she listened intently for a minute before she went off.

"Look I don't know who this is, or why you seem to think that something is funny about you calling my establishment and not saying anything. I am going to have this call traced and I will find out who you are and I will have charges brought against you for harassment. So just keep calling."

Cara didn't know if she could have the number traced, but she would definitely look into it. She couldn't afford to have the number of "Every Occasion" changed. The number had been the same since they had been in business. She had a lot return customers and those return customers made a difference. She wouldn't risk her business to the satisfaction of a prank caller.

She looked at the wall clock in her office and it read five thirty p.m. It was a Friday and most of the time Every Occasion closed at two p.m. on Fridays. This Friday Cara was going out of town with A.J. when she locked the doors of the office.

"I want to call it our weekend getaway because we have been working hard and we need a little time off."

A.J. had told her about the weekend he had planned a month before. She stood up from her desk to put files away. She smiled thinking about the weekend ahead. Just as she was turning off her computer A.J.'s sister Margo came into her office with a smile.

"My brother is here ma'am. So are you ready for your weekend? I heard its going to be nice."

Margo had graduated from college, and just as her brother suspected she wanted to become a partner of Every Occasion. Shaia decided to step down from her position so that she could raise her daughter and help her mother with the boarding house and soup kitchen. Margo was trained to fill her shoes and she filled them very well from the beginning.

Cara reached in her drawer for her purse. She smiled at Margo. "How did you hear that this weekend was going to be nice?" Cara walked across her office to the window to close the blinds. "This is Every Occasion ma'am and in our new venture booking vacations and such I had a hand in that. So I know you will have a nice weekend."

 Margo returned her smile and they both went down stairs so that they could close the office. On the wall was a board with a schedule of events for the weekend, Cara attempted to glance at it. Margo stepped in front of it,

"Don't worry about this Cara, we have it covered."

 It would be the first time in six months that Cara wouldn't be there to make sure everything ran smoothly for upcoming events. She was a little nervous, but she trusted Margo. She had trusted her for many years so she told herself to relax.


"I know you got it."

Margo nodded.

The women grabbed their keys and they shut of the lights in the office. Margo followed Cara out the front door. Cara smiled at the man standing beside his car in front of the building. He greeted her with a deep hello and she greeted him with a kiss after she set the security code. A.J. gave her a tight hug.

 "Are you ready sweetheart?"

 He whispered against her ear, his lips just barely touched her ear sending a shiver down her spine. She was so ready for more than the weekend. She wanted to tell him that she was ready for him to make love to her. They had been dating for almost a year and they had decided that they would wait to make love. Cara felt good about the relationship because they had decided to wait, but it was getting a little harder each time they were together.

She nodded. He opened the truck door for her, and he watched her slide inside. When he got into the drivers side of the truck he kissed her deep. The kiss sent a stirring at the core of her and she wanted to moan out loud to let him know what he was doing to her.

"You gotta stop man."

She pulled on her seat belt and crossed her legs, her black skirt rose up her legs, exposing her thighs. A.J. swallowed hard,

"You don't have to play hard like that, I wanted to show you how much I missed you."

He tore his eyes away from her thick thighs and cranked up the truck.

Cara leaned back against the seat and she didn't bother to adjust her skirt. She wanted to tease him. A.J. kept his eyes on the road.

"I missed you to."

She said as she looked out the truck window.

A.J. drove them straight to the airport. They didn't pack anything at all.

"We'll just get whatever we need when we get to where we're going."

Cara nodded okay. She was nervous about getting on a plane, she had only been on a plane once before and she wasn't too thrilled about taking another trip. She was also nervous about the cruise that would be there weekend get-a-way. She had never been on a cruise and she had never wanted to go on a cruise because of some of the negative things she had heard about them. When she shared this with A.J. he told her that she should quit worrying and live a little.

"That's what I thought I have been doing all this time."

He kissed her forehead and he promised her that he would hold her hand. He even sang the song by Shai called "Comforter" which made her blush if nothing else. She didn't think that anything would help her nerves except getting it all over with as quickly as possible.

When they boarded the plane just as he had promised, A.J. held her hand. He ordered her a double shot of rum and coke soon after the take off. The drink helped her relax a lot, she smiled and they talked. He never let her hand go.

As soon as they got on the boat, Cara sent Shaia and Terra and their parent's a picture message, *"We made it!"*
 *"Great!! Enjoy yourself. I love you."*
The cruise ship was leaving Fort Lauderdale, Florida headed to Nassau, Bahamas. The  temperature was about eighty five degrees and Cara still tipsy from the flight slipped into a blue bathing suit and sarong. She was ready to dance, she had noticed that the ship had a couple of little clubs on its lower deck. Dancing and sipping a little more would be the only thing that would keep her mind off of being in all of that water in the middle of the ocean. Soon no land would be in site and she was very nervous about that.
A.J. slipped into casual shorts and a button down shirt. Before they left the cabin he gathered Cara up into his arms and he kissed her. Cara sighed and smiled, she grabbed his hand to lead him away from the cabin because if they stayed she wouldn't be able to keep on her swimsuit, and she was sure A.J. wouldn't be able to keep on his shorts.
They danced, they played the slots and relaxed well into the next morning. A.J. had to carry Cara in his arms back to the cabin because she had sipped until she was well past tipsy. Once in the cabin he lay her on the bed and then he lay down beside her. She turned to face him and then she whispered how glad she was to be with him. She kissed his neck and the sides of his face and when she started nibbling on his ear it took everything in him not to strip off her clothes and make love to her right there, but she was drunk and to have sex right now wasn't what they had agreed on.
He wrapped his arms around her, stilling her roaming hands and he rocked her to sleep. They arrived at the port of New Providence Island at eight a.m. The itinerary that

they had been given upon boarding stated that they would be touring Ardastra Gardens after brunch and then Junkanoo expo that afternoon he hoped Cara wasn't in bad shape when she opened her eyes or they would be stuck on the ship for the whole day. Surprisingly Cara rose with a smile on her face.

"I love waking up next to you."

She confessed to A.J. he said,

"Likewise."

They took turns taking a shower, they got dressed and then they went to brunch hand in hand. They went to tour the beautiful island. Cara was glad that they had come because they learned so much. The weekend cruise turned into a nice little get a way for them both. They fished, they rode the Ferry boat, they ate seafood and they mingled with others on the cruise.

On the last day, Cara was surprised when A.J. woke her up with a kiss on her forehead.

"Wake up sleepy head."

He whispered in her ear.

She opened her eyes to see him knealing beside the bed. She giggled. "What are you doing?"

He didn't say anything at first, Cara sat up in the bed worried that something was wrong. When she sat up she noticed that he was fully dressed.

"What's wrong?"


He could tell that she was becoming worried so he smiled to help ease her worries. "This is our last day here so I wanted to get up early just to enjoy our last morning in Nassau."

Cara swung her legs to the side of the bed, she stretched and then she went to take a shower. After her shower she dressed in a long yellow linen maxi dress, and she put a white straw hat on her head and then she joined A.J. he took her by the hand and then he led her to the lower deck where they were serving breakfast. They were seated and shortly after they were seated a waiter came to their table with a covered dish in which he placed in the middle of the table in front of them and then he placed grits, omelets, bacon and pancakes in front of them as well with a carafe of orange juice. The waiter removed the lid from the dish and announced that it was fresh fruit.

A.J. sat close to Cara, he wanted to feed each other the fruit. She smiled, not noticing the twinkling thing amidst the fruit as he picked up an orange and then held it to her lips. She then in turn picked up a piece of mango and held it to his lips, he bit into the juicy fruit and then he kissed the juices from her fingers. Cara giggled, feeling so in love with A.J.

 While they fed each other Cara found a ring on the dish.

"O my goodness A.J, look someone lost their ring!"

He looked at her in surprise for a moment, then he held up his hand to signal for the waiter to come to the table. When he got the waiters attention, the waiter came over to the table with a smile asking if everything was okay.


"It seems that someone has lost their ring, in our fruit dish." The waiter looked shocked, he started to apologize and say that he hoped that he wouldn't lose his job for not checking the dish before he put it in front of them.

"There is no excuse, may I see your manager?"

 A.J. picked up the ring from the dish, he inspected it.

"O, yes sir."

The waiter walked away from the table in a hurry. A.J. watched him. He inspected the ring and he commented,

"Wow, this is a beautiful ring."

Cara agreed, but she was worried about the waiter getting fired because of it.

Soon the manager of the kitchen was at the table expressing his apologies for the misunderstanding. Cara didn't quite get how there would be a misunderstanding about someone losing their ring on a dish. She didn't say anything she let A.J. handle the situation. The manager kept apologizing repeatedly,

"I'm sorry sir, we thought that this is what you wanted."

Cara still had no idea what was going on until A.J. stood up from the table and then he got down on one knee in front of Cara. He had the ring from the dish in his hand. She covered her mouth then, the waiter and his manager still looked surprised.

"Cara Williams, I have waited and waited for the perfect time to ask you and there just doesn't seem to be a perfect time to ask, so I am just going to ask you right now, will you marry me?"


A.J. held his breath as he looked in to Cara's hazel eyes which had filled with tears. She covered her mouth, and she looked at all the people around her who were looking at them.

"Yes, A.J, I will marry you, I love you."

He reached for her hand so that he could remove the promise ring from her finger that he had given her just six months before. He slipped a platinum marquise cut diamond on her finger to replace it. Once the ring was secure on her finger she stood to her feet and A.J. stood to his, he hugged her and the onlookers clapped and cheered.

"I love you too, and I always have."

Was his reply, he didn't want to let her go as they stood kissing and hugging each other tight. Congratulations was in order, it was now her season of love.

# *Sticking to a plan*

Back in Virginia, everything went back to normal with Cara, running Every Occasion with the help of A.J.'s sister Margo and Cara's cousin Terra soon after Cara returned home from her weekend cruise and announced her engagement. Margo insisted that she make her wedding planning an absolute top priority around the office. Margo was excited about having Cara as her sister in law, because she had always felt close to her like she were the sister that she never had. Cara didn't make her wedding top priority, but she did devote as much time to planning as she could when she could. She was thankful that she had the expertise of wedding planning under her belt. She had set a side a date to go try on wedding dresses and then to have a cake tasting.

There were so many things that she needed to do.

She knew just who to get to help her. Sunday after church when they all sat down for dinner at her childhood home she asked her mother to help her, with planning.

"Mommy I know I could get Shaia, Margo or Terra to help me. I think I'd rather have your help."

Felicia couldn't contain her tears.

Her dream had always been to see her daughter happy in her life and she didn't doubt that her marriage to A.J. Ealy would bring her daughter the happiness that she deserved.

Felicia could hardly contain her happy tears when Cara called her from the ship to tell her about how A.J. had proposed. Felicia didn't want to fall to pieces again as the family gathered at the table for Sunday dinner so she took a deep breath before she

answered yes. Before she could ask her daughter where her future son in law was when the doorbell rang.

Bo stood to his feet to go get the door while Shaia fed their baby who was now six months old and sitting in a high chair at the table. He opened the door for A.J. who had been in Georgia since coming back from the cruise. He carried a rose in his hand. Bo gave A.J. a handshake as he said,

"I guess congratulations and welcome to the family is in order."
Felicia had come to see who had rang the bell said,
"Oh, this young man has always been apart of this family. We should toast cheers to the fact that we can finally acknowledge it as being official."
 A.J. hugged Felicia and they all walked into the dining room. Eight pairs of eyes were on A.J. as he always did he greeted everyone and he walked over to Cara. He kissed her cheek. Pam asked if he wanted to eat.
 "No Ma'am, I have to return to my office in Georgia tonight. I just wanted to spend a little time with my sweetheart before I head back. Everyone at the table looked at each other with smiles, saying o how sweet. Cara felt like they were all in high school as she stood up from the table with her near empty plate in her hand. She started toward the kitchen but her mother took the plate from her and told her to go on.
Cara grabbed A.J.'s hand and they went out to the picnic table in the backyard. He hugged her before they sat down.
 "Aww baby, you have to go back so soon?"


Cara had truly missed him. He sighed. Work had been hectic, especially since he had began the expansion project to bring his company to Virginia.
"Yes, Cara it's been a bigger challenge than I thought it would be, but I am finding it runs a whole lot smoother when I'm right there to oversee it all." Cara nodded in understanding. Ever since they added travel planning to the list of services they offered at Every Occasion she had to spend a lot more time to make sure everything ran smoothly as well.
They had planned to get married as soon as he was able to transition his company. The plan was six months. On one hand Cara could look at that as a long time, but on the other hand she knew that time would fly by and six months would not be enough time to get everything together.

"We do what we have to do babe."
She straddled his lap and kissed the side of his face.
"When are you heading out?"
A.J. looked at his silver Bulova watch and then he sighed again.
"I have a meeting early tomorrow morning with some developers. I need to be on the road soon to get everything in order."
Cara pouted, then she kissed his face again.
"Drive safely and call me when you get there?"
A.J. looked into her beautiful eyes,
"I love you future Mrs. A.J. Ealy."
Cara smiled,

"I love the way that sounds Mr. Ealy."
They spent a few more minutes on the picnic table in the backyard just talking. After thirty minutes A.J. picked Cara up as he stood to his feet.
"Can't wait to carry you over the threshold girl, and I'm going to pick you up and carry you just like this."
He carried her back inside the house just like they were in a movie with her holding on to his neck with her head resting against his chest.
He put her down and together they walked to the front door. They kissed goodbye and then Cara returned to the dining room with her family. Bo and Terra's father had gone somewhere together leaving Connie, Pam, Shaia, Terra, Josh and Baby Lauryn at the table. No one was eating; everyone was just talking.
"So Cara, are you excited?" Her Aunt Connie asked while she bounced her grinning grandbaby on her knee.
"I don't know. I don't think its really hit me yet, what this ring means."
Cara looked at her hand. She had thought about how many times she looked at her bare hand as she planned weddings for other people. She thought about how many times she had to answer the embarrassing question that she was asked so often while sitting behind the desk at "Every Occasion."

The new question would soon be, so when is the big date. Have you picked a dress, and she could go on an on non stop about the questions. She looked at the ring on her left hand as she stood among her family and she smiled.
"I think I am Aunt Connie."

"I'm glad."
Her Aunt Pam smiled at her. She joined her family at the table, happier than she had ever been."

# *Not just yet*

Baby Lauryn was six months old and Shaia finally decided that she wanted to go back to work at Every Occasion. She had planned to start off only working half of a day, Lauryn would be attending a five star "Day School." The establishment was highly recommended, but Shaia was still nervous about leaving her baby girl.

Shaia kissed her baby on her forehead and then she passed the happy baby to her mother who had volunteered to take her to school. Shaia had dressed the baby in a purple osh kosh b gosh short jumper and she had put matching purple bows in her jet black hair. She straightened the baby's bows when they didn't need to be straightened. Connie shook her head at her daughter,

"Shaia you know that you can stay home with this baby. Bo wants you to stay at home with her, you aren't going to be able to work worrying about this baby."

Connie say the unshed tears in her daughter eyes.

Shaia took a deep breath and she smiled at her mother.

"I know mama. I need to go back to work because before Bo and I got married I made a big deal about each of us contributing to this household equally."

Bo believed in being the sole provider for his family because that is the way the men in his family had done.

Shaia straightened her robe and took a deep,

"I know I can stay home Mama, but I am able to work so I will work. I know my princess will be in good hands. Thank you."

Connie gave her daughter a reassuring pat on the back before she told Lauryn to wave goodbye to her mommy as they walked out the front door.

Shaia had to turn her back so that she wouldn't be tempted to tell her mother to bring her baby right back to her and then she would call Every Occasion to tell them that she wouldn't be in today because she had to take care of her baby girl. When she heard her mothers van pull out of the driveway she locked the front door and then she headed to her bathroom to take a shower. It was eight thirty a.m. and she had promised that she would be at the office by ten.

The night before she had laid out a sleeveless lavender blouse, with a deep purple skirt and matching shoes to wear to work so she didn't have to go thru her closet in search of anything to wear. When she got to the bathroom she looked in the mirror and smoothed down her hair, she had decided to get her stylist to cut her hair short, and she loved it.

Her husband loved it to. The night he came home after she had it cut he wanted to make love to her on sight when he saw her. He had told her that the hair cut made her look "damn sexy." Shaia was sure that if Lauryn hadn't been in her arms, he would have stripped her out of her clothes right where she stood in their living room.

Remembering that as she picked through the jewelry in her jewelry box in search of pearls to wear with her outfit.

When she had all of her clothes and accessories laid out on the bed she went to the bathroom to start the shower and when the water was at a comfortable temperature she slipped out of her robe and gown and then she stepped in to the shower.

She reached for her sweet musky scented shower gel and she squeezed a reasonable amount on to her loofah. She started to lather the gel against her skin, as she

hummed a lullaby she had often hummed to Lauryn at bed time. She had to laugh at herself because she couldn't think of any current songs to hum the tune to because for six months everything in her life had been about Lauryn.

Shaia was deep into her thoughts and didn't even notice the shower door inch open slowly until she felt the chill of cooler air causing goose pimples to form on her naked skin. She spun around to see what was going on and to her surprise her husband stood there naked in front of her. She loved looking at his muscled chest and arms and she loved the way he made his member jump to salute her when she looked at him.

"Hey baby."

He greeted her before he bent down to claim her lips with his. He took the loofah from her hands.

"Let me help you."

He started guiding the loofah across her skin leaving a trail of white suds.

Everywhere the loofah touched he caressed with his hands causing Shaia to moan. She had missed his touch. With the new baby they didn't spend as much quality time as she would have liked. Soon his caresses were followed by kisses from his lips. Any words that Shaia had wanted to speak were caught in her throat and they came out as soft moans.

Her husband shut off the water in the shower and then he picked her up without a thought of drying her off, and he lay her down on the bed. The satin sheets soaked up the wetness from their skin.

"I missed my wife."

Bo mumbled between kisses and caresses.

"I missed my husband."

She replied as she closed her eyes while he took his time kissing and caressing her from head to toe. She forgot about the time until she heard her phone vibrating on the night stand. She opened her eyes, and Bo knew that she was thinking of Lauryn, so he leaned over to look at the screen of her cell phone to see that the caller was a 1-800 number.

He recited the number from the screen to her and then he asked her if she wanted to get it. He withdrew his lower body from hers and then fluidly pushed his manhood into her causing her to shudder and moan.

"No."

"Do you want me to keep going?"

He withdrew his manhood from her once more, she wrapped her legs around his waist to pull him back in as she moaned

"Yes."

Shaia could control the trembling in her legs as Bo delivered faster strokes. He whispered in her ear.

"Yes, what?"

"O, baby please keep going."

Bo worked her into a frenzy, she was close to exploding when he cupped her hips to hold her in place as he delivered powerful strokes that had her seeing stars. They climaxed together, and he collapsed against her chest kissing her face.

"Stay home today."

He demanded. Shaia looked at the clock on her nightstand and it read nine fifteen. She had forty-five minutes to get to Every Occasion if she intended to go in.

"But, baby I said that I'd be in today by ten. Mama took Lauryn to Day School, and I'm all prepared to go to work."

Shaia knew she would feel guilty if she didn't go in.

"Your husband needs you, he took the day off just to be with you, they will understand."

Bo rolled Shaia onto her stomach and then he started kissing her shoulders, and the back of her neck. She could feel his manhood throbbing against her back side. She didn't want to tell him no, and she didn't want to be a no show at her job either.

She sighed as he entered her from behind, and she didn't know what to do. She looked at the clock it read nine twenty five and time definitely wasn't standing still. She reasoned with herself that it had been a long time since it had been just she and her husband alone together, and she wasn't ready to leave her husband just yet. She reached for her cell phone to text Cara. The text read,

*"Cara, I will be in tomorrow. Sorry last minute will call you later."*

She then dropped the cell phone on the floor beside of the bed and she closed her eyes as her husband held her hips as he made love to her from behind.

# *Same mistakes*

Terra kissed her baby boy in his forehead before he got into the backseat of his grandfathers car. It was the day of her interview and her father had volunteered to take Josh to school. He had brought Terra breakfast from the corner diner. "I want you to go in there and wow those people my love." Timothy Baxter looked at his beautiful daughter, he remembered the first time he had held her in his arms almost twenty eight years ago and he remembered promising his mother that he would always be there for his grey eyed baby doll, no matter what. Timothy Baxter gave Terra his support in every way that he could, just as he promised.

He would do that until the day he died. He gave his daughter a hug and then he got into his car, his grandson and the love of his life Pam waited.

Terra closed the door, she carried the tray of food to her breakfast nook and she sat down to eat. She opened the tray and inside was a toasted bagel, scrambled cheese eggs and bacon. It was her favorite breakfast meal. Her cell phone chimed. She had to get up to get it. When she picked it up, the display told her that it was Keith calling. She wondered why he was calling it wasn't his weekend to get Josh. She answered,

"Yes."

"Hey, I know Josh is on his way to school, I wanted to catch you before you headed to work."

Keith had been great with Josh since she had made the initial introductions over six months before. He picked him up from school each afternoon and helped him with his homework and then every other weekend he would pick him up on Friday to keep him

until that Monday. That arrangement had been working fairly well for the both of them. Terra and Keith hadn't talked much; all of their dialogue was about Josh.

She didn't know what to say to him and she couldn't think of what he wanted to say to her beyond apologizing for not being there for she and Josh in years past.

He cleared his throat,

"Do you mind if I stop by, there's something I want to talk to you about."

Terra looked at the clock on her microwave. She had three and a half hours before her interview. Then she thought about the man, who had fathered her child. The man that she thought she had been in love with. The man she had kept a secret from her family, and the most important person in her life; her son.

"I have to go in by eleven, if you can come by before then that would be fine." Keith smiled to himself, thinking he had an opening.

"Okay, I won't hold you up, I will make it quick."

Terra ended the call and then she sat back down to her breakfast. Thirty minutes later her doorbell was ringing. When she looked out the peephole she saw Keith standing on the other side of her door. Terra was surprised by what she felt, looking at Keith standing before her dressed casually in a baby blue button down shirt and khaki pants.

She opened the door to let him in, the smell of his cologne enveloped her as he stood there looking at her. Terra became nervous; she remembered where she would always end up when he stared at her. She would always melt into his arms, and today she didn't want to do that. She moved away from him and asked him what was up.

He cleared his throat,

"I need you Terra. We need to be raising our son together."

Terra looked at the man in front of her sideways.

"You don't need me to take care of your son Keith."

The sexy man in front of her had tears in his eyes.

"I've made a mess Terra, and I gotta make this right. I gotta make this right for my children."

Terra didn't know what to do, she wanted to comfort him, but at the same time she wanted to tell him to leave.

"Keith, you have made things right over here with me and Josh. You acknowledged your son. You have too much going on in your life right now and I don't think that is good for anybody until you clean it up."

She was referring to Michelle and she was referring to his brothers' wife and the son that they had together. Terra still had feelings for her sons' father, but she couldn't deal with the drama he had created in his life.

"I messed up, I don't know what to do, all I was trying to do was keep my brothers family together."

"What about my cousin? Don't you feel guilty for interfering in her life?"

Keith really did feel guilty and his guilt was eating him up right at that moment.

Terra looked at him,

"I won't lie, for six years I have wanted you to say that to me. I have wanted you to say you wanted us to raise our son together, I have finally learned to accept that you

and I won't be able to do anymore than what we are doing together right now. I believe its best that it stays that way."

Terra had stood her ground and Keith looked defeated. He knew that Terra had been upset with him, but she had always come around to seeing things his way. As she stood in front of him at that very moment he knew things had changed.

He wished he could go back and do everything over, but in life there were no chances for do overs. He stepped into Terra's space to give her a kiss on her cheek.

"I'm proud of you Terra, see you this afternoon."

She nodded okay and then she opened the door for him to leave. He walked out the door without looking back.

Sandra Jones stood at her kitchen sink washing dishes when she saw Keith walking up to her back door. It wasn't his weekend to pick up Miles so she didn't know why he was there. The last six months had been hell for her. Malek had served her with divorce papers soon after Miles was discharged from the hospital.

Malek hadn't stepped a foot back in the house that they had shared. He had told her that he didn't want anything from her except to have his last name back. He had given her the house and the van. He agreed to pay half of the mortgage and utilities, and he would pay her child support.

She had been laid off from the hotel shortly after that, so she was unemployed she was living off savings and Malek's help until she was able to find another job to support her family.


Things were hard all because she didn't correct the mistake that she had made almost nine years before. Keith stood on her doorstep looking at her through the window. She threw her dish rag down and then she opened the door.

"What do you want?"

"How are you Sandra?"

He avoided the daggers she shot at him with her eyes by looking past her into the house.

"How does it look like I'm doing Keith? I lost everything."

She had been singing that same song since Miles came home from the hospital. "You haven't lost everything, you have your health and you have these kids."

Sandra put her hands on her hip, she had gained over forty pounds during her pregnancy, the baby was four months old and she hadn't lost a pound. She had gained more weight.

Sandra dropped her hands from her hips and then she pulled her messy hair back into her usual ponytail never minding the knotted edges of her sideburns and the knotted hair at the nape of her neck. Sandra didn't care. She started doing the dishes again, ignoring the man standing in her kitchen.

Ever since Miles had come home from the hospital, her mother came over as often a she could to help out with the children, while everyone else in her family that had heard about what had happened had distanced themselves from her. Sandra had been a goody two shoes, and a know it all. Some of her family members expressed that she got what she deserved for acting like she was better than...

She felt so alone.

"What do you want? You know Miles is in school."

Keith wasn't sure why he had come to visit his brothers ex wife. He was honest with his reply,

"I don't know."

"Wow, Keith Jones doesn't know? You haven't come up with any bright ideas on how to get your brother to come back to his family? Wait a minute you must have decided that I really wasn't better for your brother than Cara Williams either?"

Sandra had started to blame Cara for her problems. She began to cry; she couldn't hold back her tears as snot ran from her nose, she could see Keith looking at her with pity and disgust. Sandra didn't care how she looked.

Baby Anya started to cry, the baby monitor was mounted on the kitchen wall. Sandra threw her dishrag back down in the sink and then she walked out of the kitchen, telling Keith to let himself out without even looking back at him.

Keith hung his head, and then he turned to the door to let himself out of what used to be his brothers house.

A.J. was trying to get everything in Georgia running smoothly while Cara worked hard on the sixteenth birthday party for her clients' son. Things didn't seem to be looking that good in Georgia without A.J.'s presence. One night he expressed his concerns to Cara while they were engaged in their nightly chat. He was worried that he may still be working on transitioning even after he and Cara were wed.

"You gotta do what you gotta do babe, the Georgia plant is your baby. They need you."

Cara had just walked into her apartment, she placed her keys on the counter and then she went to look in her freezer for a quick frozen dinner to throw in the microwave.

"My lady needs me too. I don't want work to affect what's going to be home. I want us to focus on each other after our wedding."

"Aww, that's sweet, babe I would relocate for a little while."

Cara had thought about the possibility of moving to Georgia until A.J. had his business the way he wanted it. She was confident that Margo, and Shaia could handle Every Occasion with out her for a little while.

"That's good to know that you would be willing to do that for us sweetheart. I love you for that. I miss V.A."

Cara found a banquet frozen dinner that she wanted to eat and she popped that into the microwave.

"You only miss V.A.?"

"Baby you know I miss you, I'm ready to get you into that big beautiful house. I want to make love to you in every room, and I'm ready to fill those rooms up with our babies."

Cara could feel herself blush even though she was alone in her apartment. "It'll workout just the way it's supposed to babe, be patient."

"That's why I love you so much girl, your optimism, your encouragement."

A.J. looked at the picture of him and Cara that he kept beside his bed. It was the photos they had taken at the movie theater back in college.

"I love you too A.J."

They told each other goodnight and then they ended the call. Cara checked the locks on her door and then she reset the security code on the security alarm. She ate her food and then she got in the shower. It was only eight o'clock but she was tired and she anticipated the next day to be an even longer day.

Between clients she had to try on dresses, and go on a cake tasting with her mother. She also needed to finalize some last minute details of her wedding. She knew that the four months left would soon be two months left and then her wedding day would be only days away. She slipped into her pajamas, and before she could get into bed her phone rang. She picked up to see that she had six missed calls all from an unknown caller. She sat down on the side of her bed and she called her mother and father to see if they were all okay and then she sent text messages to everyone else to let them know she was powering her cell phone off for the night and if anyone needed to reach her to call her house phone.

She thought about changing her cell number because she had long grown tired of the calls from the silent caller and the unknown caller. She also thought about changing her cell phone to a message line used only for business purposes. She fell asleep with that on her mind.

The next day Cara got up bright and early. She, Margo, Shaia, Erica and her mother were going to get fitted for their dresses. Since Terra was on assignment for her job she would get fitted the next day.

Cara looked at herself in the floor length mirror, the first gown that she tried on she knew would be the gown she wanted to wear on her special day. Margo commented,

"My brother is going to love you in that dress. You are so beautiful."

Everyone agreed. Her mother looked at her only daughter with tears in her eyes.

"O, mommy stop with the tears, you are going to make me cry."

Felicia fanned herself,

"Sweetheart I can't help it. It has been my dream for you to marry a good man like A.J, I watched both of you grow up into the people that you are now and I am so proud of you both."

Soon tears flowed from all the women in the dressing room. Margo suggested they all go out for drinks after trying on the dresses. Cara thought about the last time she had gone to a bar, and where she had ended up afterwards. The memories that she had weren't pleasant ones.

When Erica started talking about how long it had been since she had been away from her babies to have a drink Cara decided to go along with them. Felicia had to go back to work, so she kissed her daughter and told the others she would see them later.

Cara's next appointment was scheduled at three p.m. it was only one thirty so they had plenty of time to sit down at the bar across the street from Every Occasion. Cara walked into the bar amongst the ladies guarded. She resolved not to have an alcoholic beverage; she would order a cranberry juice.

When the four women sat down at a little table next to a window a waitress came over to take their drink orders. Margo looked at Cara sideways when she ordered a cranberry juice instead of alcohol.

"Is there something you want to share with us sis? Cranberry juice?"

Margo was insinuating that Cara's reason for ordering no alcohol was because she was expecting. Cara corrected her,

"I have two more clients that I need to be sharp for. Pregnant no ma'am I am not."

"I'm just saying, I know my brother wants to have a house full of kids and since he can not live without you, I figure you and he may have got a head start?"

Margo was fishing. Cara laughed,

"Your brother and I are not sexually active nosy little sister. We are waiting until we are married and we want to wait for at least a year before we have kids."

Shaia and Erica looked at Cara like she was crazy.

"What's up with the time line? Who does that?"
"We do that, and plus I have a client that requires me to be so sharp this afternoon, so I don't need any alcohol to dull my senses."


The women laughed over drinks. Cara was having a decent time until she looked up at the door and she saw Malek walk in with his apron thrown across his shoulder.
"You know what y'all, I should be working on this file before my client comes."

Cara stood to her feet. Erica looked at her glass of juice,
"Cara you took only a sip of your juice though."
Cara pulled a five dollar bill from her purse and put it on the table underneath her glass. Shaia looked at her sister wondering what was going on, but then she saw Malek as he stepped through the doors. She spoke up in Cara's defense.
"I have met this lady and she does keep you on your toes. See you in a few sis."

Cara thought she had been able to avoid Malek completely until he saw her as she walked out the door, he put his apron down and he followed her out the front door.
"Hey."
He called out to her, she walked away from him faster stepping into the street as a car passed. He grabbed her arm and she pulled away, scowling at him.
"What's going on?"
"What do you mean what's going on? Nothing is going on."
Cara walked quickly across the street, Malek followed.
"You been avoiding my calls?"
Malek accused.

Cara didn't like his accusing tone, she raised her eyebrows and crossed her arms as she faced him,

"Why are you calling me? Is it you that's been playing on the phone, not saying anything?"

Malek raised his brow now.

"Nah, I left you a message or two. I don't have time to play Cara."

Malek followed Cara into her office.

"Can you please go Malek? Why are you here?"

"So we aren't friends?"

"I haven't spoken to you in over six months Malek. Friends keep in contact with each other. No I don't think we are friends."

Malek didn't expect that from her, he backed up,

"We aren't friends Cara?"

"No, and honestly I don't believe we ever were. Can you please excuse me; I have a client that I need to prepare for."

Malek's feelings were hurt, he couldn't say another word, he just watched her walk up to her office, and then he walked back across the street to the bar, so he could start his shift.

Cara couldn't believe that she had let Malek get to her; she wanted to hear A.J.'s voice to calm her nerves. She normally didn't call him in the middle of the day, if she called him she worried that he may think something was wrong. She would tell him that she just missed him.

After all she hadn't seen her fiancé in three weeks. She dialed his number, and then she pressed speaker so that his voice would fill her office. A.J. picked up on the first ring,

"Hello sweetheart."

A.J. had been conducting an interview so he was sitting behind his desk looking out the glass window of his office at his staff. "I miss you." Cara cooed honestly, bringing a smile to his full lips.

"I miss you too babe. I may be able to make it home this weekend to spend some time with you."

"Really, maybe I can come to visit you, my calendar is clear for this weekend." Cara looked at her desk planner.

"That would work sweetheart. Use your key, I will be home by five thirty and I will bring us something to eat. I'll plan a nice weekend for us."

A.J. thought of all the things they could do that weekend. Cara interrupted his thoughts when she said,

"We don't have to do anything special babe. I just want to be near you."

That was Cara's truth. She told him that she had a client in thirty minutes and she had to answer the other line. He told her that he loved her and then they hung up.

When Cara answered the other line silence greeted her from the other end and she was not in the mood for the silent caller today. Hearing A.J.'s voice had calmed her, but this caller was working her nerves right back up. She slammed the phone down, and opened her desk drawer to search for the phone book.

She was going to call the phone company to see if she could have the calls she had been receiving blocked or traced. She had no idea that someone else had been receiving silent unknown calls too. The phone technician told her that someone would deliver and set up the equipment the following day.

The next morning Cara opened up Every Occasion early so that she could let the phone technicians in to set up the equipment on the phones. It was eight a.m. and Cara wouldn't have her first client until eleven a.m. So after the technicians were done she thanked them and she sat down at her desk to refresh a few files.

While she refreshed the files she looked at the picture of her and A.J. that she kept beside her computer. She sighed as she remembered when the picture was of Eric and her. She remembered how clients would see the picture and they would ask her when she planned to have her wedding.

Cara was often embarrassed because she didn't see a wedding date in sight. She smiled now because her wedding date was in sight. November fifth was fast coming and she was so excited about it when clients asked she couldn't contain her happiness.

As she waited for the Chinese food that she had ordered, she walked around the first floor of the office. She fingered the flower arrangement that A.J. had sent to her the day before, the card that was with it said he couldn't wait to see her. She missed him; she remembered how A.J. had walked her to school almost everyday for a month after they played truth or dare.

They never talked about the kiss or liking each other or anything out of the ordinary. What they shared didn't need words, even as kids. She remembered shortly

after A.J. moved out of the neighborhood and started a new school, his father passed away.

Cara was right there by his side until A.J. distanced himself from everybody and Malek walked into her life and when he did he took her attention.

The front door of the office beeped as it opened alerting Cara that she had a visitor. The young Asian man looked at the bag that he had in his hand and he read Cara's name off the ticket. She handed him a twenty dollar bill, thanked him as he handed her the bag of food. "Keep the change."

He thanked her and then he went back out the door, the door beeped as he went out. Cara sat down at the desk and she removed her Lo mein noodles, Bourbon chicken and egg roll from the bag. As she spread the chicken over the noodles the door beeped again, she had just taken a fork full of the food into her mouth, but almost spit the food out when she looked up and Malek was standing in her office. Cara stood to her feet throwing her fork down onto the plate. She had had enough of Malek.

"Look, I need for you to understand that we are not friends, we are not lovers. We are nothing Malek and there is absolutely no need for you to keep showing up here at my office or any where that I am. We are done."

Malek looked Cara from head to toe. He had never seen her look better, clad in her orange sleeveless blouse and black pencil skirt that hugged her hips. She was so sexy to him and she was even sexier to him when she was upset.

"You keep saying that. I hear you, but I want you to know that I am free to be yours now Cara. My sham of a marriage is over. We have waited all these years to be together, our chance is now."
Cara couldn't believe what she was hearing. After college she had never waited for Malek and her to get back together. She had accepted that it was over and that it was never meant for them to be. Malek must have been delusional as he stood dressed in all black, with his fresh hair cut. He didn't look like a man that had mental issues but to keep after Cara, he must have them. Cara could have vomited because she was so upset.
"Malek, I have moved on. You had a wife and kids. We made a mistake, its over. We are done Malek. I'm sorry."
She didn't know what else she could say. Tears threatened to spill from her eyes. She looked at the clock on the wall. Her client was due in thirty minutes and she needed Malek out of her space.
"My marriage was a lie Cara. The relationship, before the marriage was all a lie orchestrated by two people that don't give a damn about anyone else as long as they get what they want."
Malek stood there like he expected Cara to change her opinion.
"Malek, what we had temporarily was also a lie. I'm getting married in four months Malek. I am going to marry a man who has always known he loved me, and no one could tell him that he couldn't love me. That is the kind of love I want and deserve."
The tears had begun to fall from both of their eyes.


"I am not going to let you jeopardize my happiness, just because you decided you wouldn't let anyone dictate your life for you. I deserve more than that."
Malek closed the space between them by stepping closer to her. He reached to touch her face, she swatted his hand away.
"No."

Malek reached for her again,

"I'm sorry for everything, wish I could take it all back Cara. I can't do that, what's done is done, but if you tell me right now that you love this dude, and you never loved me. Then I will leave you alone, I promise I won't bother you anymore if that's what you want."

Malek actually looked like he thought there was hope. Cara wanted him to understand that there was none.

"I love A.J., A.J. makes me happy. I want to be with him."

Malek put his hand down as he backed away from her.

"Did you ever love me Cara?"

The door beeped open behind him. They both swiped at their tears. Shaia had come in with Cara's client behind her. Cara was thankful that they had come in because Malek left without another word. She hoped that that would be the last time she saw him.

Cara cleared her throat,

"Good Afternoon Ms. Grimes are you ready to talk about your reception."

Cara pasted a smile on, as she walked past her sister and to her client.

"Follow me upstairs."


Ms. Grimes followed Cara to her upstairs office.

Shaia watched them walk up the stairs, she looked out the door and at the doors of the bar where Malek worked. She wanted to know why he kept just showing up at Every Occasion when he didn't have an Occasion, or any other reason to darken the door steps. She had noticed the look on her sisters' face whenever he popped up and she didn't like it.

Before she could make up her mind to go over to say something to him the phone rang.

"Every Occasion this is Shaia."

She got the sound of a phone being slammed down in her ear. The phone rang again as soon as she put the phone down. Shaia had fixed her mouth to dare a caller to hang up but she was greeted by Margo's voice.

"Hey Shaia, I stopped at the grocery store and I got a flat. I will be there as soon as triple A comes."

"Okay, are you sure you don't want me to come get you?"

Margo whispered into the phone then,

"No this sexy man is waiting with me."

Shaia laughed.

"Well be careful and call me if you need me."

Shaia ended the call and then she went to gather up her sister's uneaten food from the desk to put it in the microwave. The smell of the food almost made Shaia gag. She hurried to place the food in the microwave and then she rushed to the door to stick her nose out for air. She then knew that she was in trouble.

## *Meant to be*

At two o'clock p.m. on Friday, Cara left Every Occasion, headed to Georgia to be with A.J. It had been almost a month since she had seen his smile, smelled his cologne kissed his lips and she missed him. She called him as soon as she got into her car. He promised to meet her at his apartment as soon as he got off of work.

He had given her a copy of the key to his apartment to have incase she were ever in town and he was away from home. Cara listened to sounds of old school music from the nineties as she cruised along ninety five south. She started reminiscing when the song by Total called "Kissing you" started to play. She sang along as she remembered those days when A.J. would wait for her outside on the front porch so that they could walk to the bus stop together.

She remembered how her mother would stand on the porch with her arms crossed against her chest.

"You kids have a good day."

She would say, as A.J. would take Cara's backpack and put it on his shoulders while she only had to carry her notebook, or her band instrument. When they got to school he would walk her to class. They never had a title, they were just friends and everybody accepted that.

Cara had many memories of growing up with A.J. and each memory seemed to be tied to a song that played on that c.d. she was listening to. There was only one song that she could relate to Malek, and she was ready to turn it when it came on. She didn't want to be reminded of anything dealing with Malek.

She pressed a button on her steering wheel to answer the call. "This is Cara." She answered. There was no response. She took a deep breath thinking that it was the silent caller again. She heard a rustling sound and then her father's voice filled the car.

"Hey baby girl."

Cara smiled at the sound of her father's deep raspy voice.

"Hi Daddy, how are you?"

Deon Fletcher sat back in the recliner in his one bedroom apartment. He looked at the picture of his two little girls on the small end table beside him. The picture was of Shaia and Cara when they were babies and then in a photo beside that was a picture of the two women presently.

He was proud of the women that he had known as his daughters for the last year. He didn't feel like he could ever make up for the time that he had missed with them as they were growing up but he was trying his best to make every moment count with them now. "I'm fine sweetheart; this old man just had his baby girl on his mind so I decided to call you up."

"I'm fine. I'm headed to Georgia for the weekend." Cara admitted. She had packed an overnight bag the night before without a second thought. Her father chuckled to himself before he said,

"Won't you be glad when that young man will be within arms reach of you everyday?"

He had been counting the days that he would be expecting to walk his youngest daughter down the aisle to "give her away," when he had only just met her.

"Yes, I will be so glad daddy. A.J. and I spent so much time together when we were kids its crazy how we can hardly find the time to spend with each other now when we are about to get married."

"November fifth will be here before you know it sweet heart. So how is everything going at the office for you ladies?"

Cara sighed before she answered because it had been heavy on her heart to tell someone about the phone calls that she had been receiving at the office and on her personal cell phone. She didn't think it was really much to worry about and she didn't want anyone else to worry, so she wouldn't tell anyone about the calls today she thought as she stopped at a red light.

"Everything is going well. Shaia came back to work yesterday. She barely made it through half a day."

Cara laughed, the light turned green and she lightly tapped the accelerator moving forward. Traffic was extra light heading toward ninety five south, she thought that she would arrive in Atlanta in no time.

"Your sister has been with my sweet granddaughter every single day, all day and night for six months. I really didn't expect her to go back at all."

Shaia had shared with her father that her husband Bo didn't care if she didn't return to work. He would rather she stay at home with their child, but she believed that she needed to go on back to her job because she wanted to continue contributing to the household. Deon Fletcher had become so close to his children he thanked the lord daily because they didn't have to accept him at all but they had.

He added,

"It's about time you add to the number of grand babies, I am getting old you know."

Deon Fletcher would be fifty five the day after Christmas.

"Daddy, I think A.J. and I need to get this wedding out of the way first."

Her mother had also been making little comments about grandbabies as well.

"I know sweet heart, I'm just teasing. I'm going to let you concentrate on that road, you be sure to call me when you get there safely, I love you."

"Love you too Daddy."

Cara pressed the button on her steering wheel to end the call. She pressed play on her disc changer. Old school music from her childhood filled the car. Cara began to reminisce more as the sign that said she had just ninety miles until she reached the state of Georgia came into view. She smiled because she was almost there.

Back at the Jones house; Sandra Jones cleaned herself up a little. She changed into a plain blue sweater and a pair of slacks, she combed her hair back into a neat ponytail, then she called her mother to ask her if she would come over to watch the kids so that she could run out to get groceries. Having just gone to the grocery store a few days before she didn't know what she would pick up this time but she knew she had to use that excuse to get out of the house.

Twenty minutes later her mother let herself into the house, she placed her purse on the kitchen counter and then she walked into the living room to let her daughter know

that she had arrived. When she saw her daughter walking back and forth in the hallway she began to worry.

In her nervousness, she looked at her daughter and asked,

"Didn't you know that you needed something from the store earlier today? Here it is close to rush hour, and folks are getting off of work and they are trying to rush home, its going to be busy Sandra."

Sandra sighed, she told her mother that it was okay she knew exactly what she needed to get and it wouldn't take her long to get it. Her mother sighed as she looked at her daughter with worry. She felt sorry for her daughter because of her situation. It was an ugly situation for everyone involved and, she didn't understand what had happened with it all but she vowed that she would be there for her daughter and grandkids in anyway that she could be. She didn't like the situation but she refused to treat her daughter any differently. She clasped her hands together noting that she needed to come over to dust the furniture in the living room,

"Where are my grandbabies?"

Sandra was thankful that her mother wouldn't press her further, she may just crack at that very moment.

"Anya, is swinging in the den, Mikayla is watching cartoons in the den and Miles is in his room playing his Playstation, I will be back shortly Mom. Thank you."

Before her mother could say anything else Sandra had grabbed her keys and she was out the door. Sandra had grown tired of seeing the pity in her mothers' eyes when she looked at her. So she tried to avoid looking directly at her mother or being in her mother's presence for a long period of time.

Sandra jumped into her van and then put the keys into the ignition. She looked into the rearview mirror, when she looked at the reflection of her eyes she decided that she was going to head to The Five Spot. She knew that Malek, her soon to be ex-husband would be in the middle of his shift.

She knew that his schedule hadn't changed, for the last two years he worked every Friday, Saturday and Sunday at the bar from two p.m. to two a.m. She knew that he would be right there behind the bar when she walked in. It was four thirty when she pulled away from her home, and it was five minutes after five when she pulled into a parking space around the corner from the bar.

Malek was mixing a drink when she walked in. She hadn't seen him in two months. He had refused to visit the children while she was at home. So she had to arrange for her mother to keep the children while he visited. Sandra had to find something to do outside of what used to be their home. It was hard.

Sandra sat down at the end of the bar, Malek looked up from where he stood mixing the drink and he did a double take when he saw Sandra sitting there. He couldn't hide his frown, his displeasure at seeing her. He couldn't help thinking to himself what was it that he ever saw in her to make her his wife. He had to get rid of her so he whispered to his co worker who was also working the bar to give him a few minutes to take a break.

His coworker nodded okay. Malek moved to the end of the bar where Sandra sat on a barstool, with her hands steepled.
"Where are the kids?"
He asked her through clenched teeth.
She had the nerve to look surprised that he was speaking to her.
"They are at home with my mom. I came to talk with you."
Malek looked around him,
"Sandra, look I'm working."

"You won't answer my calls."
She reminded him. She had been calling him everyday since Miles had come home from the hospital. Malek had ignored all the calls and the text messages, after he determined that his kids were okay. He took a deep breath,
"You only need to contact me if it has something to do with my kids."
Sandra wasn't much of a drama queen, but lately each time she had come into his presence she had a problem keeping her emotions in check and she would start crying at any moment and to avoid making a scene at his job, he told her to follow him outside. Malek tossed his black apron to the side and then he walked outside. Once they were outside, he couldn't help looking across the street at the office of Every Occasion.
It was just past five o'clock and he knew that there was no one inside. He averted his eyes from the building to Sandra. He could barely stand the site of the woman in front of him because she was now his nightmare; everything involving Sandra was a constant

reminder of everything that had gone wrong in his life. He frowned at the woman in front of him not trying to mask his disgust of the woman that had birthed his two children.
"Look, I don't know why you came here. I just don't know why you keep,"
before he could finish the sentence she sobbed,
"Malek, I know we can get through this. I'm sorry, I didn't tell you about Keith and I, but that's all I didn't tell you about. I didn't know, I didn't know."
She started to chant. Malek looked around, he touched her arm to guide her away from the bars entrance. He led her across the street and a few doors away from Every Occasion.
"Sandra, for the last time, we can't get over this. I can't get over this. We were never meant to be to begin with, and I don't understand how you can't see that fact as plain as day especially since you and

my brother had to orchestrate a plan to keep me in your life. It's pathetic."

Sandra flinched, she wasn't expecting his anger. She had expected his anger to have dissipated by now.

"Well Malek, answer this, how can you spend almost ten years with someone you don't love?"

Malek looked at Sandra, she looked back seeing that his face showed no emotion as he answered,

"I stayed because of those kids. Miles and Mikayla were enough to make me stay. They mean everything to me, you know I got up most mornings thinking to myself that they are the reason I breathe. For them I was okay."

They stood on the sidewalk staring each other down, not saying a word until Sandra broke the silence.

"Until Cara Williams, you were okay."

Malek rubbed his head in irritation,

"Cara doesn't have anything to do with this, so don't try to bring her into this. You and my brother Keith are the reason why all this is what it is. Your plan, his plan just blew up in your face ten years later and Cara Williams just happened to be passing through when it blew up."

Sandra Jones could only think of things changing when her husband came home one day telling her that he needed space. It didn't matter that they had been arguing about little things every time he walked into the house for the months leading up to him making the decision that he needed his space. She didn't think of the times that she had argued with him in front of the children for something that should have been discussed in the privacy of their bedroom.

Sandra didn't think that the kids were affected by her behavior and her attitude, no Sandra Jones wasn't thinking of those things, Sandra didn't see what he saw. He had to step back for a moment.

He had decided to step away before he ran into Cara that night. He had feelings for Cara, and for a brief moment his judgment had been clouded by his feelings for Cara.

Cara had walked away from him the moment he decided to go back home to Sandra, and the bombshell that awaited him at the hospital the night his son had become ill had drove him completely away from Sandra. It wasn't about Cara.

Sandra couldn't help herself; she didn't know what had happened between her husband and Cara. She didn't know exactly when it happened, but she knew that something had happened. Cara Williams wouldn't go away; everywhere she looked she saw the woman's name. First in the newspaper clipping that Keith had given her, and then on the portfolio that the woman named Cara had given her when planning her mother in laws birthday party and then she saw the woman's name on a card in her husbands wallet. She even saw Cara's name on the side of a car passing by.

"Are you still seeing her?"

Malek couldn't believe Sandra, she had the nerve to be acting like a woman scorned.

"Sandra, I am going to say this once, Cara has nothing to do with what has happened between us, I know you aren't thinking clearly and you can't see your error in all this. You need to blame someone else. I don't care who you blame but, it's all on you. Now go home to those kids. You worry about those kids and leave me alone."

Malek literally sneered at Sandra. He walked away and she looked after him. Before he crossed the street he told her to stop showing up at his job before he had her slapped with a restraining order.

Sandra couldn't stand in the forty degree cold weather that she felt now, standing there without a coat. She didn't feel the cold when she stepped out of the warmth of the

house or the van. She didn't feel anything until she watched her husband walk away. She walked slowly around the corner back to her van with tears streaming down her cheeks, with her shoulders slumped in defeat.

When she got inside the van she pulled out her cell phone and she called her mother. She told her mother that she would be there in an hour. She disconnected the call before her mother could ask any questions. She needed help, because this couldn't be her life.

She drove across town to the apartment that her husband had once shared with his brother Keith. When she pulled up into the parking space in front of the apartment she only saw one light. Keith's car was parked outside, so she knew that he was inside.

She exited her car, at first she knocked on the door lightly, but then she began to knock harder. She must have knocked for five minutes before Keith Jones finally came to answer the door with a scowl and no shirt.

"What are you doing here Sandra?"

She pushed past Keith and she stood in the middle of his apartment with a wet face.

"I don't know what to do."

Keith grabbed his shirt from the back of the couch, he pulled it over his head before he asked Sandra what she was talking about.

"He won't have anything to do with me. He told me the only reason he has stayed with me for over nine years was because of the kids."


Keith looked at how disheveled the woman was standing in the middle of his living room. She looked bad, she looked even worse than what she had looked like when he had visited her. He felt sorry for her and he took some fault in the drama that had unfolded in her life but at that moment he wasn't in the mood to deal with anyone else's problems. He had his own problems to deal with. He had only one answer for her.

"You need to go home and get yourself together San."

"Keith, you gotta help me."

She was demanding him. There was nothing he could do.

"Sandra, let it go. Let him go. I can't help you." Malek wouldn't even speak to his brother even though his mother begged and pleaded for them to work through the problem that he had created. Sandra stared at the picture of Keith, Malek and their mother on the coffee table. She had never seen that picture. That picture made her think of Cara.

"Is he still seeing her?"

"Her?"

Keith pretended he didn't know what Sandra could be talking about.

"Is he still seeing Cara Williams?"

She could visualize the sexy dark skinned woman standing in front of her husband dressed in a sheer pink negligee. She could picture her husband Malek picking the woman up in his arms and laying her on their bed. She swallowed hard, shook her head to get the vision out of her head.

Keith hadn't spoken to his brother in several months but he knew through Terra that Cara had moved on with her life and that she counted her brief time with Malek as a mistake that he knew she regretted. In defense of Cara, the woman he had tried to defend his brother from he said,

"Cara Williams has moved on with her life and she isn't looking back."

Sandra wiped at her eyes with the sleeve of her sweater.

"How do you know? Has he told you that? Are you with her?"

Keith wanted to tell Sandra that Cara was a strong woman. He wanted to tell her that he believed, she would never end up in the kind of mess that Sandra had ended up in.

"Let me suggest this, accept that your marriage is over."

He advised with no sign of remorse.

"If I do, then she has won."

Keith raised his brows,

"Sandra, it isn't a competition. When Malek met Cara, he had already decided he was done with you."

Sandra didn't want to hear that. She needed to blame someone other than herself. Sandra turned around on her heels and she left the apartment without saying another word. Keith stood in his doorway watching her turn the ignition in her van and reverse out of the parking space. He hoped that Sandra would just let it all go.

It was six thirty and Cara had just gotten out of the shower at A.J.'s apartment. She had messaged A.J. the moment she had arrived in Georgia. He messaged her back

that he was on his way to the restaurant to pick up their dinner. Cara dressed in some black tights and an over sized long sleeved tee that A.J. had left at her apartment. After she dressed she went back to the living room and then sat on the couch. She turned on the television to channel surf until A.J. arrived. Cara curled up on the couch and soon drifted off to sleep.

Almost thirty minutes later A.J. stepped into his apartment. He watched the rise and fall of his fiancés chest as she lay curled up on the couch. He couldn't resist giving her a kiss. He placed the bag of carry out plates on the kitchen counter along with his keys and then he walked slowly over to the couch. He loved the woman lying there on his couch sleeping peacefully. He couldn't believe that soon she would be his wife and she would have his last name. He got on his knees beside of the couch and he kissed her gently on the forehead. Cara sighed as she opened her eyes. She smiled when she looked into the eyes of the love of her life kneeling before her with a smile.

"Hello sexy." He greeted her.

"Hi, you."

She greeted him with a soft kiss on his lips. She stretched not realizing that she had been tired and felt like she had rested for hours when indeed she had only just laid down twenty minutes before. He asked,

"Are you ready to eat?"

"Yes, I will fix our plates while you go get a shower and get relaxed."

She touched the stubble on his chin, and then she kissed him again. His stubble tickled her lips. She got up from the couch as A.J. slipped off his coat.

"Did you have a long day babe?"
She asked him as he kicked off his shoes and then picked them up from the floor. "Yes, I had a long day, as a matter of fact I had the longest day that I think I have ever had."

A.J. looked tired. She could see it in his eyes.
"We can eat, and I can give you a massage."
Cara suggested as she washed her hands at the kitchen sink and then she started to open up the Styrofoam carry out plates that were in the bags that A.J. had just brought in.
"I would love that."
A.J. felt like he was lucky to have a fiancé like Cara as he peeled off his layer of clothes while walking into his bedroom.
While he showered Cara reached up into the cabinets in search of dinner plates so that she could transfer the food from the Styrofoam carry out plates from the restaurant.
The aroma from the macaroni and cheese, the barbecue chicken, beef ribs, collards and corn bread wafted up to Cara's nose making her stomach growl. She couldn't wait to sit down to eat. She had just realized that she hadn't stopped to eat all day and she was indeed hungry.
Ten minutes later A.J. walked back into the kitchen, clad in grey sweat pants and a football jersey. Cara was standing at the refrigerator, searching for something to drink. A.J. walked up behind her, and he scooped her up into his arms and he held her, he

inhaled the scent of her. He thought to himself he had indeed been missing her. He kissed the side of her face and then he found himself nibbling on her ear. Cara felt weak all of a sudden, she melted into his arms.

He turned her to face him and she stood with her back to the open refrigerator.

"Cara, I missed you."

He kissed the side of her neck and then he trailed kisses to her throat. Cara was about to loose her balance.

"Baby, you gotta stop."

She started begging as his hands slid underneath her shirt and he caressed her breasts, causing her nipples to harden and strain against the fabric of her bra. A soft moan escaped her lips. Cara knew if she didn't stop him, there would be no turning back. They had spent a year vowing to wait until their wedding night to make love again for the first time in ten years, but his kisses felt so good at that moment Cara was having second thoughts about waiting.

She grabbed his hands which were now tugging at her waistband. He slipped his hands inside the back of her tights and he cupped her butt in his hands.

She began to beg,

"Let's eat baby."

A.J. began to massage her buttocks with his large hands. Her legs got weak, she felt as if her legs were about to give out and A.J. must have felt her slipping, because he picked her up, she wrapped her legs around his waist and her arms around his neck. Cara

was trying to avoid his hot kisses turning her head as he kissed her chin then the side of her mouth.

"Let's eat baby."

She begged, not really wanting him to stop, but needing him to stop.

"You must be hungry."

She nodded. Cara was hungry for food before he got out of the shower, but now she had an appetite for more than food. A.J. continued to kiss her neck, as he held her, he backed up from the refrigerator, and he carried her to the kitchen table where she had placed the food. He let her down slowly, and he saw that she had her eyes closed.

"I'm sorry babe; I get so weak when I see you."
Cara hugged him,
 "Don't apologize babe, I am so happy knowing that you want me."
 He beckoned her to look at him.
"Baby, I want you in so many ways I can barely contain myself
when I am around you. I can't wait to call you my wife, and don't
you forget that. Now let's eat."
He gave her one last kiss and then they sat down at the table to have
their dinner. While they ate they talked about their busy work week.
        "It seems like the weeks are getting longer and longer the
closer we get to November fifth, don't you agree?"
A.J. looked into Cara's hazel eyes, as she nodded in agreement.
"Thirty five more days, and I will be where I feel like I was meant to
be.


Cara smiled at A.J. and A.J. smiled back. He caressed her hand as
they finished their dinner with apple pie a la mode for dessert.
She put there dishes into the dishwasher and then she took him by
the hand.
"Do you think you can handle a massage now Mr. Ealy?"
Sexual tension still lingered between them. A.J. took a deep breath,
and then he smiled at Cara.
 "I think I can handle a massage now future Mrs. Ealy, just go easy
on me."
Cara wanted to play it safe, so she massaged his neck and shoulders
as he sat at the kitchen table. When she was done they got up and
they went to sit down on his couch in front of the television. They
decided to watch movies on comedy central, and it wasn't long
before they both fell asleep in each others arms on the couch.

The next morning Cara awake lying between A.J.'s legs, with her
head on his chest. She looked at him sleeping and she knew she
wanted to wake up to him for the rest of her life. She kissed his chin
and then she got up, she washed her face and hands so that she could

prepare breakfast. When she peeped into his fridge she didn't see anything to make a decent breakfast with so she decided she would go around the corner to the market.

After she took a quick shower she got in A.J.'s truck and entered nearest market into his GPS. The GPS led her directly around the corner from his apartment. When she got to the market she picked up eggs, bacon, pancake mix and your basic breakfast foods, along with a bell pepper and an onion.

As she looked at the pepper that she had picked up for the omelet she had planned to make, she decided that she wanted to cook dinner. She decided to cook stuffed peppers. So she grabbed four more peppers from the produce section and then she went around to the other departments to collect the other ingredients that she needed. Cara also grabbed other foods that she knew A.J. liked that he could throw in his microwave after he got off of work.

She could tell from all the menus on his refrigerator that he lived on take out. As she stood in line to pay for the groceries she thought about how she was going to change that.

When she made it back to his apartment as she was making her second trip to the get the groceries from his truck, she noticed a young woman about her age come from out of her apartment as if she were looking for someone. The apartment was directly across from A.J.'s apartment; their doors faced each other, so there weren't too many places that the woman could look.

The female was wearing a silk night shirt that revealed the tops of her breasts and her thighs. She turned around and she looked directly into Cara's eyes as she came up the stairs. Cara could tell that the woman had no intentions of opening her mouth to speak so Cara spoke first.

"Good Morning."

Cara could tell that the woman was surprised that she was speaking. After the woman took a moment to collect her thoughts she stammered,

"Good Morning, you must be A's little sister Margo."

The woman took note that Cara reminded her of Malinda Williams from one of her favorite movies "The Wood," except Cara had hazel eyes and she was more curvaceous than Malinda who had a smaller frame.

A.J. had always favored Omar Epps with those beautiful expressive eyes. She had always been in love with that man on television, and with the one that used to be her man.

It was Cara's turn to be surprised that the woman mentioned Margo, and this woman had called her fiancé by a nickname.

"I'm Cara."

The woman didn't have anything else to say, she just went back inside of her apartment. Cara shrugged her shoulders and then turned her back to go back into A.J.'s apartment to start on breakfast. She had no intentions of giving the woman anymore thought, although she wondered what or who she could have been looking for. Cara put the groceries away and in an hour she plated two cheese omelets, bacon, pancakes and she had filled two glasses of orange juice for she and A.J.

A.J. still slept peacefully on the couch. Cara smiled as she looked at her man. It was her turn to wake A.J. She kneeled on her knees beside the couch,

 "Wake up sleepy head."

She patted his chest. He didn't budge so she shook him gently.

"Wake up babe, time for breakfast."

Cara kissed his cheek and she couldn't help but giggle as his whiskers tickled her lips. Her giggle caused his manhood to stiffen more; he let out a low groan that sent a tingling feeling between her thighs. He opened his eyes and he smiled.

"You cooked me breakfast?"

 He stretched.

"Yes, I cooked you breakfast. Go wash your face, brush your teeth and come eat." He reached and wrapped his arm around Cara, pulling her close against his chest. "I can really get used to this Cara."

"I want you to."

She admitted. A.J. kissed her cheek and then he got up to wash his face. They sat down to have breakfast, and then after breakfast they took a walk around the corner from his apartment to the park. They walked hand in hand through the park and they fed the ducks at the pond.

"You know A.J. I talked to my dad on my way here for this visit and he said oh you know I am ready for you to have a grandbaby for me. I said daddy can we get married first?"

They laughed. A.J. told her that his mom had said close to the same thing.

"I'm ready for a family Cara. I'm ready to slow down with work and I want to concentrate on my wife and kids."

He wrapped his arms around her waist and he pulled her closer to him as they began to walk again.

"I'm even more ready to have fun making babies with you."

He stopped walking so that he could kiss her. The kiss he gave her was a soul stirring kiss that Cara was glad that they were in public instead of at home alone. What she felt she didn't think she could squeeze her thighs together and then run away this time.

When they stopped kissing, Cara noticed the same woman that she had seen earlier at the apartment across from A.J. walking toward them.

A.J. acknowledged the woman by speaking her name,

"Hey Sabrina, what's going on?"

A.J. squeezed Cara's hand. The woman named Sabrina didn't even bother to acknowledge Cara who was standing in the crook of A.J.'s arm.

"Hey A, what's up?"

"Working hard as always, meet my soon to be wife Cara. Cara this is Sabrina. We met and dated briefly when I first moved here five years ago."

Cara admired A.J.'s honesty. She could tell that Sabrina didn't expect the formal introduction in fact Sabrina sounded a little salty when she said,

"Yeah, we did date very briefly. Now I just moved in the apartment and I hardly see you."

A.J. nodded.

"I have been working overtime so that I can hurry up and get to my sweetheart."

Sabrina nodded slowly, avoiding looking at Cara as A.J. leaned down to kiss her again. Sabrina looked as if she had had enough, so she nodded her head as she backed away from where they stood.

"Well congrats, and I guess I will see you around neighbor."

She gave A.J. a tight smile and then she walked off.

The rest of the weekend went well, except on Sunday when it was time for Cara to drive back home. She had a flat tire and an issue under her hood that caused her car not to crank.

A.J. put down her hood, and he told her to take his truck, he would have his mechanic to work on her car when he could.

"I love you babe."

He told her as he gave her one last hug and kiss before she headed back to Virginia. He watched Cara get on the road safely and then he pulled out his cell phone to call his mechanic to get him to work on Cara's Impala.

## *Counting down*

For the next few weeks leading up to the wedding Cara and A.J. delved deep into their work. Cara and Margo gathered up extra decorations to take to the party that they were hosting for a sixteen year old. The party was being held at a small club called "The Basement."

The party was scheduled to begin at ten p.m. that night. Cara and Margo took pictures of the space before anyone arrived. This party was special. One day a woman came into the office of Every Occasion, with her heart set on giving her son a decent party for his sixteenth birthday.

 "My son has been through a lot, and I have been through a lot this last year. My son has come along way from where he was two years ago. He was in the streets, getting into trouble and he got shot. My son almost died. When we nursed him back to health he vowed to turn his life around and I want this party to signify the beginning." Cara's heart went out to the woman after hearing her story. The woman told her that she wasn't expecting to get her services for free by telling her the story she just wanted to share her son's story. Cara was touched by the story. After deciding on a location for the party she discussed deposit and total price of Every Occasion's services with her client just like she would normally do. A contract was signed and Cara took the woman's deposit.

After the deposit she wouldn't accept another dime from her.

When she discussed it with Shaia and Margo they were okay with giving the birthday party for just the deposit. They paid for the club, they paid for the D.J., as well as the food and anything else they needed for the party.

As Cara and Margo stood back to look at their work, the D.J. brought in his equipment. It was nine p.m. and as he came in two teenage girls followed him in. One was dressed in a short hot pink mini skirt that barely covered her butt, and the other girl wore a long tight lime green dress that had a thigh high split.

Margo gave them a faint smile wishing they were somewhere else other than an event sponsored by Every Occasion. She would definitely pull the young girls to the side to explain to them why the way they were dressed wasn't at all cute, it was actually made them look bad. Margo just asked them if they were there for Ellijay's party. One of the girls looked at the other, she rolled her eyes up toward the ceiling and she smiled.

"Yes."

The other girl whispered loudly to her friend,

"what does it look like."

Loud enough for Margo and Cara to hear, they exchanged looks with each other. Margo smiled back at the young girl,

"Well, the party doesn't start until ten and we weren't letting anyone in until Elijay gets here, so we need to ask you ladies to wait outside."

Cara smiled at the girls and looked at the door. She didn't care for their lack of respect for adults at all. When one of the girls began to complain about it being cold outside Cara shook her head, looking at the way they were dressed. The two girls were

dressed like they were going to a club in the middle of summer when it was the end of October.

"Well, we can let you stay inside, but just stand at the door."

Cara could tell that the girls didn't like the idea of standing by the door. Margo considered them lucky to have Cara's pity because she would have told them they still needed to stand outside until the party began.

She and Margo sat at the small bar while the D.J. did a sound check after he had finished setting up his equipment.

"If I tried to wear something that little out of my Mama's house, I wouldn't even make it to the front door girl."

Cara shook her head as she looked at the tiny skirt the teenaged girl wore.

Margo shook her head,

"Girl my Mama wouldn't let me bring anything like that into her house. She monitored every stitch that I spent money on."

The two young women shared a laugh. The D.J. started to play some old school mixes and the two women got out on the floor to dance. While Margo and Cara danced the two young girls looked on. The D.J. got on the mic,

"Big ups to the owners of Every Occasion tonight for putting this party together, yeah what's up Cara, what's up Margo, I see you." Margo and Cara put their hands up as they danced to Notorious B.I.G.'s

"One more chance."


It was fifteen minutes to ten, and as if on cue, teenagers started coming in thru the door. They all stood against the walls until the birthday kid arrived at exactly ten p.m.

Elijay was a tall and handsome young man. He wore a green button down collared long sleeve shirt, with khaki pants and timberland boots. Cara noticed that the scantily clad girls moved close to the D.J. booth as soon as the room started to fill with teenagers. She also noticed that the girls kept their eyes on Elijay.

Elijay was smooth, he greeted everybody that came thru the doors. He looked as if he were expecting someone so he didn't even look in the direction of the half naked girls. They seemed to be trying hard to get his attention by doing little dances and talking loud.

Elijay had his attention on a cute girl who stood with her friend close to the bar. When he spotted her he asked the D.J. if he could borrow his microphone. The D.J. told him that it was his party so of course he could get the mic. Elijay cleared his throat, the D.J. lowered the music so Ellijay didn't have to yell.

"I want to thank everybody for coming out tonight to celebrate my birthday with me, it means a lot."

He paused as he looked over the crowd. He spotted his mom who was standing beside another woman that Cara recognized. The woman standing there was Sabrina, the woman that lived near A.J. in Georgia.

"I want to thank my mom for always having my back. I don't think I would be here if it weren't for this lady. I love you Ma. I want to thank my friend Nadia for pushing me too. Can a birthday boy have a dance with you?"

At that moment it seemed like the Basement got quiet. Everybody looked at the girl standing at the bar. She was dressed in pink, so she stood out. The girl blushed as she looked at Elijay. Elijay handed the microphone back to the D.J. then he walked the short distance from the D.J. booth to the bar where the girl was standing. He extended his hand to her and she timidly took his hand and joined him to dance. The D.J. started playing

"Make me Better" By Fabulous ftg Ne-Yo.

"Let's give a birthday shout to our boy Elijay. Thank everybody for coming out tonight to celebrate."

The D.J. gave more shout outs.

Margo commented on Nadia and Elijay,

"They are so cute."

Cara agreed, then a familiar voice whispered in her ear,

"Do they remind you of somebody?"

Cara spun around to look into the eyes of A.J. He smiled and hugged her.

"What are you doing here?"

Cara was surprised to see him.

"Ms. Kelly invited me to this party."

"Really? I didn't know you knew Ms. Kelly or Elijay."

He nodded.

Ms. Kelly and Sabrina walked over to where they stood. Ms. Kelly gave A.J. a big hug while Sabrina stood looking at Cara and Margo with her arms crossed.

"Ms. Kelly this is my fiancée Cara Williams and my little sister Margo."

The woman beamed,

"Well, you two make a good couple. I congratulate you on your coming nuptials. You both have made a difference in my sons' life and I just want to thank you for it because you didn't have to do any of it."

Ms. Kelly was near tears. Cara grabbed the woman's hand.

"Are you okay Ms. Kelly?"

Cara looked at the woman with concern. Ms. Kelly began patting Cara's hand. "I'm fine sweetheart; I just get emotional when I talk about what my baby has been through."

Sabrina didn't say a word she just looked on with her arms crossed against her chest.

"Yes ma'am he has come along way,"

A.J. gave the woman another hug. He explained to Cara and Margo that he became Elijays' mentor after meeting the teenager almost two years before in a program for young teenage boys who needed positive male role models in their lives. Cara nodded.

She watched Elijay and Nadia hold hands after a song was over and they stepped over to the bar to get something to drink.

"He has applied for early college admission and he is taking college courses for credit just like you advised him. My baby is going to do something great with his life. I can't thank you enough for stepping in to help. Honey, you have a good man."

Ms. Kelly said to Cara before she kissed A.J. on his cheek and then she turned her attention to a teenager that she recognized from her neighborhood. Sabrina walked away from them.

A.J. walked over to the bar, when Elijay saw him a big smile spread across the young mans face. He gave A.J. the pound and then he embraced him.

"What's up A."

"Came to check out your birthday celebration, I couldn't miss it."

"Thanks for coming man. Thanks for everything; my manager had a fit about letting me off because it's a Friday night."

Elijay had a job at the local car wash that he worked at every weekend and on teacher workdays. The young man had really turned his life around.

"Do you have to work tomorrow man?"

A.J. had a surprise for his mentee.

"She went ahead and gave me the whole weekend, my mom is having a dinner for me at her church tomorrow and I'm trying to convince this girl right here to go to the movies with me, since it's my birthday weekend."

He cut his eyes at Nadia who stood behind him as he talked to A.J. Nadia pushed her hair which was in a simple dubie wrap behind her ear and she smiled.

A.J. laughed, he squeezed Cara's hand.

"Well, I am going to come get you and Ms. Kelly tomorrow morning around twelve, so be ready alright?"

Elijay nodded and turned around to give his attention back to Nadia. The couple returned to the floor when Chris Brown and Jordin Sparks song "No Air" flooded from the speakers.

A.J. pulled Cara back to the middle of the floor to dance close. Cara wrapped her arms around his neck and rocked with him, she looked around his arm as she could barely see over his shoulder and she locked eyes with Sabrina.

Sabrina didn't smile. She just stood against the wall with her arms crossed. Cara wanted to ask A.J. about the nature of the relationship between them. She sensed a lot of dislike from Sabrina, when she didn't even know the woman nor did she know anything about the past that she had shared with A.J.

As A.J. held her close to him, she thought it really didn't matter. She probably would never see this woman again after her dealings with Ms. Kelly were done. The woman lived in Georgia, so she didn't think she would ever see this Sabrina again after A.J. had moved from his apartment in Georgia.

No, Sabrina didn't matter.

Thirty minutes later it was eleven p.m. and the cleaning crew that Every Occasion usually used to clean up after most of their events came in. After they were greeted and given instructions on when to start clean up, Cara and Margo grabbed their coats and then walked toward the door with A.J. following close behind.

A.J. walked between his sister and his fiancé to where they had parked their company van. The van was black with the logo of Every Occasion on the side of it in gold.

A.J. opened the door for Cara to get inside, she sat on the seat with her legs on the side of the seat, A.J. stood between her legs and she held the sides of his face to give him a quick tongue kiss. He backed away from her, when she started nibbling on his lower lip.

"Baby, you know you are so wrong for this, especially since you won't let me stay at your place tonight."

"You are more than welcome to stay babe, I have boxes everywhere but that doesn't mean you can't come."

A.J. groaned as he thought about Tim and a couple of his other friends would be waiting at the Pecan Tree hotel and suites for his bachelor party.

"You know the boys will be waiting for me at the hotel for my party later, but first we are going to meet at the bar across the street from your office."

Cara pouted; remembering that tonight was the night of his bachelor party and tomorrow would be her bachelorette party.

"Aww, I guess I will see you tomorrow then?"

A.J. gave Cara another long tongue kiss, before gently pushing her legs to the front of the car seat, and moving away from her so that he could close the door. The sexual tension between them was so thick, he knew if he didn't leave now, he would follow her home. He walked to where his car was parked; he got in and then put the keys in the ignition. He cranked up his silver mustang and then followed Cara in the Every Occasion van to the office. He tapped his horn at her as he turned the corner and into the parking lot of The Five Spot.

A.J. recognized one of his co workers cars, he also recognized Bo's car, parked in the parking lot. He pulled into an empty space and then he got out straightening the collar of his leather jacket.
When he stepped into the bar the first person he recognized at the bar was Bo. He hadn't seen his business partner in months.
"Hey, Mr. Oden what's happening?"
He shook Bo's hand when he turned around on the bar stool to acknowledge him. "Man, I'm working hard right now. I've taken on a few new clients and they are putting me to work man."
"Yeah? Let me know if you need any help with any of that."
A.J. sat down at the bar beside Bo. He looked around to see if the rest of his friends were anywhere near, not seeing anyone.
"So, where did Ray, Tim and Phillip get off too?"
"They said they had some last minute things to pull together at the hotel, so they told me to wait here for you until they got back. They have been gone for about fifteen minutes now."
A.J. nodded his head. He waited patiently for the female bartender to come ask him what he would have to drink.
A.J. noticed that Bo had two glasses in front of him and he was signaling for a third.
"So how is everything at home man? Cara sent me a recent picture of Lauryn and she is getting so big man. Is Shaia ready to have another little one?"

Bo shook his head a little.
"Man another little one is on his or her way whether Shaia and I are ready or not."
The bartender finally made it over to them. She offered to take Bo's order but he pointed to A.J. so that she would take his order first.
A.J. ordered a double shot of gin and juice, and he ordered one for Bo.
"Whoa, how does Shaia feel about it?"
Bo dropped his head before he answered his friend.

"Shaia, doesn't think I know but she is all to pieces about it. We hadn't planned to have kids back to back. She is just getting back to work and everything has been just like she pictured it. This new pregnancy though, she has been having bad morning sickness and its already taking a toll on her."

A.J. nodded in understanding.

"Well if I can do anything to help y'all I'm here." A.J. started downing his drink.

"Thanks brother in law, you good people man."

Bo threw back his third drink. He was starting to feel the effect of the drink, his eyes had become glassy and he told A.J. that he was cutting himself off because he wanted to enjoy the bachelor party. While the two men talked they didn't notice that the bartenders had switched.

The female bartender had taken off her apron and disappeared to the back of the house. Malek Jones was back on the clock after taking a late lunch break he took the female bartenders place.


When he came on to stand behind the bar he thought he recognized the two men sitting at the end of the bar but he wasn't sure until he got up close to them. When he was able to get up close to them he recognized both Bo and A.J.

The men hadn't recognized him. Malek listened to them talk intently. He learned that Cara and A.J. would be exchanging vows the next Saturday. He also heard A.J. say that he was excited about it but nervous all at the same time.

"I love that woman. I have loved her since we were kids. This past year, I have learned so many things about this woman that I am almost upset with myself that I didn't ask her to marry me sooner and take her from all those sorry dudes she found herself tangled up with."

Malek flinched. He wanted to know how A.J. had known Cara when they were kids. He wanted to know how close they had been and when they became close. He felt that maybe A.J. was to blame for

Cara's change of heart from the very beginning. Malek's chest got tight as he continued to eavesdrop on the men's conversation. The more he heard A.J. talk about Cara and the more times he heard Bo agree or say something positive he felt his heart start to race.

Tim, Ray and Phillip came back into the bar, they sat down and signaled for him to take their drink orders. Luckily his co worker had come back and she was able to fill most of their orders. A.J. ordered another double shot of gin and juice so that he would feel carefree when he stepped into the hotel. Tim had told him that he had gotten some strippers to dance at his party. He didn't care to look at another woman but tonight would

be the last time he saw another woman's body up close and personal. He wasn't a dog, he was a man that was about to get married to the love of his life.

The strippers didn't mean anything to him but he was still a man so he would go and be entertained at his party.

Malek couldn't help himself, he had to say something to A.J. before he left the bar. When the men got up to leave it was eleven thirty and so he told his co worker that he needed a break to make a phone call. He walked a few steps behind the men as they all got in a big dark colored truck. Phillip was the designated driver to the hotel. He and A.J had been good friends while they were in college. Phillip had met Cara a few times over the years and he agreed that she was a good person. Phillip was genuinely happy for his friend.

Everyone except Tim and A.J. had gotten into Phillips Ford Excursion. They both wanted to check to make sure that their vehicles were locked before they left them there until the next morning.

"Hey, can I holler at you for a minute?"

Both Tim and A.J. turned around to see Malek standing beside the building with his hands in his pockets. Tim wondered what Malek had to holler at them about. He hadn't talked to him since they were in high school. When A.J. turned around, Tim remembered that in high school Cara used to be Malek's girlfriend and he hoped that Cara wasn't the topic of conversation. He knew that Malek was talking to A.J. But he stood outside the truck waiting for Malek to say what he had to say so that they could get to the party waiting for them at the hotel.

"Yeah?"

A.J. had just turned to face Malek. The two men just stood there looking at each other. No words between the two.

Tension was thick in the air. Tim told A.J. that they needed to get going, but before he could get the words that their was someone waiting for him out of his mouth, Malek charged at A.J. knocking him into the side of Phillips truck.

You could hear the men curse in surprise, because they had been oblivious to what was going on. They were talking about the strippers.

A.J. pushed Malek away from him with so much force Malek stumbled backwards onto a vehicle causing its' alarm to go off.

"Man what's the problem?"

A.J. was a grown man and he had been able to avoid confrontation very well as a kid growing up. That didn't make him a pushover, so he wasn't too happy about the way Malek was coming at him right now.

Malek was so pissed off that he couldn't form the words that he wanted to say. He couldn't even think as he charged at A.J. again. At that moment Malek didn't care that he was outside of his job, and he could lose everything he had worked hard for. At that moment he didn't quite know what he was fighting for. Tim tried to talk A.J. into getting into the truck and letting Malek cut the fool alone. Normally A.J. would walk away from any altercation, but tonight with the liquor in his system he saw red. He was tired of this dude trying to stand in the way of his future. A.J. balled up his fists, and as Malek charged him he swung hard hitting the man with a two piece. Malek fell back against the car again. A.J. was about to grab him up and hit him again but Bo, and Ray had jumped out of the truck to get A.J. in the car while Tim kept Malek from running up on A.J. again.

"What's this about man?"

A.J. yelled at Malek while Tim and Bo pushed Malek back, he was trying to get around them.

"You know what this is about. You just can't leave her alone you gotta marry her?."

A.J. stepped back from the truck to correct Malek,

"What you and Cara had, has been over for years. She made her choice and she didn't choose you man. It's over so stop acting like all this happened yesterday. Get yourself together and move on."

Tim didn't know the whole story of Malek and Cara he knew that they were a couple in high school. Tim knew enough of the story of A.J. and Cara to say that the wedding was going to happen the weekend coming and their life together was just beginning.

If Tim didn't know any better he would think that Malek had been drinking. Malek began to cry out loud until the manager of the bar and a few patrons came running out of the building to see what was going on. Malek's eye was swelling, and he had blood coming from the corner of his mouth.

"She loves me."

He said as Tim backed away from him. Bo and Ray had gotten back into the car with A.J.

"She loves him."

Tim shouted to the man, as the manager and the other bartender asked Malek if he had been mugged and if they needed to call the police.

Malek wiped the blood away from the corner of his mouth. He was embarrassed. "No, I'm good."

He insisted.

The camera in the back of the building that was pointed toward where they stood in the parking lot would show that he had started it all by charging at A.J.

The manager insisted that Malek tell him what was going on. Malek apologized to the patron who had just disarmed the alarm of the car that he had fallen against when A.J. pushed him off of him he told his manager that everything was okay. He didn't want his boss to know that he had started it all.

Phillip pulled out of the parking lot. He asked his friend if he wanted to go to the emergency room to get his hand wrapped because from the moment he got inside the truck he was holding his hand.

"No, go on to the hotel, I have a party to attend."

He hated that the man couldn't seem to grasp that Cara didn't want to be with him. He couldn't grasp that Cara was going to be his wife. Malek had had his chance at a life with Cara and he chose to go on with his life and he got married to someone else. A.J. felt sorry for the man, but he wouldn't allow him to disrupt his present or his future.

"You good man?"

Bo asked, he knew of Malek and he couldn't believe the dude had acted out like that. A.J. sat in the front seat beside Phillip staring out the window, wondering if he had to keep dealing with Malek going off like that.

"Yeah, I'm good."

A.J. didn't know if he could handle it as well as he did tonight if Malek approached him with that foolishness after he pulled this stunt tonight. In the back of his mind he worried that he may have to beat the man down to keep him from coming back at him.

Phillip pulled up to a twenty four hour Walgreen's to get an ace wrap for A.J.'s hand.

Ray went into to purchase the wrap and Tim helped wrap his hand while they were headed to the hotel.

It was twelve fifteen when the five men walked up into the presidential suite on the sixth floor of the hotel. The front room was a wide open space with leather couches and end tables beside each couch. There was a big picture window that looked over the city. There was also a wet bar, and on the bar were bottles of liquor and cartons of juice chilling in ice if anyone wanted to mix a drink. Bo grabbed a glass and poured some gin into it followed by a little bit of orange juice. He handed the drink to A.J.

"You need that man. Relax and enjoy yourself."


A.J. wasn't really feeling the party anymore. He wanted to go back to Cara's apartment and hold her in his arms. His hand was aching. He looked at his friends and they seemed to be excited. So he just sat back in the chair as they instructed, he tossed back two more drinks and then Tim called the strippers to come into the room.

Tim and Bo were both married so they stood back while A.J., Phillip and Ray got their eyes full of the curves and tricks of the strippers who came to entertain them that night.

Cara got up the next morning bright and early. She and her mother would be going to pick up her wedding dress. She had invited her mother over so that she could take them both to The Waffle House for breakfast. Cara jumped into the shower, by the time she got out of the shower she could hear her mother calling her from the front room. She had given her mother a key to her apartment for emergencies and incase she ever lost her own key.

"Good Morning Cara Boo."

Cara smiled as she got out of the shower. Her mother hadn't called her by that nickname since she was in middle school.

She called back to her mother as she dried off,

"Good Morning Mommy."

Felicia called back to her as she spread Styrofoam containers of food across the kitchen counter.

"I stopped by The Waffle House on the way here and got us some All Stars hun."

Cara said okay, as she lotioned her body and then slipped into a pair of black skinny jeans and a pink shirt that Margo had given her as a gift. It was a t-shirt that read bride. Cara put on all of her clothes except her shoes before she joined her mother at the kitchen table. "Thank you, Mommy. How are you doing?"
Felicia looked at her only child.
 "I am excited. In six days my baby is getting married to a wonderful man who will vow to make her happy for the rest of her life. I am very excited."
Cara looked at her mother with wonder. Cara wanted to understand what made her mother so emotional about her relationships. She wanted to ask her mother the nature of her relationship with her father Deon Fletcher. So many things were unspoken about her mothers past and Cara wanted to take the opportunity to ask her about it today while they were alone.
"Mommy why have you never gotten married?"
Cara asked. She had been trying to figure out a way to ask her mother that question for a long time. She finally concluded there was no other way to ask the question except to just ask. Her mother put her fork down and she looked her directly in the eye.
"I think I missed my chance. Before I became pregnant with you Cara, I was seeing this wonderful guy. He was hardworking, responsible, smart, handsome and sweet. I let someone else get in the way of our relationship. She messed up our trust, our understanding of each other. We fell apart. I ended up in the arms of Deon Fletcher. He

was a bad boy that I had heard about once or twice. I was mesmerized by his beautiful eyes, while I was hurting for the love I had thought I lost. I got pregnant with you, and the guy that I used to date, he never left my side. He stepped up like he was your dad. He helped me with you and he made sure I had whatever I needed. I pushed him away. I didn't think I deserved to have a man in my life like him. Especially when he discovered that he had a calling on his life. He asked me to marry him, he wanted to adopt you. As soon as he started to change his life, the rumors started. The rumors about us hurt him, hurt me. The rumors hurt our families. I told him that I couldn't marry him because I thought I would be protecting him from what people had to say. He told me that he didn't care and that he just wanted to be there to protect us. I wouldn't let him. Twenty years later here I am wishing I had made a better decision."

By the time Felicia finished talking she had tears streaming down her cheeks.

Cara was touched, she felt like crying herself after hearing the story. She started to ask her mother who was the man and if her mother could contact him. She didn't remember anyone except her grandfather. Before Cara could ask any more questions, her cell phone rang. When she said hello into the phone the caller hung up.

"What happened to him Mommy?"

Felicia looked at her watch like she wished she had somewhere else to go.

"He's still around."

"Is he seeing someone?"

Cara hated to see her mother alone.

"No, I don't know. We haven't talked in a while. I miss him, sometimes I think if I hadn't been a coward that we would be together right now."

Felicia looked away from her daughter as she wiped away her tears with a napkin.

"It may be twenty years Mommy, but it may not be too late."

Felicia didn't know. Pastor Williams was a different man and she was a different woman. Their time had passed. She didn't want to her daughter miss her happily ever after.

"I don't know hun. You just make sure you hold on to A.J."

Cara knew that she would hold on to A.J. She didn't know what she'd do without him in her life. She was counting down six more days.

Cara and her mother Felicia went to down town Virginia to a wedding boutique to pick up her wedding dress and shoes. Felicia watched her daughter stand in the floor length mirror to try on her dress. She couldn't contain her tears.

"My baby is so beautiful."

Felicia's dreams for her only daughter were coming true. After the wedding boutique they went to the jewelers to pick up Cara's earrings and necklace then they decided to walk the mall to get outfits for her honey moon.

"Mommy, I can't remember the last time you and I went shopping together. I miss it."

Cara could remember a time when her mother would take her shopping out of town malls once a month. She would dedicate the whole weekend to shopping and doing whatever Cara wanted to do. Sometimes Terra and Shaia would come along. Cara missed spending time with them as well.

"Mommy, you never told me the name of the guy that you were seeing before you met my dad."

Cara stopped to look through a store window that displayed a pretty skirt suit that she could wear to work at every occasion. She thought about going into get it while she waited for her mother to answer.

Felicia debated about revealing more about her past to her daughter. She wanted to be honest about her past but at the same time she wanted to protect it.

"I know hun."

"So I guess you aren't ready to disclose that information, I understand."

Cara pointed to the ice cream shop. Her mother nodded, she had a taste for strawberry cheesecake ice cream.

"While we are being honest with each other about our pasts, what happened between you and Malek?"

Felicia had been hearing rumors that Cara was the reason that Malek had left his family. She didn't want to believe it, she wanted to believe the other rumor that she had heard that his wife had had a child by his brother and she had hid it from him. Cara ordered their ice cream knowing what type of ice cream to order for her mother and then they sat down at a table to eat it.

Cara sighed before she answered.


"I made a mistake. Malek and I saw each other maybe twice, he told me that he was officially separated from his wife. I still had feelings for him, and I was on the rebound from Eric. I regret it everyday that I allowed myself to fall into his arms, and his messy life. I didn't break up his home; his home was already broken when he ran into me."

Her mother was disappointed with what Cara had just said. She had hoped that none of the rumors were true to any extent. She had one more question for her daughter and then she was done with talking about the past.

"Have you talked to his wife?"

Cara looked at her mother sideways not sure why she had asked that question.

"No. His wife came to me trying to accuse me of breaking up her home, but her home was already broken. It had nothing to do with me Mommy. I was just passing through and I got caught in the middle for a split second."

Cara looked down at her cell phone she had received a text message from A.J. "Be sure to stop by the front desk at the apartment before you go up. I love you."

### *Surprises*

Cara and her mother finished shopping and then they went to their childhood home to hang up Cara's wedding dress in the closet. Cara would be moving from out of her apartment in four days, she would be staying at her childhood home with her mother and Aunt until her wedding day.

A.J. had arranged for a moving van to arrive to her home on Wednesday morning. The moving van would deliver her things to the home that he and Cara would share after their honeymoon. Cara was excited. Felicia waited while Cara punched in the security code to her apartment building. When she was buzzed in she stopped at the front desk. The young man greeted her by name, "Good Afternoon Ms. Williams."

"Good Afternoon Mr. Jeffrey, I was told to stop here at the desk, you have something for me?" Mr. Jeffrey smiled as he reached in a cabinet. He pulled out a white envelope and handed it to Cara. "Thanks."

Cara looked at the envelope, her name was written in cursive on the outside of it. She pulled out a card, and when she pulled the card out of the envelope a large key with a clicker attached to the key ring fell out. She looked at her mother and then she read the card. It read, *"Dear Cara, you are my everything. I love you, and I will spend everyday showing you that I love you. This is only the beginning my love. My mechanic who has been working on vehicles for over thirty years took a look at your vehicle. I know you love the car but there were so many repairs that needed to be done to get it to where it*

*should be it would have been more to fix it then what it is worth. I can't have my wife riding around that way especially when she doesn't have to. I want you to drive this vehicle, let me know if you like it. If you don't like it, then we can go find you something that you do like. In the back parking lot of your building is a vehicle waiting for you. I love you and I will talk to you soon. Six more days love."*

 Cara looked at her mother and then handed her the beautiful card that was decorated in beautiful peach roses. She covered her mouth with her hand as she walked to the front door and then started walking around the building to the back parking lot. Felicia followed close behind her daughter with the card in her hand. Before Cara reached the parking lot she saw a black Lexus truck with a big red bow on it. She laughed as she pressed the button to unlock the doors. Felicia smiled at her daughter. Cara got inside the truck, the smell of leather greeted her. She inhaled with tears in her eyes.
"Baby what's the matter?" Felicia stepped to her daughters side, looking at her daughter with concern. "He never stops amazing me with his show of love Mommy. I can't believe it sometimes."
Felicia nodded her head, she was happy for her daughter. She watched her touching the interior of the car. She watched her daughter start dialing her cell phone to call A.J.
"Thank you so much, I love it, but I love you more. You didn't have to do this."
A.J. knew that Cara would tell him that he didn't have to get her the truck and he knew he didn't but he wanted to show her his love.


A.J. talked to her for a few more minutes, he was at Tim's apartment laying down on the couch. He had a bad hangover from the night before, but he managed to meet Elijay and his mother as well as deliver the truck to Cara's apartment before she made it back in. Tim had hired three strippers. The strippers danced and performed sex acts to music until the sun was about to come up. He hadn't expected the night to turn out the way it did, he was actually miserable as he sat there with a fake smile plastered on his face while the women wiggled and gyrated close to his face. He made it clear that he didn't want to be touched so they respected his wishes. He didn't want to be there so he drank more than his limit on gin and juice to numb the ache in his hand, and to show his friends that he appreciated the thoughtful gesture of giving him the bachelor party. That was a moment that he desperately wanted to end, but it wasn't in his character to get up and walk away.

Tim's wife Erica had left early that morning to get the bachelorette party set up for Cara. She took their two children to her sisters' house, planning to pick them up later that night when the party was over.

"Hey, man we need to be getting on the road to Georgia, you gotta pack that apartment up and something tells me that you haven't even started. A.J. had rented a pod for all of his things. The pod had been delivered to his apartment in Georgia and on Monday he would have it delivered to the house he would share with Cara in Virginia. He planned to let Cara furnish the house any way she wanted to and then he would put his things from

his apartment into the apartment in the back of the house. He was sure he wouldn't spend much time there in the future but he wanted to furnish the apartment all the same.

Tim jiggled the keys, he was ready to start on the task at hand. He was glad that he could help his best friend out but he was ready to relax with his family.

A.J. lie faced down on the couch, his head had a dull ache, as did his fist. He thought about putting packing and moving his things off to another day, but out of respect for his friends time he got up slowly from the couch. He slipped his feet into his shoes and then he followed his friend out the door and to his truck.

"I appreciate everything you doing right now man. Thank you." Tim put the keys into the ignition of the truck and he nodded. "Dude, you have always been there for me, I feel like I owe you."

A.J. leaned his head against the passenger seat, in which he leaned all the way back to a reclining position. "You don't owe me anything man. Friends have each others back."

Tim backed out of the parking space and then he maneuvered the truck out of the apartment complexes parking lot and onto to the road. They were headed toward Georgia.

Cara arrived at the newest mid day club in V.A. at exactly six o'clock that evening. The building had several suites. The suites were reserved by different persons or groups of people for their small parties. Cara's bachelorette party was being held in Suite B. Cara stepped into the doorway of the suite. Her mother, sister, sister in law, her aunts , her cousin and her good friend all sat on a long white contoured couch at an oblong glass table that was decorated with silver confetti, the floor was littered with silver balloons

and streamers. On the table were three bottles of champagne, champagne flutes that were half full, and gifts for Cara in silver and white gift bags and wrapped gift boxes. Margo stood to her feet when she saw Cara. Margo raised her glass of champagne as did everyone else at the table. "To the future Mrs. Ealy."
Cara's mother handed her a champagne flute. Cara took the glass from her mother and with her smile she nodded to her family. "Yes, Yes."

Four hours later Cara returned to her apartment leaving her gifts in her truck. It had been a long day and all she wanted to do was get in her bed. She opened her door and then kicked off her shoes. She pushed her shoes into a corner with her foot and then she turned around to close the door. Cara jumped, grabbing her chest when she noticed Malek standing quietly in her door way.
"What the hell is your problem?" Cara could have slapped the smug smile on his face, but she noticed that someone else had given him a black eye and a fat lip.
"I knew if I buzzed you, you weren't going to let me up, so here I am."
Cara crossed her arms against her chest. "You shouldn't be here."

A.J. ignored Cara. He walked past her into the apartment, observing all of the boxes lining the walls. The apartment no longer looked like the place his high school sweetheart lived in. The pictures had been removed from the walls, no curtains hung from the windows and the bookcase held no books. "So you are really moving out."
Cara sighed as she looked at the man she had once cared so much about. He had become the man that she hated to see coming.


"I am getting married next weekend, and I am moving into a home with my husband."
Malek looked at Cara. He wished that he could say something that would get her to change her mind about going on with her life without him. He had watched A.J. drive a truck into the parking lot and he had watched him place a big red bow on the windshield. He knew that the truck was a gift for Cara.
"So are you with this dude for the gifts that he can give you? It seems like he is trying to buy your love."
Malek watched Cara's nose flare.
He knew that he had struck a nerve with her. The whites of her beautiful hazel eyes turned red.
"Look, anything that A.J. can buy me, I don't have a problem buying those things for myself. I don't know why you are doing this right now but I don't have time for it, please leave before I call security to get you."
Out of desperation grabbed at Cara's arm.
"Cara this dude ain't perfect."
He tried to pull her to his chest so that he could hug her and hope that she felt something for him. Cara pushed him away with all of her might, pushing him hard against the door frame. He winced. Cara didn't care. She wished she could black his other eye.


"I didn't say he was perfect, neither am I. I need for you to get out now before I call the police."

She shouted, not caring what neighbor may have heard.
Malek straightened his back and stepped into the hallway.
 "You are making a mistake Cara."
Cara slammed the door in his face after she told him that it was her mistake to make. She could have reminded him of how he had not been by her side after she had a miscarriage. She could have reminded him of all the times he wasn't there when she called to bring up the point that he shouldn't think he was the better man by any means.
In tears Cara locked the door and set the security code. She decided she was going to leave her things and go to spend the nights at her childhood home earlier than she intended. She would leave everything behind the next morning and she would count down the days to her wedding there. She didn't want to have any more surprise visits from Malek Jones.

Back in Georgia, Tim finished putting the last few boxes into the pod. He and A.J. had accomplished a lot. They planned to finish the next morning. A.J. had gone to bed while Tim sat stood at the door for some fresh air. He was sipping on a beer. It was two o'clock in the morning and he heard the soft click of heels on the pavement below. He followed the sound and saw a woman walking down the sidewalk headed toward the stairs that led to the apartment across from A.J.'s apartment.

The woman wore a red mini skirt that left nothing to his imagination, as did her red bikini top tied around her neck. The bikini top revealed full brown breasts. He had to look away, because her breasts bounced with every step she took up the stairs and he felt himself getting aroused.
When the woman got to the top of the stairs and stood at the apartment door she produced a set of keys. After two tries of unsuccessfully unlocking the door she dropped the keys on to the steps. Tim instinctively wanted to ask if she had it, but the words

caught in his throat when the woman bent over in the mini skirt "mooning" him with her beautiful round bottom upturned. He didn't know if she even noticed him standing there.

 If she had noticed him standing there surely she wouldn't have exposed herself anymore than she was already exposed in the barely there attire that she had on by bending over.

He stood stuck there watching this woman and he was surprised when she turned around and looked directly in his face. She smirked and then she went into the apartment shutting the door behind her. It was dark and her facial features were illuminated by her porch light. He recognized her as one of the women he had paid to strip at A.J.'s bachelor party. She was the wildest one of them all and it seemed like she had become obsessed with A.J. the moment she stepped into the hotel room.

He was a little baffled. He closed the door and stepped back into the apartment. The couch was the only piece of furniture left in the apartment besides the bed in the other room.


Tim had known his A.J. for over twenty years, but he had to ask his friend if he was ready to leave his past behind and marry Cara, the love of his life.

# *The Wedding*

November 4th, the wedding party gathered at Zion Hill Baptist church for a rehearsal dinner. Everyone was in the dining hall except Cara and A.J.

Cara was at her childhood home sitting in her mothers' old room at the window seat trying to read a book that she couldn't keep her mind on and A.J. was in sitting in his car outside his mothers house thinking about going to see Cara.

He didn't believe in the superstition that it was bad luck for the bride and groom to see each other before the wedding. He didn't think Cara believed it either. A.J. wanted to see her because he hadn't seen her in a week. A.J. was excited knowing that the next day by three o'clock would mark the beginning of their forever together.

He pulled up the red brick house and he saw Cara's truck. He knew that she was there. He could have just called but he needed to see her face. He got out of the car, walked up to the front door and tapped on it.

He could hear someone coming down the steps. He saw the curtain move, and then the door opened. Cara stood there, with a smile on her face that made him melt.

She opened the door to come out onto the porch.

"Hi, Ms. Williams."

He reached for her and she stepped into his space.

"Tomorrow you will be Mrs. Ealy."

She smiled even more.

"Yes, I will be Mrs. Ealy. If you are going to back out Mr. Ealy this is your chance."

Cara looked up into his eyes.

"I'm not running anywhere babe. If you are trying to back put now is the time." Cara shook her head no. She reached for his hand to hold it, and he winced. She became concerned.

"Babe, what happened?"

A.J. hadn't told Cara about his run in with Malek. He knew she would probably get upset because he hadn't told her. He hesitated before he told her that his fist connected with Malek's face a week ago. A.J. wanted there relationship to always be based on honesty so he told her how it all happened before he went to the hotel for his bachelor party.

Cara bit her bottom lip, she couldn't get upset because she hadn't told him about Malek showing up to her apartment the night of her bachelorette party. She remembered his black eye, and for a split second she wondered who had given him the black eye, but he had upset her so bad she didn't even care.

"He showed up to my apartment last Saturday night. He told me that I was making a mistake and that you weren't perfect."

Cara reached up to touch her scarf. She had gotten her hair done for the wedding that morning along with her feet and nails.

A.J. touched her chin because he wanted her to look directly into his eyes.

"Baby, I need you to tell me things like this."

"I know, I was just so upset, I wasn't thinking about anything else except getting away from that apartment. I'm sorry. I wasn't trying to hide it."

He knew she wasn't trying to hide anything. He hugged her and kissed her forehead. Her mother's car pulled into the drive way. He knew that her aunt was probably going to run him away from the house, so he kissed her lips and told her goodnight. "I love you."

A.J. was walking down the sidewalk waving at the people that he had known since he was in elementary school; the people that would be called his in laws tomorrow.

Felicia smiled and waved at A.J. as he got into his car and pulled off. He was upset, he was tired of Malek. Apart of him wanted to go to the bar where he had no doubt the man was working, but he knew that nothing good would come of the meeting.

He would be marrying Cara tomorrow, no matter who didn't like it. He went to his childhood home, where his mother was waiting in the door way.

Saturday Morning, November 5th
Everyone was up and about in the Williams household. Pam had been feeling well, so she decided she would cook a big breakfast everyone. Everyone kept asking Cara if she was nervous yet, and Cara's truthful reply was no. She hadn't been able to sleep that night because she was so excited. Her big day had finally come. She counted the hours left before she would become Mrs. Ealy.


After breakfast everyone gathered there things and headed to the church by twelve p.m.
Cara stood in the floor to ceiling mirror looking at her reflection. She stood in just a robe, after her make up was done she would put on her dress for pictures. There was a light tap on the dressing room door. Come in she called, her father Deon Fletcher peeped in the room.
"Hey daughter, are you decent?"
"Yes daddy."
When the man walked completely into the room he whistled.
"Daughter you are beautiful."
"Thank you."
Cara gave her dad a hug. Terra who had just finished her make up told her she was going to step out for a minute.
Deon Fletcher was dressed in a white tuxedo with a emerald green bow tie. The man had tears in his eyes as he looked at his daughter.
"I am so blessed to be here right now, to have the opportunity to watch my beautiful daughter walk down the aisle."
Cara corrected her father,
"I am blessed to have my father to walk me down the aisle."
He nodded,

"Yes, yes. Both my daughters have respectable, intelligent men in their lives who are their equals, I am so proud of you and your sister."

Cara's cell phone chimed, interrupting the intimate moment between father and daughter. The cell phone was on the dressing table beside the mirror. The display told her that it was Margo. Cara pressed send to answer putting the call on speaker phone so that she wouldn't destroy her make up by holding the cell phone near her face.
"Hey sis, are you ready for help getting in your dress?"
Cara looked at the time displayed on the phone. It was one o'clock.
"Yeah, I'm ready."
Cara started to feel butterflies in her stomach. In an hour she would be getting set to walk down the aisle with her father to the wedding march. She ended the call and looked at her father. He smiled.
"It's almost time baby girl. See you in a few minutes okay?"
Deon Fletcher blew his daughter a kiss and then he left the waiting room. Cara looked at her dress hanging beside the mirror. It was almost time. Her cell phone chimed again, and without looking at the display Cara pressed send to answer thinking it was Margo again.
"Hey."
She answered.
There was silence. At first she didn't think anything of it, but as she held the phone and no one said anything after a few minutes her heart sank. The silent caller hadn't called in a few days and whoever it was chose her wedding day to start calling again. Cara was determined not to let anyone ruin her day. She was about to hang up when an unfamiliar voice said,

"You think you're going to have your happily ever after when you have destroyed someone else's? You may have today but I promise you that you will not have forever BITCH!"
The caller slammed the phone down. Cara almost dropped the phone. She wanted to cry, she couldn't believe someone had resorted to threatening her on her day. She wanted to cry, but she took a deep

breath when Margo, Shaia, and her mother came into the dressing room to help her into her dress. While they fussed over her, Cara drew blanks in her mind trying to figure out who the caller could be. She couldn't hold back the tears that threatened to fall from her eyes. Shaia noticed the tears,

"O girl, don't mess up your make up."

Everyone joked about her makeup. Cara tried to think positive. She went through the motions after that, posing for pictures with her family and when two o'clock struck she joined her father outside of the sanctuary.

"Are you alright sweetheart?"

Her father asked once more.

Cara didn't dare speak for fear of a sob coming from her mouth. She nodded and then she looped her arm in his.

"I have dreamed of this day since I was little. Today is my day."

At two fifteen the wedding march began to play, the sanctuary doors opened and Deon presented his daughter to the family and friends who had gathered to witness the nuptial of A.J. and Cara.

Pastor Williams tried to hold himself together as he watched the man walking the beautiful young woman that he had watched say her first words, take her first steps and ride her first trike.

He stood there with missed emotions as he watched his nephew- the little boy that he had played catch with when his father was away on business. He took a deep breath to steady his fast beating heart as they approached the alter. He cleared his throat as he looked at all the family and friends that had gathered there.

A.J. and Tim stood at the front of the church. Tim stepped back beside the bridesmaids that included A.J.'s sister Margo, dressed in a Chartreuse Blue gown, holding a bouquet of white lilies, beside her stood Erica and then Terra the maid of honor, and Nashaia was the pregnant matron of honor.

They all waited for the little flower girl which was Tamika's daughter from Hope House…. She tossed chartreuse and white petals down the aisles for Cara to step upon as she joined her groom. Her beautiful white gown hugged her curves and then flowed into a beautiful train that followed her every step. She stood before the Man of cloth and her groom face covered by a white cage veil. She was so beautiful every woman that wasn't married took note of the beauty of it all.

Cara and Ahmad joined hands. He looked into the hazel eyes of the woman that he knew he loved from the moment he gave her the first now and later. He knew by the

way she thanked him with a smile, he knew when she always answered his questions even if they were dumb and unnecessary. He knew he loved her when he kissed her while playing the game of truth or dare as a teenager. He knew each time he saw the sadness in her eyes that he wanted to be the one to make her smile.

Even though she walked away, he knew that one day he would ask her and she would say yes. He knew that one day she would say yes to becoming his wife. He knew that being a dear friend would lead to something more. Here they stood, reciting their vows and professing their love for one another in front of their family and friends and the Man of Cloth.

Pastor Williams opened his bible and then he began,

"Dearly beloved, we are gathered here today to witness this man and this woman join each other in holy matrimony. I am so proud of my nephew for taking that step and I know that our Lord is pleased."

A few of the church members said Amen, and clapped a little. As soon as it was quiet again Pastor Williams turned to Cara and asked her to repeat after him,

"I Caraya Williams take you Ahmad Ealy to be my lawfully wedded husband, before these witnesses, I vow to love you and take care of you as long as we both shall live. I take you with all your faults and strengths as I offer myself to you with my faults and strengths. I will help you when you need help and I will turn to you when I need help. I choose you as the person with whom I spend my life."

Cara had prepared a few of her own words to say to him, she took a deep breath and looked deep into his eyes,

" A.J. you have always been right there for me and I am so glad that you were. You always made me feel good about myself and I thank you for that. I am so glad that you chose me to share your love with. I love you."

A.J. squeezed her hand as she concluded her vows and then Pastor Williams gave him the go ahead to recite his vows. He slid the band on her finger and then brought her hand to his lips.

"I am so glad that I chose you too, I knew along time ago that you would be the one to complete me. I felt lost when we were apart, when we are together I feel so complete, I knew that I couldn't be without you. I am going to spend the rest of my life being your everything."

A.J. mouthed I love you, then the couple turned to Pastor Williams so that he could continue the ceremony. He said a few more words that neither he or Cara heard. He asked if there were anyone that objected to the union of that man and that woman to speak now or forever hold their peace. No one said a word when he paused. They didn't hear anything else until the Pastor told him that he may kiss the bride.

Ahmad lifted her veil and looked into her tear filled eyes.

"I love you Mrs. Ealy."

He leaned down and gave her a kiss that sent a stirring in her soul. She wrapped her arms around his neck as he wrapped his arms around her waist. The on lookers clapped. When they finally separated Pastor Williams announced to the church,

"Mr. and Mrs. Ealy."

They then joined hands and walked back down the aisle past clapping family and friends. Some stopped them for hugs, others shouted congratulations.

When they reached the open church doors, Cara was surprised when she saw a white limousine waiting at the curb. A.J. looked down at his wife's beautiful face.

"I love you Cara."

He led her down the steps and to the limousine.

"I love you too, are you sure you don't want to skip the reception?" Cara said it jokingly but seriously at the same time. A.J. looked back at their family and friends who had gathered outside to share their moment.

"Nah lets stay long enough to take pictures, do a toast and dance and then we'll skip out."

Cara nodded and tilted her head for a kiss from her husband. He leaned down to kiss her then they turned to wave to their family. The photographer snapped photos of them. They couldn't contain their smiles of happiness as they stepped hand in hand to the waiting limo. When Cara looked at her family and her friends, she was convinced that this was **Her Season Of Love, and no one could do or say anything to change that.**

The Sequel…. Happily Ever After…Coming soon

www.ingramcontent.com/pod-product-compliance
Lightning Source LLC
Chambersburg PA
CBHW022150170626
46807CB00005B/2143